ALSO BY APRIL GENEVIEVE TUCHOLKE

Seven Endless Forests

THE BONELESS MERCIES

APRIL GENEVIEVE TUCHOLKE

FARRAR STRAUS GIROUX · NEW YORK

An imprint of Macmillan Publishing Group, LLC
120 Broadway, New York, NY 10271
fiercereads.com

Library of Congress Cataloging-in-Publication Data

Names: Tucholke, April Genevieve, author.
Title: The Boneless Mercies / April Genevieve Tucholke.
Description: New York : Farrar Straus Giroux, 2018. | Summary: Four female mercenaries known as Boneless Mercies, weary of roaming Vorseland, ignored and forgotten until they are needed for mercy killings, decide to seek glory by going after a legendary monster in this reimagining of *Beowulf*.
Identifiers: LCCN 2018003350 | ISBN 978-1-250-21150-7 (paperback) | ISBN 978-0-374-30708-0 (ebook)
Subjects: | CYAC: Fantasy. | Mercenary troops—Fiction. | Euthanasia—Fiction. | Monsters—Fiction. | Mythology, Norse—Fiction.
Classification: LCC PZ7.T7979 Bon 2018 | DDC [Fic]—dc23
LC record available at https://lccn.loc.gov/2018003350

ISBN 978-0-374-31283-1 (International edition)

Originally published in the United States by Farrar Straus Giroux
First Square Fish edition, 2020
Book designed by Elizabeth H. Clark
Square Fish logo designed by Filomena Tuosto

1 3 5 7 9 10 8 6 4 2

To all those who seek glory

The story's been sung, the story's been told,
She burned the dead, and kept the gold,
Out goes the fire, in comes the cold,
She was the last of the brave, the last of the bold.

—"Song of the Lone Girl,"
from the *Blood Frost Saga*

This is a story of heroes,
of Mercies and witches, of marshes and Merrows,
of reeds and thorns, of women and giants,
of bravery and friendship, of an age that's ending,
and one that's about to begin.

—ESCA ROTH,
Jarl of Blue Vee, from the poem "The Boneless Mercies"

I shall gain glory or die.

—SEAMUS HEANEY,
trans., *Beowulf*

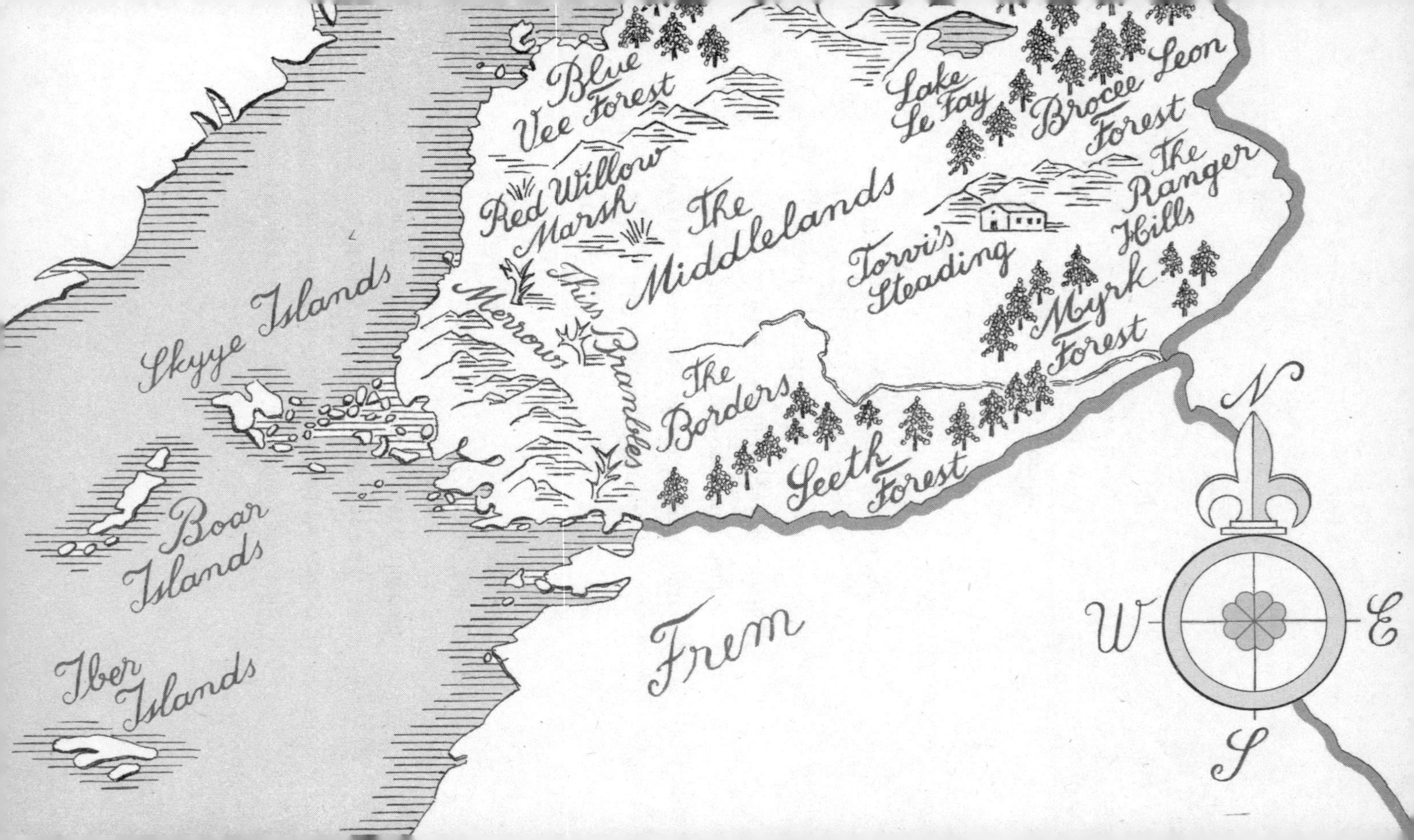
Blue Vee Forest
Lake Le Fay
Brocee Leon Forest
Red Willow Marsh
The Middlelands
Torvi's Steading
The Ranger Hills
Skyye Islands
Merrows
Thiss Brambles
Myrk Forest
The Borders
Seeth Forest
Boar Islands
Iber Islands
Frem
N
W
E
S

VORSELAND
Finnmark
Wild Ice Plains
Faroe Glaciers
The Far North
Elshland
Quell Sea
Green Wild Forest
Skal Mountains
Imp's Ear Peak

THE WITCHES

ONE

T*hey say dying makes you thirsty, so we always gave our marks* one last drink.

I reached for the flask of black currant *Vite* I carried in my pocket and put it to her mouth. "Here," I said. "Drink this, lamb."

She took a long sip. I pulled the flask away and wiped a drop from her lips. They felt plump and warm under my fingers, like a red plum in August just picked from the tree. I called all our marks *lamb*. Even the big ones with thick beards and hands the size of boulders. Even the mean ones with cold, shriveled hearts and dried blood under their fingernails. This *lamb* was neither.

She was covered in black silk, head to toe. The silk clung to her curves and moved lightly through the air as if woven from soft summer breezes. I wanted to touch it. I wanted to wear it. Our thick Vorse wool and furs and leather kept us warm, but they were utilitarian and plain next to her delicate dress.

"You're from Iber." Runa stared at the woman's clothing as well.

The woman nodded. "I grew up with soft white sand instead of snow. The sun shone bright and brazen, and women had fire in their blood."

She'd hired us herself. She wanted to die. Her husband, children—all dead from sickness. How she ended up in a dark, sod-roofed house on the other side of the Black Spruce Forest, I didn't know.

The woman in silk was tall, taller than me, taller even than Runa. She had deep brown eyes and pointed ears like the Elvers in Vorse fairy tales. She took another sip of *Vite* when I offered it, and then slipped a gold coin into my hand.

"What's your name?" she asked.

"Frey," I said. I didn't ask hers in return.

She sighed and leaned against me, her soft arm against my hard shoulder. I pulled her black hair away from her cheek, gently, gently, my knuckles across her skin. Her hair felt heavy on my palm, and it bore scents of the south. Myrrh and frankincense.

"We will do it quick, lamb," I said. "As promised." She looked up at me. Her smile was swift and kind and sad.

I motioned to Ovie in the shadows near the cold hearth, and she came forward, taut but quiet, like a snow cat on the hunt. Juniper, our Sea Witch, began to pray in the corner by a pile of hides and an old loom. Trigve stood by my side, and Runa simply watched us from the doorway.

Ovie handed me her knife—it was better made, sharper than mine. I took it and slit the woman's neck. A flash of sharp silver, and it was done. The woman kept her eyes on mine until the end, never looking at the knife. I caught her as she fell to the floor.

Juniper finished her prayers and came over to us. She put her hand on the mark's chest, and her curls fell over the dying woman's cheeks. Juniper's hair was blond, with a faint shimmer of pale, pearly sea green, the same as all the witches of the Merrows.

We waited for the mark's breath to slow. Slow, slow, and stop forever.

"I bet she was fierce when she was young." I closed each of her eyelids with a gentle push of my thumb. "Fierce as the Iber sun. I wonder if she was banished here, to the frigid north, for some fierce, heroic deed . . ."

Runa looked at me, sharp.

She said it was dangerous, this way I had of thinking about our marks after they died, imagining how they had lived, dreaming how their lives had played out, the twists and turns they had taken. She said all that dreaming was either going to get me into trouble or turn me soft.

Runa wasn't soft—she would have made a good Mercy leader. She could have gone off and started her own Mercy pack. Though when I admitted this once to Juniper, she'd just shrugged and said leadership took imagination as well as strength.

Runa stood then and began to explore the cold, empty house. I knew she was looking for food and clothing and weapons. I caught her halfway down a shadowed hallway leading to more dark rooms, old bearskins hanging in the doorways.

"Leave it, Runa. The job is done. Let's get out of here."

She'd glared at me, mouth tight above her pointed chin. "There might be something hidden—treasures from the south, desert jewels we could sell for enough gold to book passage aboard a ship . . ."

"No." Ovie's deep voice echoed down the corridor. "We will not steal. Leave her things alone, Runa."

Trigve and Juniper stood silent behind Ovie, though Juniper fidgeted, at war with herself. Her thieving urge was strong. Siggy had told us time and time again that the gods were watching and that they would punish a Mercy who took anything other than coin from a mark.

And yet . . .

I cut a lock of the Iber woman's hair before we left. I slipped Ovie's dagger under her head, metal scraping the cold stone floor, and sliced.

Runa had taken things in the past from our marks: simple, useful things. She kept a strong coil of hemp rope in her pack and all other sorts of stolen odds and ends: strips of leather and metal hooks and pieces of old wool and vials of potions and tonics. Runa usually did as she pleased, and I admired her for it.

Afterward, we waded into a nearby stream to wash the blood from our hands. We tried not to get blood on our clothing. Whenever we met people on the road, their eyes flashed to our black cloaks . . . and then to the old red stains on our plain wool tunics. It reminded them that one day their blood might be staining our clothing as well. People didn't like to think about this.

The woman in silk hadn't wanted us to burn her. She'd asked us to leave her there in the forest, with the worn front doors of her home left wide open. The wolves would come and take care of everything after nightfall.

"That's how they do it in Iber," Trigve said. "I've read of it."

Walking away and leaving the woman's body to be torn apart by beasts in the night took all my discipline, all my steel. I ached to set her body on fire and let her soul drift up to Holhalla while her flesh turned to ash. Or even to put her safe in the earth, six feet deep, as the Elsh did with their dead.

How someone preferred to die said a lot about how they'd lived. The woman in black silk had wanted to die bloody.

And if she'd wanted a wild death, who was I to take it from her?

They called us the Mercies, or sometimes the Boneless Mercies. They said we were shadows, ghosts, and if you touched our skin, we dissolved into smoke.

We made people uneasy, for we were women with weapons. And yet the Mercies were needed. Men would not do our sad, dark work.

I'd asked my mentor, Siggy, about our kind one solstice night, when the light lingered long in the sky. I asked when the death trade had begun, and why. She said she didn't know. The bards didn't sing of it, and the sagas didn't tell of it, and so the genesis of the Mercies was lost to time.

"Jarls rise and jarls fall," she whispered, her dark eyes on the last orange streaks of light flickering across the horizon. "The Boneless Mercies remain. We have roamed Vorseland since the age of the *Witch War Chronicles*. Perhaps longer. We are ignored and forgotten . . . until we are needed. It has always been this way." She paused. "It is not a grand profession, but it is a noble one."

I didn't answer, but she read my thoughts.

"This isn't a bad life, Frey. Some have it much worse. Only fools want to be great. Only fools seek glory."

TWO

Sleep eluded me, as usual. It lurked just out of reach like a gaunt North-Fairy from the sagas, shy and hollow-eyed.

Ovie's short, lithe body was nestled into mine, our feet toward the dying fire. I could feel her deep breaths matching my own. We were nine or ten miles outside a town called Hail. There would be death work for us there, if we wanted it. Based on the near-empty money pouch at my waist, we did. The Iber woman's coin would be enough to get us food and ale at the inn on the following day—a nice change from river water and snared rabbit.

I rested my cheek on top of Ovie's head. Her cords of thick white-blond braids smelled like snow. All of her smelled like snow. Snow and a hint of Arctic Woad. Every few months she dyed the ends of her hair with leaves from the fragrant northern woad plant until they turned as blue as the winter sky. It suited her.

We all believed Ovie was the oldest among us, maybe nineteen, maybe twenty, though she never told me her age. Something in her stillness made her seem wiser.

But for all her wisdom, at night Ovie nestled into my arms like a child.

Juniper once speculated that Ovie did this because she had nightmares, possibly about the time she lost her eye.

Behind me, the Sea Witch moved in her sleep. She was curled up with her back against mine, her thick curls making a pillow for the both of us. Unlike Ovie, Juniper smelled faintly of salt, specifically the Flower Salt that the Fremish harvested from the ocean and dried in the sun. I'd tasted some once in a Great Hall, the flakes sprinkled over a roast leg of venison. We'd been allowed to take part in a feast as payment for our services—the sick son of a servant, dying too slowly for the jarl's liking.

Runa was off by herself, as usual, her long legs stretching into the shadows. The rest of us always slept in a pile, our Mercy-cloaks wrapped around our bodies. The cloaks were well made and thick—they served as our blankets and our beds.

Sleeping all together in a pack like dogs, keeping one another warm at night . . . I'd grown to rely on it. I knew what it felt like to sleep alone. I remembered the long, solitary hours I'd spent on the open road after I'd run away from the Bliss House. Sleeping under trees, curled into myself, no one to run to, nowhere to go. It felt like a heartbeat ago.

I heard someone stirring. Trigve rose to his feet and set another log on the fire.

Trigve wore his hair long, like some Vorse men, dark strands tied back with leather straps or left streaming over his shoulders.

People often mistook Trigve and Runa for brother and sister, though their personalities were as different as snow and blood.

Trigve had been born three weeks before the festival of Ostara, in winter's last throes, and his mind ran strong and quick and cheerful, like a winter wind coming off the sea and stirring up the snow. He was even-tempered but deep, with a healer's compassionate heart. He was the most lighthearted of us, lighthearted as the Quicks, the famous archers who roamed the Seven Endless Forests.

Juniper had it in her, too, this lively spirit, but not Runa, and not Ovie.

Juniper had once said that Runa and Ovie understood darkness and carried it with them, but Trigve rejected darkness and turned to the light. The Sea Witch had looked at me then, hands on hips, eyebrows raised, as if to say, *And which are you, Frey, dark or light?*

We'd found Trigve last winter sitting beside an overturned caravan, the only person left alive in the village of Dorrit. He had no family, no home, like the rest of us Mercies. I'd lost my own parents at twelve from the snow sickness. My father had been a fisher and shipbuilder, and my mother a weaver. After they died, my father's brother sold me to a Bliss House, where I washed clothing and cleaned floors until I was old enough to provide another service. When the Bliss Mistress, a red-haired woman who looked kind but wasn't, told me I was ready to move from the kitchen to the bedroom, I crawled out a window and ran. I ran until I found Siggy.

Autumn had already come again—the nights were growing cold and raw. Summer in Vorseland was bright, and short, lasting ten to twelve weeks, no more. I dreaded the coming of winter—the prior one had been especially hard. We saw no fewer than six blue bodies on our travels, frozen in the snow near the ash of long-dead fires. I often worried our flames would go out some night—one strong gust of wind, and then all of us freezing to death in our sleep. But Runa had a way with fire—she could get sparks sparking on wet wood on the coldest night and make the flames last until dawn.

"You have a glint," Juniper said to Runa once, a few days after she'd joined us Mercies—the Sea Witch was the last girl Siggy recruited before she died.

Runa just shrugged and pulled out the little wooden box that contained her flint, steel, char cloth, and tinder.

"What you call a knack, the Sea Witches call a glint." Juniper raised her arm and put a fist to her heart. "A glint is a spiritual gift from the goddess Jute. It shouldn't be taken for granted."

"What makes you think I take it for granted?" Runa leaned over and blew on a spark until the tinder nest caught fire. "Why don't you just pray for a fire if you're so devoted to Jute? It would save me the trouble."

Juniper shrugged. "Prayers are tricky. And they are about giving, not receiving."

Runa gave Juniper a long look. "Are they, now?" There was a snap to her voice, though her expression was mild.

Juniper simply smiled in return, and that's when I knew Siggy was right, that this tiny girl with big ears and wide gray eyes would be a good addition to the Mercies. She was a sweet, earnest contrast to Runa's deeply rooted skepticism.

Not that Ovie or I prayed much, either—the average Vorse citizen was not overly religious, as a rule. Supplication did not come easily to us as a people. Some exceptions existed—like the Gothi nuns, the Sea Witches, and a handful of pious jarls—but in general we did not turn to it unless in dire need.

When I did pray, it was to Valkree, the beautiful, silent, mysterious goddess of Boneless Mercies and all rover girls. It was said she had a special fondness for us. Siggy had taught me to pray when she'd first taken me on—it was part of my Mercy training. She'd taught me how to pray, just as she'd taught me how to slit a throat quick and clean by practicing on rabbits and squirrels, just as she'd taught me how to be patient and silent by tracking wolves and foxes back to their dens.

But the praying seemed to me more about fear and adoration than strength and function, and I'd never been one for passive worship.

Juniper whispered something in her sleep, and I felt her hair move across the back of my neck. She was the youngest of us, fifteen, and the smallest, too. But she held her own. She moved as light as air and was almost shameless when it came to theft.

She could steal the shirt right off your back, and you wouldn't know it until you felt the cold breeze shoot down your spine. When Ovie's traps failed, Juniper came through. She stole chickens at night, creeping past shaggy guard dogs without a sound. She once stole a sleepy red cow with gentle brown eyes when the farmer's back was turned. We had fresh milk for a week before we traded her to a cobbler for fleece-lined leather boots, a pair for each of us. Those boots kept our feet from freezing last winter and were the reason we still had all our toes.

I thought of my own theft—the Iber woman's hair tucked into my pack. A person was never truly dead as long as someone, somewhere, remembered them. Memories made you immortal. This was why men went to war. Why they had climbed in their longboats and raided Elshland, before the gold dried up. They risked their short, mortal lives for the everlasting glow of immortality. A chance to be a hero in a bard's song.

Runa said war was stupid. Juniper flinched at the wasted lives, at all the lost stories. Trigve said war was heartless. Ovie said nothing about it at all.

But I understood it.

I wanted to change my fate, to force it down another road. I wanted to stand in the river of time and make it flow a different direction, if just for a little while.

If I stayed on the Mercy path—this path of sad, inglorious, quick-and-quiet deaths—only the Mercies would hold Frey memories in their hearts after I died.

Siggy had said it was honorable to live an unknown and undistinguished life. She said it took courage. I disagreed with her on this, and other things.

I did not want to die like the woman in silk, alone in the woods, alone in the world, joy gone, love gone, spark gone, one last sip of *Vite*, chin up, neck slit, body down, a pool of blood, a midnight meal for hungry beasts.

I wanted to be known. To be sung about. I wanted men and women to hoist me onto their shoulders, to shout my name into the rafters.

I was a Mercy-girl with no family, no home, no fortune, and yet my blood sang a song of glory.

Juniper said the gods liked to humble people who dream big dreams. But the gods had never done much for me, and I wasn't afraid of them.

I stretched my arm over Ovie, searching in the dark for Trigve's warm fingers. I squeezed his hand. Sleep often shunned him, like me.

When I finally did drift off, my dreams were turbulent. Wolves howling into crisp winter air. White, sinuous moonlight on a black field. Oily red blood spilling across gray stone.

THREE

W*e walked slowly through the village of Hail the next* morning, to let them see us, the people with death on their minds. It was market day, and busy, but the villagers parted to let us through. None made eye contact—no one wanted to be seen trying to catch the attention of a Boneless Mercy. They gave us a wide berth, so the edges of our cloaks wouldn't graze them as we passed.

People knew us by our Mercy-cloaks—tightly-knit wool, dyed black and embroidered with raven feathers. Ours glistened with the golden linseed oil we rubbed into the cloth to keep out the rain and snow.

A girl couldn't take on or carry out Mercy-work in Vorseland unless she wore a Mercy-cloak. Doing so could invoke the wrath of an overly zealous jarl—otherwise, anyone could buy a small, Mercy-size dagger from a village market and simply start trading in death. The cloaks were trickier. I'd had our four commissioned two years ago from a tailor's daughter who wanted us to kill her father—he drank too much, beat her, and who knew what else.

Runa said it was a vengeance kill, not a Mercy-kill, and hence not our business. Ovie said it would mean trouble if it was found out. But I didn't care. I saw the girl's bruises, deep purple across her cheek. I knifed her father as he pissed that night outside the tavern, a harsh slash to the gut. He writhed on the ground in the mud, blood pouring.

That daughter-beater screamed his way into a slow, painful death, and I was glad of it.

Siggy used to say that Mercies shouldn't enjoy killing. But the daughter-beaters, the wife-beaters, the ones who were cruel to animals, the ones who were brutal and selfish and hard . . . I liked killing them. I took pleasure in it.

Eventually we drifted into the Hail Inn—roaring hearth fire, sturdy wooden tables, cheery, bearded barkeep who didn't care a bit about our Mercy-cloaks after he saw our coin. I ordered beef stew and bread and a pint of dark ale for each of us. We found a table in a dark corner away from the fire, Runa and Juniper on one side, me between Trigve and Ovie on the other. A skinny serving girl brought us steaming bowls and bubbling mugs, and I was in high spirits, grateful to be someplace warm and lively, grateful not to be eating on the cold ground again.

Runa did not share my good humor. She ate three bites of her stew, then set her spoon down with a thud. "I'm done with Mercy-killing."

This was an old argument. One we'd been having since the day Siggy died. There was no penalty for quitting the death trade—we didn't pledge ourselves to a jarl like Vorse warriors. Mercies were more like the hedge-fighters of Elshland—wandering mercenaries who took work when they could find it and slept under a hedge when they couldn't. We lived without the comfort of a jarl's Great Hall and the food and shelter it provided . . . But we were free to come and go as we pleased, which had its advantages.

Ovie, for her part, didn't mind the death trade, though I knew she wanted to travel to distant lands and see the world. Runa didn't mind the endless wandering but hated bringing death. Juniper ached to stand still—she'd been raised by the Sea Witches in a cove by the Quell Sea and knew what it meant to have a home and a family.

None of us was content.

Occasionally I wished my parents had left me some small, isolated parcel of land at the far end of some quiet jarldom. As a farmer, I could have done as I pleased, more than most, at least. I'd be at the mercy of no one but nature and the gods.

I'd seen the occasional Vorse female farmer in our wanderings. She tilled the earth, cultivated it, harvested it, season after season, year after year. I imagined it was a hard life, filled with harsh sun in the summer and freezing wind in the winter. And farm-women often looked half-starved and weary beyond reason. But I would have taken that life in a heartbeat over being a Mercy.

No, that was a lie.

I would have stuck it out as a farmer for one season, possibly two, and then sold the steading. I was a wanderer through and through. Siggy saw it in me from the first, and she was right. I would never choose to sink my youth into the dirt, my back growing bent, my skin turning rough. I wanted more than this. A lot more.

"I'm done with Mercy-killing," Runa said again, louder this time.

I looked at her. *"Once a Mercy, always a Mercy."* It was something Siggy used to say whenever I asked her if she'd ever thought of leaving the death trade. "We've seen too much death not to carry it always in our hearts, whether or not we wear the raven cloaks."

Runa slammed her fist on the table, and ale sloshed over the rims of our cups. "And if we joined the Quicks, they'd say, '*Once a Quick, always a Quick.*' Wouldn't you rather this be true?"

"Runa." Ovie's voice was soft but deep, her eyes narrow. "Don't."

Runa blinked and started in anyway. "I want to do something else. *Anything* else. Let's join the Quicks."

The Quicks moved through the Seven Endless Forests, living off the land. They were single-minded and focused when hunting but jovial and carefree at night beside the flames. We'd stumbled upon our fair share of Quick bands in our travels across the Vorseland Borders, following the death trade. They often let us share their fire.

Boneless Mercies were required by Vorse law to keep their hair long—it was the standard code for us death-bringers, as important as our cloaks. But the Quicks cut their hair short to keep it out of their way, to stay silent, to stay *quick*. It was said they were blessed by the gods, and jarls believed they brought luck to any forest they wandered.

Many jarls were also required by ancient Vorse law to pay the Quicks a sizable amount of gold to keep their forests free of thieves and brigands, an easy feat for the skilled archers. This gold allowed the Quicks to purchase sturdy boots and well-made cloaks. It allowed them to maintain a series of secret, well-stocked shelters across Vorseland, from caves to tree huts to camouflaged longhouses deep in the forest, invisible except for the thin plume of smoke rising from the roof.

I pushed my bowl away and rested my chin on my hand. "We've been over this, Runa. The Quicks will not take us in. I've asked each band we've come across, and they've all turned me down, every one. They want carefree wanderers, slow to anger, quick to laugh. They want skilled archers, silent on the hunt but loud and boisterous at night beside the fire. And we are death-traders."

Runa shrugged. "We will learn. They can teach us."

"And why would they bother?"

Juniper's gray eyes shifted from me to Runa and back again. She kept a handful of small seashells in a pocket of her tunic, plucked from the shores of the Merrows, and she began to fiddle with them. She did this whenever she was worried. I heard them softly clinking under the table.

Runa closed her eyes and sighed. "Then let's just form our own woodland band. We can head into the nearest Endless Forest and never leave."

I shook my head. "The Quicks have gold, and shelter—they can weather the worst of the winter storms in relative comfort. What would we do when a snowstorm hits, and we have no secret shelters and no coin?"

Runa took a sip of her ale, and then wiped her mouth on the back of her sleeve. "Fine. Then let's join the Sea Witches."

Juniper looked over her shoulder at Runa. "You can't. I've told you this already. The Sea Witches won't take in outsiders. Mother Hush wouldn't even let me adopt a stray dog once because he wasn't born on the Merrow shores. Though in the end, I kept him anyway. I fed him fresh fish and sang him the dog-prayers . . ."

"Is that why they exiled you?" Runa's anger had switched in a heartbeat from me to Juniper.

"They didn't exile me."

"Then why are you here with us? The Sea Witches protect their own—you must have done something truly terrible for them to banish you."

I set my mug down. "Back off, Runa."

Next to me, Ovie finished her ale in one long swallow. Quickly, silently, she pulled out her dagger, reached across the table, and put it to Runa's throat. "Leave Juniper alone. She's a right to her secrets, just like all of us."

Trigve opened his mouth to protest, but I put my hand on his arm to keep him still. I wanted to let this play out.

"*I* don't have any secrets," Runa hissed, her eyes meeting Ovie's over the blade.

"We all have secrets," Juniper whispered.

"Yes." Ovie pulled her blade away again, leaving a thin line of blood on Runa's throat.

Most Vorse preferred not to speak about their past. They thought it unlucky. Often when a character in a saga spoke of their childhood, it meant they hadn't long to live.

Besides, Siggy used to say, the path to the death trade was paved with sorrow, and sad stories are best left alone. So we didn't pry, even Runa . . . until now.

Runa wiped the blood from her neck with a flick of her thumb. Ovie was the only thing in the world that seemed to scare her. Still, her fire had only been tamed, not put out. She leaned back and crossed her arms. "So we can't join the Sea Witches. Then how about we take up with the Gothi nuns?"

I shook my head. "The nuns can't enter the convent without a large donation to their god, Obin. Besides, they deal in the death trade even more than us. I can't see you washing dead bodies and preparing them for burning, Runa. And what if some jarl wants to make a vestal sacrifice to Forset, and the nuns send you? What then?"

Runa didn't answer. There was a long pause among us, our table cloaked in stillness, surrounded by the hum of the bustling inn. Juniper fidgeted. Trigve's foot brushed against mine. Ovie was silent, simply waiting to see what I'd do next.

Runa's gaze met mine. "Well, what would you suggest then, Frey? If you don't like any of my ideas, then why don't you come up with one of your own? I know you hate Mercy-killing as much as I do."

I leaned back and crossed my arms, just as she had, and said a silent prayer to Valkree to send me a new idea, an alternative path.

The front of the inn began to stir. A tall man with long red hair had risen from his table and now stood near the fire, telling a story. It was too loud to make out his words, but eventually the room began to hush. Spoons rested quietly in bowls, bodies went still, all eyes turned to the tale-teller.

He was telling a story about the Blue Vee Beast.

I'd heard of the beast. We all had. Rumors of blood, darkness, death. A creature that came in the night and slaughtered whole villages in Blue Vee. Men, women, children. A few weeks of quiet would pass, a month . . . And then the butchery began again. Some said the creature ate the corpses, and some said it dragged them away to its den, and some said it took only the girls, and some said it took only the boys, and some said it took only the heads and used them in dark snow-magic rituals.

". . . and in the morning they found the bodies, headless,

lifeless, strung up in the trees by their feet, the youngest still a babe. Roth's men had them taken down and burned, but the village is a haunted place now, and the ghosts of the dead roam after nightfall." The red-haired man's voice soared across the inn. "Jarl Roth is offering a hundred gold klines to anyone who can defeat this beast, but who here will swear him their blade?"

Roth was the jarl of Blue Vee, and half his warriors had been slain fighting this beast. He'd called in aid from neighboring jarldoms, but few answered. It was a difficult place to reach on foot—one had to cross the dangerous, fetid Red Willow Marsh or take the narrow Ribbon Pass over the Skal Mountains. The Jade Fells lived along the Ribbon Pass, and they were a wild people from the far north, brutal and fearless. It was said they ate the hearts of their dead.

A person could sail up the coast and avoid these dangers, but raiding longboats required two dozen strong men at the oars, and only jarls could afford their own single-mast, clinker-built vessels. Enough gold could book a person passage on the rare merchant ship that landed on the Blue Vee coast, but if any of us were that wealthy, we wouldn't risk our lives trying to slay a monster.

The people near us began to whisper. They called Blue Vee a cursed place and speculated on what would happen if no one was able to kill the beast. Would it go back to the far north and leave the rest of Vorseland alone? Or would it move farther south?

The red-haired man raised a fist in the air, and the firelight glinted off the bronze band on his wrist. "Who here has the heart to seek out this monster and bring it down?" He pointed at a broad-shouldered man near the door. "Do you, blacksmith? Will you add your strength to Roth's and put an end to this horror?"

The blacksmith, a handsome, bearded man of around thirty, just shrugged.

No one here would answer Roth's call. I'd seen a similar scene play out a dozen times in various inns throughout the last few months.

And yet . . .

I looked each of the Mercies in the eye. "I say we turn west and try for the Blue Vee Beast. We hunt it down, fight it, slay it, and claim the reward."

Ovie said nothing. Juniper said nothing.

"Blue Vee?" Runa rubbed her palm along her jaw and eyed me warily. "That's your plan to get us out of Mercy-killing? We slay the sick and old, Frey, not bloodthirsty beasts. What makes you think us Mercies can kill this thing? A creature that trained warriors haven't been able to destroy?"

Even as she said it, I felt my heart beat faster, blood buzzing through my veins.

I wanted to fight something that fought back.

I wanted it more than I wanted a home and a family. I wanted it more than I wanted food and warmth and gold.

My eyes met Runa's. "Trained warriors kill loudly. We kill silently. And that is how you hunt a beast."

"*Quiet.* Both of you." Ovie nodded toward a group of men in the opposite corner playing a dice game. "They're listening."

We left the inn and napped off the stew and ale under a large oak tree at the edge of town, stretched out on grass that smelled clean and floral. I woke before the others and lay still, staring up, arms crossed under my head. The sky was stark blue, and it was one of those perfect, early-autumn evenings.

But the oak's leaves were beginning to change color. A sign of things to come.

Winter.

Short days, long nights. Little food. And the cold. Always, always the cold.

Mercy-work was best done after the shadows set in. The people with death on their minds found us as the sun began to set.

An old woman, stooped and twisted as a bone-white juniper tree. *"Come to the house at the southern crossroads, the one with five windows. Bring poison. I can pay."*

The blacksmith from the inn, dark eyes deep and melancholy. *"Come to the smithy, climb the outside stairs, and knock twice. My grandmother is eager to see Holhalla."*

A father, thin and weary, with forlorn brown eyes. *"Come to the hut by the tall pine, straight north. Skin-eating disease."*

And one last request, just as the fat orange sun sank below the sky. A girl, no older than twelve, with long black hair and green eyes.

"I need a vial of Blue Seed."

"Why?" Runa asked. "We aren't Potion Peddlers. We *use* poison, we don't sell it."

Blue Seed poison was squeezed from the seeds of the black pine—it was hard to make and hard to get, but it brought a fast and painless death. A smaller dose would also empty a woman's womb, if that was her wish—this was lawful in some jarldoms, but not all. Laws changed as often as jarls died and new rulers took their place. Young women sometimes approached us for "Small Seed," as they called it, clutching their bellies, eyes afraid. I told them to seek the Potion Peddlers . . . but I also suggested they use Wild Carrot Oil in the future to prevent a similar event.

The black-haired girl started shaking under Runa's hard gaze, thin shoulders twitching in her black wool dress. "My father went off into the Red Willow Marsh and never came back. My mother took a new husband and he's . . . . He's not kind to her or to me. I want him dead."

"That's a vengeance kill, not a Mercy-kill." Runa's voice was a little softer now.

Juniper walked forward and put her arm around the girl's waist. She moved a strand of her hair and whispered a prayer in her ear.

My eyes met Ovie's. We'd done vengeance kills in the past. To get our Mercy-cloaks, yes, but it hadn't stopped there. Vengeance kills were forbidden, and things would go badly for us if it was discovered. Still, they were far more satisfying than Mercy-kills.

Ovie nodded. She agreed with me on this.

I slipped my hand into my leather satchel, pulled out a vial filled with oily blue liquid, and gave it to the girl. "Take it," I said. "And remember, our Sea Witch sees all and knows all. If I find out you used this potion on anyone other than your stepfather, we will track you down and send you straight to Hel. You are putting us all at risk. Understood?"

She stared at me for a moment, nodded, then handed me two coins before running off into the night.

The Potion Peddlers followed strict laws and never sold to children. Sometimes they wouldn't even sell to us. Siggy never would have given the girl the poison.

I wasn't sure if this had made her a strong Boneless Mercy, or a weak one.

We went to the crossroads first, then the blacksmith's. Old and sick. Simple tasks. We left the skin-eater job for last.

The house was nothing but a stone hut, built next to the tangled roots of a tall, ancient pine tree, upper branches reaching out vast and strong over a small black lake. The thin man from earlier answered the door, bloodshot eyes, shaking hands.

His wife had thick blond hair and small hands. Her skin was covered in weeping sores. She sighed when she saw us, whether with sadness or relief, I couldn't tell. Her husband took her in his arms and held her. A few moments passed, and then he lifted her chin with his palm, exposing the red blisters on her ashen neck.

"It will all be over soon, lamb. No more pain, just peace." I gestured to Ovie, and she handed me her knife. Sharp blade, thin neck, one slash and it was done. The woman went still.

Next came the son. Trigve led the father outside as we climbed the ladder to the loft—he'd seen his wife through to her death, and that was enough for one man.

The boy was ten at most, with wavy yellow hair and a brave, intense look in his blue eyes, even as he lay dying on his bed. Juniper dropped to her knees and began her prayers.

Ovie took one look and shook her head. "No. I'll not stay to watch this." She spun around, went back down the ladder, and walked out the front door.

I turned to Runa.

"He's just a boy." Runa's voice was deep and raw and sad.

I nodded.

Runa and I were the only ones fierce enough to take children. Yet we both held back every time.

"Just do it," the boy shouted from the bed, fire in his voice. "I want to reach the Great Hall of the Slain while there's some fight left in me." He raised his fist into the air, and a sore burst and leaked blood down his arm.

The boy's bravery about broke me. Even after all I'd seen, even after all the death.

Juniper's prayer-whispers stopped.

"I'll take him," I said. "You did the last two children, Runa."

Runa moved her dark braids behind her shoulders. Her hair was a true Skyye black, like many Vorse people whose ancestry could be traced to the Skyye Islands, and it shone a violet-blue in the firelight beaming from the nearby brazier. "No. I'll do it. Blood is blood and bone is bone and death is death. It's all the same."

Juniper started her prayers again.

Runa's Mercy-knife was smaller than Ovie's but just as sharp. She went to the boy and, despite what she'd said about death being death, reached forward and gripped his small arm in hers, forearm to forearm, like warriors before battle.

People said the skin-eating disease was contagious, but that didn't stop her.

The boy's fingers tightened on her skin until the knuckles went white. He tilted his chin back . . .

And it was done.

His body went limp, blond head sagging against the pillow.

FOUR

I don't think we should sleep here." Juniper narrowed her eyes as she stared up at the large rock.

I'd decided to build our fire that night next to a lonely, free-standing stone, fifteen feet around, twelve feet tall, jade-colored moss growing up its sides. We were a few miles outside Hail, in a dip of land near a group of spruce trees and an empty field.

Trigve helped me gather wood, and Runa got it lit, like always. I could taste autumn on the air. There was still a tang of life, of green and growing things, but a nip was sneaking in—the bite that would stiffen our muscles and freeze our blood come winter.

"I don't think we should sleep here," Juniper repeated. She'd been off in the spruce trees, praying for the skin-eater boy and his mother. I hadn't heard her return—she moved as silent as the moon. She arched her back and put her hands on her hips, tunic wet from the ground, black wool leggings gleaming with damp.

"Why not?" Runa was quieter than usual, almost melancholy, and after what she'd done earlier, who could blame her. We all had our roles as Mercies, and we were all needed, but Runa . . . Runa came through when the rest of us failed. She had our respect, even when her temper was as sharp as her steel.

"Troll," Ovie said in response to Runa's question. She lifted her black leather eye patch and rubbed her calloused palm over the hollow.

Trigve sat down near a bed of purple heather and undid his braid. He shook his head, and his dark hair rippled down his back. "Large rocks are not trolls turned to stone. That's a myth. The warriors in the *Blood Frost Saga* named their weapons after legendary trolls, but even they knew the creatures weren't real. Trolls aren't mentioned in any of the Anglon Mystic books."

Runa walked by and smacked Trigve on the shoulder. "So you know how to read. What good does it do you?"

Trigve shrugged. "It's useful."

Runa sat down, stretched out her long legs, and began to sharpen the blade of her knife with a small piece of unglazed ceramic from her pack. "Maybe. But it can't help you hunt or kill or win a skin-fight."

Skin-fight was a slang term for Vorse one-on-one combat, fought naked, no weapons. It was sometimes to the death, but mostly not. Jarls often used skin-fights to resolve disputes between two tenants. The opponents were usually of the same gender, though not always.

Siggy had taught us the basics of Mercy-killing—where to put the knife and the angles that made the blade go swift and deep. She taught us poison and the doses that would bring death. She taught us how to pull the breath from someone with a rope and with our hands. She even taught us how to snap a mark's neck—though I believed Runa was the only one among us strong enough to do it.

But winning a skin-fight usually came down to either strength and stamina or wits and cunning. We'd seen a few in our travels—the times we'd been called to work in a Great Hall—and the fights always brought excitement to dark winter nights.

"Trolls *are* real, though."

I looked over my shoulder. Juniper was staring up at the stone again.

"They were the mortal enemies of the Winter Elvers. One of my Sea Witch sisters saw an Elver battle a troll once, in the far north, past the Skal Mountains, in the Wild Ice Plains—it was a great fight of blood and ice, lightning and thunder. I believed her, too. Sea Witches never lie. Not to one another."

I smiled. "I hope to meet your Sea Witches someday, Juniper." Something about her tales of the witches made my imagination flicker, my blood move faster.

Trigve and I started on supper. We knelt on the cold ground and shared a plank of wood—I sliced carrots with my Mercy-dagger, and Trigve cut onions. We were making rabbit ale stew again. The skin-eater deaths had given us enough coin to buy vegetables and mead.

I hated taking money from the sad-eyed man in the hut. A father, no longer, a husband, no longer. Alone.

Trigve tossed his pile of onion slices into the pot, shoulder grazing mine. "Forget what I said earlier. Juniper is right. There is something unnatural about this big rock. I feel as if it's watching me." He turned and pointed. "Look at those spots there, where the moss doesn't grow. Don't they look like eyes? And there . . . See where that part juts out, like a nose? It's eerie. Why did you pick this place to camp, Frey?"

"I thought the stone would block the wind, which it does. I didn't know everyone would worry about trolls."

"Enough." Runa was on her feet, blade in hand. "I will skin-fight the next person who says *troll*."

She reached up, undid the simple pewter clasp at her throat, and let her Mercy-cloak fall to the ground.

"Today was the last day I will do this. I meant what I said at the inn. I'm done. Done killing children, done killing weak, ailing people. Done with sadness. Done with death." She gathered up the cloak in her arm, raven feathers gleaming in the firelight. She lifted it out over the flames . . .

I jumped to my feet and pulled the cloak back from the fire, holding it bundled to my chest. "Don't burn it, Runa. You need it to keep off the cold this winter, if nothing else."

She looked at me for a long moment, then bent down, one knee forward, and seized the knife from the leather sheath around her hard, lean calf. She lifted her chin and put the edge of the blade to her neck. "I can't go on doing this. I'd rather take my own life than the life of one more innocent person. I'll slit my throat. Watch me do it."

We faced each other, eyes locked.

It was that feisty, dying skin-eater boy. He'd been the last straw.

I dropped to the ground and gently pulled the knife away from her throat. "I agree with you, Runa. I don't know how Siggy did this year after year. I don't know how she bore it."

Runa leaned forward, her face close to mine. "Did you mean it, at the inn, about going after the Blue Vee Beast?"

I opened my mouth, and then shut it again. *Had I meant it?*

I felt small fingers at my elbow, and then Juniper was there, her thin arms sliding around both of us. "People are in pain, and they need us. We help them. Isn't that enough?"

Juniper, always unselfish, always thinking of others.

I stood, and Runa followed. I put my hand on my heart, a gesture of apology. "I'm sorry about the skin-eater boy, Runa."

Runa let out a deep sigh, and her posture relaxed. "How could we have known the boy would be so young, so full of heart and life despite the sickness? Besides, we've done Mercy-kills for children before. We need the money. We always need the money."

It was true and would always be true as long as we stayed in the death trade.

Runa threw her blade onto the ground, tilted her head back, and let out a howl of frustration. "I still say we head into the nearest Endless Forest and to Hel with the consequences."

I smiled. "I love your spirit, Runa." I picked up her knife and gave it back to her with a flip of the handle. "But I do not want to starve to death in the snow this winter."

Runa gave me a long look and then nodded.

The three of us stared into the fire, not talking. Ovie slipped out of the shadows, back from checking her traps, and came to my side. Trigve stood apart and alone. I motioned for him to come over, but he shook his head. He wasn't one of us, and he knew it.

It would become a problem down the road. Even if I wanted him to stay . . . even if *he* wanted to stay. It wouldn't be enough. Not as long as we continued to roam and trade in death.

I felt something touch my cheek, and I looked up. It was snowing. The flakes were light and pretty, but it was snow all the same.

Winter.

I looked at Runa, then Ovie and Juniper. I took a deep breath and closed my eyes. I smelled juniper and pine and snow.

Trigve had been teaching me the Two-Pronged Path. It was a discipline mastered by the mystics and took years of training, but he'd accomplished the basics. The goal was to send your mind down two paths and follow them both to the end in an attempt to understand the future.

I breathed in and out. Slowly.

The first path, the path of Mercies and the death trade . . . I knew where this road led. It was filled with cold and loneliness and tedium and sorrow.

The second path, however . . . The second path was filled with sharp turns and deep angles. Dark shadows and bursts of light. It was unknown.

It was beautiful.

I opened my eyes.

I put my hand on my dagger and faced the Mercies. "It has been less than a year since Siggy died, and here we all are, at a crossroads. Siggy Mercy-killed for forty years and led with courage and love and blood and fire. But things in Vorseland are changing. I'm sure I'm not the first to notice that the other Mercy groups we meet on the road are all older. The young aren't taking up the trade anymore. It seems that orphaned Vorse girls have found a new path. And so must we. We make a decision. Tonight. Voice your suggestions now, and then we will vote."

There was a long pause. The snow fell, white flakes on long Mercy hair.

"I won't go to a Bliss House." Ovie's expression was calm and impassive. "I'd rather eat a black Snow Plum, ripe from the vine and leaking poison. I'd rather die shaking and screaming in pain, than end up there."

"Yes," I said. "So would I."

Ovie reached out and let her palm fill with the falling snow. She closed her fist, and it dripped through her fingers as it melted. "I think we should go south. We'll need to steal enough gold to book passage on a ship, and it will be a risk. But the woman in black silk said that Iber has sand instead of snow and that the sun is hot and strong and the women are filled with fire. I want to see this place."

I raised one finger. "Ovie votes for the south." I raised another finger. "And I say we fight the Blue Vee Beast and try to win our gold, rather than steal it."

I turned and met Juniper's gaze. "What is your wish, Juniper? What path do you think we should take next?"

Juniper looked up at the night sky, and her pale sea-green curls slid down her back. She held up one hand, thumb bent, in a Sea Witch gesture that meant *hold, wait, give me time.* "Let me say a prayer for guidance."

She moved a few feet away from us and knelt on the ground, eyes closed, lips moving silently.

I looked over at Trigve, sitting by himself near the fire. He would not voice his opinion.

Next to me, Runa reached up and gripped her blue-black braid in one fist. She pulled her dagger and put the edge of the blade to her scalp. "The Quicks will take us in. They will. I'll cut my hair right now. We can all cut our hair, burn our cloaks, take to the woods, and join the first band we come across. They wouldn't take us in as Mercies, but perhaps they will accept us as orphaned boys with no homes and no families and no worries. We'll never tell who we are, what we've been. I'm ready, just say the word—"

I grabbed Runa's wrist and stopped her blade for the second time that night. "They'll see through the ruse. We can't simply dress as boys and fool everyone for years on end as we move through the Endless Forests. Juniper might be young enough still, but the rest of us would always struggle to hide what we are."

"Some of us more than others," Ovie said with a half-smile.

It was true enough. Runa was built straight and tall and solid, and Ovie was compact and lean, but I was rounder in every way.

Runa eyed my chest and frowned. "We could go to the Seeth Forest, where we met that friendly band last winter, and see if they will take us in this time—"

"No." Ovie shook her head, and the firelight moved across her blond braids. "It won't work. There's a reason the Quicks hesitate to take in women." She paused. "My mother joined a band of Quicks when she was young. She was quiet and fast, good with a bow. They let her in on the understanding that she would be female in form only, that she would dress as a man and *be* a man."

Ovie paused again.

"What happened?" I asked when she didn't continue.

Her eyes met mine, and I saw sorrow, deep and sharp. "My mother lasted three years. She fell in love with another archer, and all went well until she ran out of Wild Carrot Oil in one of the Endless Forests and became pregnant with me. Women with babes can't roam through the woods with nothing but a dozen arrows in hand. Infants are unpredictable. They cry and startle prey. They remind wanderlusting men of homes and settled life. The Quicks kicked her out faster than they let her in.

Her time with them haunted her until her death—she ached to return to the forest."

I stared at Ovie, a bit stunned. She rarely spoke, and never for so long.

Juniper rose from the ground, done praying. I pulled out my flask of *Vite* and passed it around as we waited for the Sea Witch's decision.

She took a long drink of the fire liquor and then looked at me. "Jarl Roth is a man in need of heroes. We go west."

Runa swore.

Ovie nodded.

I smiled.

Heroes in the Vorse sagas like to seal a promise with blood. I grabbed the blade from its strap across my right calf and slashed my palm, deep enough for the blood to ooze.

"The four of us will go to Blue Vee and fight this beast," I said. "If we survive, we will take the gold and do whatever we please with the rest of our lives. We will be as free as any woman in Vorseland. I swear it on Siggy's flaming pyre."

I closed my fist and let the blood drip through my fingers as Ovie had done with the snow.

Trigve and I sat up late by the flames that night, talking softly while the others slept—something we'd done often in the seven months he'd traveled with us.

"So we go west." Trigve touched the edge of my cloak, rubbing his thumb along one of the feathers.

"Yes."

I squeezed my hand into a fist, felt the cut sting my palm. I reached up and unhooked the pewter clasp at my throat, just as Runa had done earlier, and let my cloak slide to the ground. I felt lighter suddenly.

Trigve threw his fur over both of our shoulders. We sat hip to hip, arm to arm, the dying fire making our cheeks glow. He'd been with us less than a year, but I knew his body like my own, through and through, blood and bones.

I looked out across the field. The snow had stopped, and the moon was bright. The night was no longer black, but a vivid midnight blue. A few more weeks of warmth, and then the snow would come for good. The easy days of green leaves and balmy breezes and plenty of food were behind us. Warm skin, deep skies, long days ending in lingering twilights . . . It would all fade into memory after the first few snowfalls.

I held up my hands and turned them back and forth in front of the fire. They were free of the marks of a settled woman: no burns from scalding laundry, no creases of dirt from a garden, no bruises from a butter churn, no calluses from cleaning stables, kitchens, floors. My palms looked . . . innocent. All the spilled blood hadn't left a trace.

I realized suddenly what day it was. I twisted to the left and looked at Trigve. "I will be seventeen tomorrow. I'm the age my mother was when I was born." I paused. "That must be why my voice is starting to sound like hers in my ears."

Trigve pulled one knee up, and his thigh brushed against mine. "You were born in the autumn?"

"Yes, on the night of our village's Lion Star festival."

Trigve's eyes went soft and distant, as they often did when he thought of books and ancient stories. "Many of the old sagas speak of lions. Our Vorse ancestors brought back tales of the great beasts from faraway lands."

I nodded. I'd glimpsed the creatures on tapestries, yellow fur, mouths open wide, white teeth sharp and bright. Ergill in *Ergill's Saga* had compared their roar to the growl of wolves and the sound of thunder.

"Siggy used to say I was a Lion-child and roaring was in my blood."

Trigve smiled. "Your old Mercy mentor was right." He reached up and started loosening my hair from its thick silver braid.

I'd kept my hair tied back ever since I walked away from a Mercy-kill with the ends of my locks dripping blood. But Trigve always freed his hair at night—he said he liked to feel the wind on it.

"Which one of your parents gave you this?"

"My father was a typical blond Vorse, but my mother was born into a family of nomadic Relic Hunters from Finnmark. She was my age when their band went south on the hunt for ancient artifacts. She met my father at a Night Market, fell in love, and stayed behind." I leaned my head back, into Trigve's hand. "She gave me her looks, and her height, and her hair the color of the winter moon."

My mother never spoke of her days with the Hunters, and my father never asked. I'd long wished I knew something about her family. Perhaps I even had kin in Finnmark. It was something I dwelled on late at night.

"Trigve?"

"Yes?"

"Are you going to leave us, now that winter is drawing near? Wouldn't you prefer a settled life of honorable trade in some Vorse village, a warm roof over your head during the long, cold nights?" I paused. "If you're planning to go soon, tell me straight. Don't linger over it."

Trigve stared at the fire, and didn't answer.

Young men were often taken into service at the Great Halls. Or they could seek apprenticeships with a village tradesman, like the blacksmith, if they looked strong enough—which Trigve did, now that he'd been eating his fill of roast rabbit every night.

Every morning I waited for Trigve to wake up, turn to me, and say he was leaving. Men didn't travel with Mercies. It made them uncomfortable, the way we killed: no glory, nothing conquered, no riches, just quiet and swift, take the few coins, and leave. But the weeks passed, and Trigve didn't move on. He never even mentioned it.

"You gave him his life-spark back," Juniper said to me, not

long after Trigve had joined us. She pressed her palms together and blew over her right shoulder, lips pursed, in the way of the witches when they set a wish out on the air. "And it's a good thing he's with us. The wind whispers a story to me of four girls and one dark-haired boy."

The fire popped and crackled as a log crumbled into ash. I leaned my shoulder into Trigve's, and shifted closer into his side.

His green eyes fell on me. "Do you want me to leave, Frey?"

"No," I said, quickly. "Never. But men don't travel with the Mercies, not for long. Some Mercies take lovers for a while—it is always temporary. The other girls have said nothing about your coming with us, but this can't last forever. I know it can't."

My voice had gotten louder as I talked, enough to make Juniper shift in her sleep and Ovie open that one blue eye of hers. She glanced over at Trigve, then back to me, and then shut her eye again.

Trigve took a breath and let it out slowly. He spread his palm across the back of my neck, then wove his fingers into the roots of my hair and gave it a gentle tug. "Remember that day last winter when you found me in the snow?"

FIVE

The first time I saw Trigve Lothe, he was sitting in the snow, next to a dead horse, on the outskirts of a dead village.

The snow sickness struck some poor town or two each year, killing humans and animals both. It would appear soon after a snowfall, sweep through, and then vanish until the next year, the next village, the next snow. Some lived, most died.

People liked to whisper that the snow sickness was a curse from the Sea Witches, but that's as far as they went. They might burn witches in other places, but not in Vorseland.

We had been on our way to the town of Kragen, following a rumor. A serving girl at the Crossroads Inn told us of an old, rich widower who had married a young, beautiful girl a few years past. Now he was ailing, and had been for months. We were going to present ourselves to the fair bride and see if she took the bait. We didn't usually go searching for customers, but the winter had been long—it had taken many people who should have been ours.

We had planned to cross through the village of Dorrit and stop at the tavern, giving us a chance to fill our bellies and get warm by the fire. Snow had come in the night, and we were cold to the bone.

"Something's wrong," Ovie said when we were still several yards from the edge of the town.

I nodded. "Everything is too quiet. Too still."

I slowed my steps, and the rest followed.

We reached the short, three-foot stone wall that surrounded the huts in a lopsided circle, and the four of us simply stood there, gazing across the white drifts, wondering whether we should enter.

Dorrit was a place like any other. It consisted of a dozen arched huts, covered in thatch. Round wooden shields were the only spark of color to break up the long stretch of white—the shields were a remembrance of the dead, and they hung on the sides of most Vorse homes, red, blue, white, green, black. I spotted the graceful curves of an abandoned longboat poking out of the snow—each village in Vorseland used to build and maintain its own ship, which the men would then use during the raiding season in spring. They would drag their boats to the broad Black Knife River, thick ropes taut against strong backs, and from there they would sail to the Quell Sea. But the golden age of the Red Sky Raids had ended thirty years ago, and most ships were like this now, unused and rotting.

The snow had stopped falling, which meant the sickness was

past. Still, we hesitated, watching for signs of life and pointing out the bodies of the dead.

The corpse of a young man, crumpled on the ground near a tall, simple statue of the battle god, Nor.

An older woman with a frozen infant in her arms, slouched in the snow with her back to a juniper tree.

A girl, collapsed by the well, curled into a fetal position. The snow was blinding under the morning sun, and at first I'd taken her for a shadow. But a cloud came up, and I saw her clearly, red hair bright against the fresh white flakes.

The Sea Witch touched the tips of her fingers to her lips, then heart. "I wish them all a quick journey to Holhalla."

A dog's howl broke the silence, and I flinched.

Runa turned and glanced at me over her shoulder. "This is an opportunity, Frey."

By this she meant that she wanted to ransack some of the houses for food and coin. The quiet homes, where everyone had died.

For all that I dealt in death, I had no desire to go among the dead, to see the victims blue with frost, expressions of pain frozen on their faces. Besides, it was the right of the Gothi nuns to go through and take what was left after they burned the dead. That was how it was done.

Runa scanned the horizon, hand to her forehead. "It won't take long. I can have this town searched before noon."

I opened my mouth, ready to argue—

And caught a flicker of movement off to the right, a bit of dark shifting in the white snow.

A young man was sitting at the far end of the village near a turned-over caravan, his back against a dead Iber horse. And he was alive.

A wind gusted through the trees, shaking the nearby pine needles in an eerie, omniscient way. It had been a calm morning up until then, no breeze, complete stillness. I heard Juniper draw in her breath—rogue winds were a sign that the gods were watching, according to the Sea Witches.

I went over to the man and knelt. He was young. My age, maybe. He had long hair, tied back, and ink-stained fingertips.

"You live," I said.

"Yes," he answered, not looking at me.

"I'm Frey." I pulled off a thick wool glove and pressed my bare palm to his cheek. It was icy cold.

"I'm Trigve Lothe." His eyes met mine now, and they were green, green like unripe juniper berries rolled between your hands until they shine. He didn't flinch at the sight of a Boneless Mercy, didn't jerk away from my touch.

I stood, and he stood, too, slowly, his limbs frozen and stiff. Snow fell from his body and drifted to the ground. He pounded his fists on his thighs to bring the blood back, then glanced over my shoulder at the other Mercies. "Where are you headed?"

"Anywhere," I said. "Everywhere."

"Can I join you?"

I didn't bother to ask the other Mercies. Runa would say no and Juniper would say yes and Ovie would say nothing at all.

"You can," I replied.

He nodded, then walked around to the other side of the caravan. He yanked on the door. It swung open and hit a pile of snow. I put my hands on my knees, crouched down, and looked inside. I saw velvet cushions and carved wooden panels. I saw a man in a red cloak, face contorted, limbs twisted.

Trigve dropped to his knees and crawled over the dead man, into the capsized caravan. When he came back out, he was holding a leather satchel and a thick wolf pelt. He threw the satchel over one shoulder, and the pelt over the other.

"Let's go," he said. "There's nothing left for me here."

Trigve followed us to the edge of the Seeth Forest, one mile, almost two, across snowy, raven-filled meadows, the road dipping down into a gully, back up again, northern spruce spreading out before us like a dark green ocean. We reached the large, thick-timbered home of the young wife with the rich, ailing husband. Trigve said nothing when I knocked, and she let us in. Said nothing when she looked at our black Mercy-cloaks and flinched. Said nothing when she showed us through the Great Hall, past two wide-eyed servants, up a flight of stairs to her husband's bed.

The young wife was beautiful, as the girl at the inn had said. Soft curves, deep brown eyes, full cheeks, lustrous brown hair.

She put her hand on her husband's shoulder, and his eyes opened.

The man's face was pinched with pain, but he was handsome still, despite his age. Thick beard, dark eyes. They looked at each other for a long moment, and I could see then that she loved him. This was a true Mercy-kill.

"Poison," she whispered.

I pulled the vial of blue liquid from the leather pouch at my waist and held it up. She nodded, one jerk of her chin. We didn't use Blue Seed often. It was expensive, whereas Ovie's steel was cheap.

When Ovie realized she wasn't needed, she turned and left without a word. Runa edged back into the corner shadows to watch. Juniper went to the bride, took her hand, stood on tiptoe, and whispered a witch prayer in her ear.

Trigve went to the bed. He slid his arm underneath the man's back, helped him rise into a sitting position, and then nodded at me as if he'd always done this, as if he'd never done anything else.

The man reached a shriveled arm out and took the vial from me. He drank it in one quick toss, head back, eyes closed. And in that gesture, I saw the man he'd been. I saw battles fought and won. I saw feasts in front of fires. I saw tender nights under furs, silken girls at his side. I saw laughter and anger and lust and grief and glory.

I saw the life I wanted.

Afterward, Juniper prayed over the body, her small arms sweeping up and down the bed, preparing the man's spirit for Holhalla.

The wife paid us well, and we bought ourselves a room at a nearby inn that night. We had venison and bread in front of a bright fire. Trigve ate and ate and ate, and then we all got drunk on Cloudberry Mead. Later we crawled up the rickety stairs and stumbled into our room. Runa curled up by herself in the corner, which left three Mercies and one bed. We tucked ourselves in and squeezed, tiny Juniper in the middle.

Trigve threw his wolf fur down on the floor by my side of the bed. And later, when we both lay awake, chasing sleep, he reached his hand up, and I took it in mine.

"Yes, Trigve," I said. "I remember that day in Dorrit."

"Would you like to know how I ended up there?"

I nodded.

"It involves a girl."

"Ah. What was her name?"

"Lilas."

"Go on," I replied a few moments later, when he stayed quiet.

Trigve's eyes met mine. "Lilas was sixteen when her parents were drowned on the Quell Sea during a winter storm. She gathered all the coin her parents had saved and made her way across the islands. She made a donation to Obin and entered a convent in Stroth. Lilas began training in the way of the Gothi nuns and was content. Until Jarl Keld caught a glimpse of her during a solstice ritual.

"Keld bought her life a few months later. The Gothi soothsayer I was apprenticed to—a man named Lars—was sent to fetch the girl and bring her to the temple so her life could be offered to the god Forset at dawn. So we fetched her."

"I hate these Gothi sacrifices," I said loudly. Juniper stirred in her sleep again.

Trigve sighed. "Yes. Lilas was a pawn for jarls and mystics, her life worth less than a prayer. But these sacrifices are the old way. They will not last much longer."

"What happened?" I knew this story would not end well.

"Lilas traveled with us for seven days, and we grew close. She was passionate and bright and full of life." He paused. "Lars had been bartering prayers for goods on our journey, and one day a farmer gave him a home-brewed bottle of apple *Vite*. That night, Lars got drunk. He was a violent drinker, and we left him alone to sleep it off. Lilas and I wandered into the village."

Trigve looked away, toward the fire, the shadows cutting across his face. I turned and kicked another log into the flames.

"We spent the night together in a bed at the inn, Frey."

I raised my eyebrows. The nuns for the Gothi sacrifices need to be untouched by man, and the world, or the god will reject the prayer and bring misfortune. Everyone knew this.

"Lars beat me when we returned to the caravan, but he beat

her worse." Trigve reached toward me again, fingers sliding through my silver hair. "He kicked her in the ribs as she crouched between the soothsayer's bed and a small wooden table. I put my hand around his red fleshy neck and strangled him with his own leather belt. The caravan was too small for him to turn around, to throw me off. He fell to his knees, and I fell with him."

Trigve paused. "Afterward, we went back to the inn and planned our future. We were going to head south—I wanted to study with the Orate Healers on the island of Santor, and she wanted a little farm by the sea.

"I woke up that night with Lilas sweating in my arms. The snow sickness came and went. She died. I placed her by a group of yew trees on the other side of the village, where the Gothi nuns would find her. When I returned to the caravan, it was overturned, the horse dead."

"I'm sorry, Trigve," I said. Compassion is best when given straight and simple.

He rubbed his hand along his jaw, where a dark stubble was setting in. "The punishment for killing a soothsayer is *vivisepulture*, which means I would have been buried alive if caught. The snow sickness hid my crime, for the nuns don't speak, and everyone else in the village was either dead or grieving. Yet I felt no relief at my narrow escape. I felt nothing. Hours passed, and I didn't move. I was slowly freezing to death."

"Why did you just stay there, among all the dead?"

"I don't know. I didn't have it in me to move on. I couldn't find the will to make a choice, to get up, to leave."

He wasn't ashamed, saying this.

The woman in black silk had been filled with this lethargy, too. Juniper called such people life-cold and said their spark was buried deep in snow that never melted.

"You brought me back," Trigve said. "I had nothing . . . And then suddenly you were there."

I was quiet for a while, thinking on his story. I pushed another log into the fire with the toe of my boot, nuzzling it into the embers. "Trigve?"

"Yes?"

"What do you think it is, this beast?"

He ran his thumb over an old bloodstain on the side of my brown tunic. "Perhaps it's a Giantine Wolf come down from the far north."

"Aren't the Giantine Wolves ignored in the Anglon Mystic books, along with trolls?"

The corners of Trigve's eyes creased, and he smiled. "A few of the wolves are supposed to be left, up in the Wild Ice Plains and the Faroe Glaciers. It's possible that a lone wolf began ranging south and started terrorizing Blue Vee. It could have caught a tundra virus and gone rabid. It hasn't happened in three hundred years or so, but it's possible."

I thought about this for a moment, and then shook my head. "Wolves, even rabid Giantine Wolves . . . They are predictable.

They have patterns. This beast feels different. Juniper would say that my heart is trying to tell me something and that I should listen to the beats. These regular attacks on Roth's villages feel like . . . vengeance."

I ran my fingertips over the tender slice across my left palm. I pressed in until I felt a sharp ache shoot down my wrist.

My band of Boneless Mercies might defeat an animal, no matter how big or rabid, but revenge belonged to something more . . . *human*.

"Juniper would not have agreed to go unless she also believed we had a fighting chance."

Trigve nodded. "True."

I turned to him and put my hands on his arms, my thumbs in the hollows of his inner elbows. "If we die in Blue Vee, then it will be a good death—a warrior's death. It is every Vorse warrior's wish to die with a blade in hand. It is my wish, as well."

We fell asleep that night, bodies wrapped together. Juniper and Ovie had to nestle into each other, instead of me.

I woke at dawn, the sunrise tickling my skin. I whispered Trigve's name. His eyelids fluttered, but he kept sleeping. Ovie smelled of snow, but Trigve smelled faintly of sweet green herbs. I breathed in, long and slow, then yawned and watched the orange-and-pink-smudged sky.

I was seventeen.

I would not die like my parents, and like Lilas, shivering and sweating in some godforsaken Vorse village. I would not have my corpse found by Gothi nuns and burned by strangers.

I would try my hand at greatness, and see where it led.

Glory.

I wanted to touch it. Taste it. I wanted it so deeply I thought my heart would swell up, claw its way out of me, and float away on the wind, cawing like a Sea Witch raven, a prayer caught in its beak.

I would travel to Blue Vee and fight the beast. And I would likely die, like all the rest. But it was a step toward the light. I would not quietly fade, lost to time, as all the Mercies had before me, throughout the countless years since the Witch Wars.

I would be remembered.

SIX

T*he morning of my seventeenth birthday was clear and cool, the* bright sun quickly melting all the snow from the night before.

Trigve was off, looking for the last of the summer blackberries—he wanted to find me a handful for my birthday. I sat on the brown-gray stump of a fallen tree near the fire and watched the sky. I looked for the witch signs Juniper had taught me—warnings of dangers up ahead, of perils on the horizon. But I saw no odd-shaped clouds, no group of crows on the wing, no eerie gusts of wind, no ominous shimmer of mist rising off the trees.

Juniper's pale sea-green hair shimmered in the sun as she poured steaming roasted chicory tea into the wooden mug we all shared. She handed me the cup, and I took a sip, smiling as the comforting, earthy brew slid down my throat.

Ovie sat down next to me on the log, knee touching mine. I passed her the tea, and she gave me a nod of thanks.

Even Runa seemed at ease, her eyes narrowed under the

bright sky. She stretched, her long arms reaching up. "This morning I am happy to be alive. I can't remember the last time I felt this."

Ovie glanced at Runa and smiled. She rarely smiled, but when she did, it stirred my heart.

Ovie was a follower of the old Vorse ways. She was stoic, and philosophical, and I admired her for it. Though, in contrast to her silence, or perhaps because of it, she held a deep attachment to the sagas, to all the old stories, told around the fire.

A crow cawed overhead. I shaded my eyes with one hand and squinted against the sunshine. It was sitting on the top branch of a tall pine.

"Crows are lucky," Juniper said, as if reading my mind. She took the mug from Ovie, held it between her small palms, and looked at me.

"Crows are messengers of the dead," Runa said, the old snap back in her voice.

Juniper tilted her head to the side, and an expression of yearning passed over her face. "Frey, we will pass the Merrows on our way to Blue Vee. We could visit the Sea Witches and get their blessing."

I stood and put my arm around Juniper. "Yes, we will stay a night in the Merrows. The witches may be able to help us—they might know more of this beast and how to kill it. It's worth the delay, though we need to get to Blue Vee before the first winter storm. The Red Willow Marsh will be hard enough to cross without hunting for the path under snow."

Runa's eyes met mine. "Either way, we risk stumbling upon the Cut-Queen's hidden reed-village and ending up tortured until we convert. Or worse."

I held up a hand. "For all we know, the Cut-Queen's followers have already mutinied and drowned her in her own marsh. I will not let you quell our nerve, Runa. Not on a morning as beautiful as this."

I turned to Ovie. She was still sitting on the spruce log, feet in the tall grass, elbows on her knees. "You've been quiet. Do you share Runa's fear of the Cut-Queen?"

Ovie ran her fingers over the hilt of the knife strapped to her ribs. "Yes. But that which doesn't kill us will make us stronger." She stood and put her hand on Runa's shoulder. "If we survive the marsh, then we will have reached the border of Blue Vee, and whatever happens next we will at least be able to feast and sleep in a jarl's Great Hall as winter sets in. We'll spend our nights warm, satiated, and in new company. Focus on this when the fear hits you, Runa."

I caught sight of Trigve over Runa's shoulder and nodded at him. He nodded back, the sun catching the green in his eyes. He set a handful of ink-colored berries on the log and came to my side. The five of us formed a half circle, there in front of the troll-stone, me at the center.

"Today begins our quest to slay the Blue Vee Beast." I put my fist to my heart and let my voice ring out strong into the morning air. "Let the gods see what we can do with a real foe—one that isn't old or heartbroken or diseased. We do this because we can. We do it because it's never been done before."

"Leap of faith." Juniper turned her face to the sky. "The gods will look favorably on this."

She chanted a prayer, one of the swift ones that praised earth, air, water, and fire. Then she reached into her pocket and took out her short dagger. She held out her left palm and made a shallow cut, echoing what I'd done the night before.

"Give me your hand, Frey." She recut my wound and pressed her bloody palm to mine. "There. It's done."

Runa took the knife and cut her palm. And then Ovie. Each pressed her hand to mine.

"Leap of faith," Runa said.

"Leap of faith," Ovie said.

Trigve was the last. I handed him Juniper's blade. He slashed his skin and pressed his warm palm to mine. "Leap of faith, Frey."

We traveled west under a vibrant sky that seemed to stretch all the way to Holhalla. Blue Vee was some hundred miles from Hail, in the Destin Lush Valley, which lay between the Quell Sea and the Skal Mountains. We'd be traveling for a few weeks, maybe more; we would make it to Blue Vee before it snowed, if the weather held.

My heart felt full, wide open, as if it had grown in the night, feasting on the promise of change. As Boneless Mercies, we'd traveled from village to village, always seeking work, no greater hope than quick deaths, a few coins, and a warm meal. Each band of Mercies had its own unofficial territory, one that criss-crossed a handful of jarldoms, and Siggy's was the mid-Borders. The High Jarl's realm sat farther east, but we'd never been there. We looped around our own region, hitting every village twice each year, and didn't stray far from this.

I was impatient to meet the Sea Witches and see where Juniper had come from, to see the Merrow sands, to set my eyes on the famous witch huts built into the branches of the Scorch Trees. Juniper's witches were Tree Witches as well as Sea Witches.

I was less eager to reach the Red Willow Marsh. We'd all heard the horrifying tales shared late at night in village inns across the Borders.

The Red Willow Marsh had always been a dangerous place. People slipped and disappeared in the mud between one heartbeat and the next. Jade-green marsh vipers slithered between white reeds, their bite bringing pain and possibly death. But within the last few years a hamlet had sprung up in the reeds as well, said to consist of all girls, led by a woman called the Cut-Queen.

The Cut-Queen's fervent worship of the goddess Fen made people shiver when they spoke of her. Made taverns filled with laughing, chattering people go silent at the sound of her name. The Blue Vee Beast was spoken of in bold, noble tones, like the ones used for the telling of the sagas . . . But the Cut-Queen was discussed in whispers. I'd seen scarred, battle-hardened warriors go quiet at the mention of the Woman in the Reeds.

We would try to pass through the marsh at night, unnoticed. I hoped to slip through and be long gone by sunrise, if luck was with us.

My boots parted thick, end-of-summer grass as we drifted over hills and past villages and farmsteads, the edges of my cloak soaking up the dew. We walked all day, not meeting a soul outside a young, dark-eyed shepherd who smiled sweetly at me despite my Mercy-cloak.

Juniper found the season's last lingonberries near a stream, and we ate them for dinner, along with a thick triangle of hard, nutty cheese.

There was a hum in the air that first night of our journey, a buzz of joy that emanated from each of us, even Runa.

I watched the Mercies as they ate, smiling to themselves around the fire. Was this how the Border warriors felt before they marched south to battle the Fremish? Was this what the raiders felt when they went to sea? Or the Quicks before entering one of the Seven Endless Forests?

We camped that night next to a thin, fast-flowing stream. There would be more and more of these little brooks as we went west, heading toward the Merrows and the sea.

I washed everyone's hair after dinner—Juniper, Ovie, Trigve, then Runa. I warmed ice-cold river water over the fire, and then used our wooden cup to pour it over their hair, lathering the soap between my palms and massaging it in until the suds were as thick as cream.

Some Boneless Mercies let themselves grow dirty and ragged, and that was their right. But we all washed with snow, when we had it, and if not, we'd find a stream. Trigve didn't bring death, like us Mercies, but he knew a bit of medicine, and he said keeping clean could keep us alive. Runa grumbled about it and said washing so often was a waste of time, but Runa grumbled about everything. Her grumbling was almost a comfort, steady and to be relied upon, like the sun coming up in the morning. And for all her talk, she secretly enjoyed it when I washed her hair, my fingers moving through her straight black mane, her pretty, scowling face pointed up at the night sky.

Juniper talked quietly of easy, pleasant things when I washed her hair. Trigve told me tales from the Anglon Mystic books. Ovie said nothing at all.

Afterward, Trigve offered to do my hair, and I let him. I sighed as he rubbed his fingers into my scalp. My shoulders melted. My heart slowed.

Juniper joined me later as I sat by the fire, waiting for my hair to dry before I went to sleep.

"Hold out your hand, Frey."

I did, and she slipped something into my palm. I glanced down at the small green vial that sat nestled in the hollow of my hand, then popped the cork and sniffed.

"Jasmine." I inhaled again, deeply. "Where did you get this?"

Juniper smiled her witch-smile, and her gray eyes danced. "I stole it from the perfumery in Hail. Happy birthday, Frey."

I heard Trigve laugh behind me. Juniper's light fingers and shameless thieving amused him.

"I hope you were careful." I dabbed the exotic, floral scent up my forearms. "I worry about you, Juniper. As far as I know, Keld is still the jarl of Hail and all else near here. He worships Forset, and you will lose a finger if you're caught."

"I won't be caught." Juniper ran her palms down her curls, which had grown bigger and thicker as they dried. "I don't steal anything that will be missed."

Runa knelt beside me and Juniper, her eyes on mine. "I have a gift for you, as well. Take it, or don't, makes no difference to me."

I took the gift. It was a finely braided leather strap to tie back my hair. I leaned forward and grabbed both girls in my arms. Juniper sank into my side, and Runa stiffened, but then relaxed a moment later.

"I also got you a present." Ovie crept out of the darkness, back from checking her traps. She was carrying a dead rabbit in one hand, fist clenched around his fuzzy gray ears.

I smiled. "Food for tomorrow's stew?"

"No. Something far better."

Ovie reached into her pocket and pulled out five small, pretty mushrooms with spotted red-and-white tops. She smiled, and her blue eye twinkled. "Sly Barbaric Mushrooms. I found them in a small patch of woods near here. How about we celebrate your birthday and the end of the death trade in the way of the witches?"

The Sly Barbaric Mushroom was rare in Vorseland, but well-known because it appeared in many of our stories, usually the ones about magic.

In a high enough concentration, the mushroom worked as a poison, much like Blue Seed. In the poem "The Fevered Mother," a wicked woman named Else killed her twelve children by feeding them a Sly Barbaric Mushroom soup.

But the mushrooms were also used as a drug. The hero of *Blood Song* took a mushroom before battle and defeated his enemies in a dream. And the young seer in *Twilight Comes the End* ate a Sly Barbaric and gave his people a prophecy that led to war.

Yet the mushroom was most famous for an old song about the Sea Witches, called "Witch on the Fly." The song said the mushroom gave the witches wings.

Juniper began to whisper the lyrics as I reached forward and took the largest mushroom from Ovie.

"The witches dined on the red-and-white Sly,

Grew black wings and soared up high,

Sailed through the clouds, and scraped the sky,

Witch on the fly, witch on the fly . . ."

We all said the last line together, in unison.

I ran my thumb over the top of the mushroom, tracing a path around the white spots. "Shall we eat these mushrooms and dance for luck tonight under the autumn moon?"

Ovie popped one in her mouth. Then Runa. Trigve and I ate ours together. He chose the smallest, giving me a wink as he plucked it from Ovie's palm. He chewed. I chewed. The mushroom tasted nutty, with a bittersweet aftertaste that hinted at the night to come.

Juniper went last. She laughed, and took the last mushroom from Ovie. "Let's fly, Mercies."

Nothing happened at first. Time passed slowly, like clouds gliding across the moon.

We were all piled together in front of the fire, even Runa. I felt languid . . . smooth and slow and tired, but not sleepy. I could smell the nearby stream, the clean, earth-and-stone scent of the water misting into the air. I turned my head and buried my face in Juniper's curls. Ovie's head was in my lap, and Runa's head was in hers, and Trigve was sprawled on his side in the middle of us all. I touched the strap of Ovie's leather eye patch. I undid her braids, one by one, and let her blue-tipped hair spill across my legs.

Juniper whispered something into the empty night air, and Runa stared at the stars.

The tingling started in my fingertips, ran up my hands and

arms, down my torso, down my legs. It felt good, instinctual, like getting warm after being cold, like eating after going hungry.

I lazily untangled myself from the girls, limbs falling away, strands of hair sliding past my skin. I rose to my feet, and one by one they followed. I felt fingers press into mine, and a gentle tugging on my arms. We all held hands in a circle around the fire.

I looked up, and the night sky *melted*, fell down on my face like a soft black cloak, a Mercy-cloak, the edges fluttering around me like the Iber woman's silk dress.

We started moving around the flames, long hair rippling down our backs. Juniper chanted and Runa whispered and Trigve sang one of the old songs, throaty and low. I could feel Ovie's breath on my cheek, though her lips were closed.

When our feet left the ground, it felt as familiar and safe as falling asleep. I arched upward, chest out, head tilted back. Up and up.

My heart hit the moon.

Trigve squeezed my hand. I felt his leg against mine, my elbow at his hip, his long hair whipping in the wind, mingling with mine. We rose higher and higher and higher.

I closed my eyes, raised my arms, and *screamed*.

It wasn't a scream of fear.

It was a scream of *blood*. Of slicing. Of skin and meat and bone. I felt the heft of a blade in my palm, slick with sweat. I smelled salt and pine resin and death. I looked down and saw a field of blood-soaked grass, a battlefield, corpses at my feet . . .

I screamed again and felt the blackness of the sky cut me open like a knife.

Juniper was screaming now, too, "*Nante, nante*," a Sea Witch word to cast off the dark, "*nante*, *nante*, *nante*—"

The stars screamed back at us, a thousand whispery wails.

Then . . . silence.

We began to sink, sliding down the night sky like silvery moons. The stars watched us as we slid, hundreds of twinkling little eyes.

Down, down, down.

We fell back into a pile by the fire, limbs and hair and skin and bones, all woven together, a tapestry of Mercies.

"*Nante*," Juniper whispered again as we drifted into sleep. "*Nante.*"

SEVEN

H*ow long do you think she's been hanging there?" I shielded my* eyes from the sun and stared up at the thick, dead tree.

"Two days, maybe three." Trigve stood at my right shoulder, back straight, expression grim.

I slid my dagger from its sheath on my calf. "We're cutting her down."

Ovie yanked her own knife from the leather straps around her ribs. "I'll do it. I'm the best climber."

We were at the Levin crossroads, a mile from town. Many crossroads in Vorseland had a hangman's tree, and this one was no different. The younger jarls now preferred skin-fights and trial by combat, but a few of the older leaders still used the trees.

The hanged girl had straight blond hair and wore a simple blue tunic. Her dangling bare feet betrayed her youth. Smooth skin, no calluses.

Juniper reached into one of her many pockets and pulled out a small piece of wood. "I'll pray."

The wood was Heart Ash—a mystical tree that grew in Iber. The Sea Witches believed it chased demons away from the dead. Runa threw Juniper the flint box, and the Sea Witch lit the incense until it smoked, wisps drifting up the poor girl's legs.

Ovie faced me and put her hands on my shoulders. I cupped her right foot in my palms and hoisted her into the air. Her arms wrapped around the gray trunk, and she shimmied up the tree, stretching out on the thick branch, crawling toward the noose, dagger ready.

Runa and I caught the hanged girl as she fell. We laid her gently on the ground. Juniper fell to her knees at the girl's side and waved the incense over her body.

"Frey." Trigve's voice was low with warning. "Someone is bound to wander by soon. What do you plan to do now that you've cut this girl down? She was left here for a reason."

"I know." I straightened and stared down each of the roads, squinting in the light. "We can't burn her. The fire will be seen."

Ovie pulled the cloth away from the girl's neck and showed us the skin underneath. The dead girl had been branded, a small circle with two lines slashed through it. This was a mark given to someone who had disobeyed a jarl's laws—oath-breaking, theft, arson, or murder.

Juniper looked up from the white-gray curls of incense smoke. "I suppose that's why they killed her."

I sighed. "Who knows why they killed her. Or left her hanging here. Brutes."

"Hurry, Frey." Trigve was staring down the main road toward Levin. "You need to make a decision."

And just as he said it, I heard hooves on packed dirt.

Men on horses meant wealth.

The shaggy Ice Horses of Vorseland were small and swift, large enough to carry children but not grown men. Only the wealthiest Vorse men could afford the tall, sleek horses from Iber—jarls, and perhaps the occasional soothsayer.

"They are coming," Juniper whispered. "Fast."

Runa gripped my shoulder, and I turned. She pointed her thumb at a small wooden marker near a dark lane lined with yew trees. "If that leads to what I think it does, we can bury her there."

The marker bore a carved face peering out between leaves and vines—the Green Woman. There was an Elsh graveyard nearby.

I nodded. "Good idea, Runa. And hurry."

Runa leaned down and picked up the dead girl, one arm under her neck, one under her knees. She gasped as she lifted her, shifted the body in her arms, and started down the lane, the tips of the hanged girl's hair kissing the earth as she walked.

We followed, quickly putting the twisting yew trees between us and the road, the autumn leaves hiding us from view.

I heard the men pass by a few moments later, but they didn't stop. My shoulders relaxed.

The lane was overgrown, neglected, unused. It opened up

after a half mile and began to wind through a small, fallow field, the clouds casting shadows across the rows of plowed earth.

The only sound was the crisp chirping of a willow warbler and the rustle of Runa's feet on the path, slow and heavy with the weight of the body.

Trigve and Juniper had brewed a special dandelion tea that morning to help us purge the last of the mushroom poison. We'd all woken up with a headache, except Juniper—she had eaten Sly Barbaric Mushrooms before, during her days with the witches.

Juniper had spent the morning watching the sky, expression thoughtful. "Five people dreaming the very same dream, one of flying and battle and blood—it's significant. It happens among the Sea Witches sometimes." Juniper sipped the dandelion tea, swallowed, and then traced her fingers lightly down her throat as if willing it to move faster. "When a group of us had the same dream, Mother Hush would always want to hear about it. Prophecies come like waves, some fierce and white-capped like a winter storm, and some small and soft, a gentle lick upon the sand. Group dreaming leads to fierce visions. It usually signifies the first step down a hard path."

Runa had just laughed. "Five people and five mushrooms will lead to all sorts of mischief."

"Quiet, Runa." My head was pounding, and her laughter made it worse. Trigve gave me the tea, and I drank deeply.

"A hard path is not always a bad thing." Ovie rubbed her palm over her missing eye. "Who knows what we will learn. All knowledge is useful."

The willow warbler began his cheerful song again, the notes soaring across the empty field. I looked over my shoulder. Ovie's cheeks were pink in the hot sun. Runa was grimacing, her feet kicking up clods of dirt with each step. There was no shade now, and we were all hot and still feeling the effects of the night before. The tea had helped my headache, but my muscles ached, as if bruised.

Runa shifted the girl again. Sweat was dripping down her face.

Trigve glanced at her, brow furrowed. "Let me take her for a while, Runa."

She shook her head. "If a man has hanged a woman," she said, "then it's a woman who should carry her body. I will do this alone."

We were almost to the copse of trees when Runa began to breathe heavily. She was strong, stronger than all of us, but carrying the deadweight of a hanged girl for half a mile was no small feat.

We reached the graveyard at last. We all stood still for a moment, none of us wanting to take the first step, walk past the first dark line of simple stone markers.

We were unfamiliar with cemeteries. They seemed wrong and unnatural . . . all the bones beneath our feet, the spirits stuck there, unable to rise to Holhalla.

There had been a battle here in this hollow long ago, Vorse

against the Green Women warriors from across the Quell Sea. We'd all heard the bards sing "Fire and Earth," the song of Levin and the ancient battle fought at dawn on a cold spring morning. The Green Women lost but were fearless in battle and valiant in defeat. They were given a plot of land to bury their dead, to send them back to the earth, as their gods commanded.

The Vorse burned their own dead nearby. Fire and smoke and shovels and dirt. This was how battles really end.

The Green Women had almost entirely passed out of Vorse memory, forgotten except for a song. But many had once thrived in northern Elshland, in a stretch of hills called the Strange. I'd never been there. Few Vorse had. It was a wild place, according to the song. A place where women once fought, and women once ruled. The ballad said the Stranger Hills were so high the clouds stroked the women's cheeks as they passed by.

I'd thought about that line often, when watching the sky.

I'd seen a tapestry of the Green Women once, last winter, in the home of a wealthy, dying widow. It had hung across one wall near a roaring hearth, and it showed a battle scene—the Green Women jumping through the air, attacking fur-clad men, swirling green tattoos up their arms and across their chests.

Something about those women had struck a chord in me.

Juniper had said it was one of the gods of fate plucking my life-strings. Meaning my path would lead me to the Strange someday, and the Green Women would play a part in my life somehow.

We dug a shallow grave for the branded girl in an empty corner near the trees. We had only our daggers and our hands, but the ground was soft from recent rain. Ovie found a large, flat stone to use as a makeshift shovel, and it worked well enough.

Afterward, we covered the top with small rocks to keep away the wolves. When it was done, Juniper knelt and said one of her witch prayers.

Runa's dark eyes met mine as we watched the Sea Witch pray. We'd left the death trade behind, and here we were, dealing with the dead again.

I wiped my dirty hands on my brown tunic, then stretched my aching back. I looked off into the distance, and my eyes caught movement—a father and a daughter, cutting barley in a nearby field, moving in a graceful rhythm.

I wondered if they had known the hanged girl. I supposed they had, in a village the size of Levin. I wondered if they had welcomed her execution or been grieved by it.

We ate a quick lunch of early-autumn apples and cheese, sitting between worn grave markers, faded symbols of the Green Women carved on each. Trigve kept an eye on the horizon, watching, watching.

Runa took a bite of apple, and then stood and rested her hand on the edge of a gravestone. "Frey, we need weapons for this journey. Not little Mercy-daggers."

It took a few moments for her meaning to dawn on me.

She began to rub her cheek with her palm, thinking. "This is the only graveyard on the western shore. We won't get another chance like this."

I nodded. "You're right. I thought I would ask Jarl Roth for weapons, if it came to that. But I'd much rather we had our own."

Ovie tilted her head to the side, hand on her knife. "Stealing from the dead is unlucky."

Juniper made a Sea Witch gesture, thumb touching forefinger—it meant "honorable theft," which was a concept she thoroughly embraced. "Runa is right, we do need real weapons. For the Red Willow Marsh, at the very least."

I looked at Trigve. "What do the Anglon Mystic books say about taking things from the dead?"

He shrugged. "Depends who's dead."

I sighed and rubbed the back of my neck. "Boneless Mercies don't steal from the dead, but we are no longer Mercies. Let's take the blades."

We once did a Mercy-kill for a Fremish family, not long after Siggy died. They had come over on a ship from Elshland and were working their way south. They were grave robbers, which was a common enough profession in Frem, almost as common as raiding used to be in Vorseland.

We met them on a hill near Nind. Midwinter, almost twilight. I knew where they hailed from as much for their soft, lilting accents as for the tiny silver owl icons they wore around their necks. Many of the Fremish wanderers worshipped a half-owl, half-human god named the Rover King—he was a nomadic deity and looked with favor on all unsettled people.

There were two older sisters in the family, and three boys younger than me, as well as the father, mother, and grandmother. They all had chestnut hair, but their eyes, down to the youngest, were a pale light blue, like Ovie's.

"You'll find no graves to steal from here in Vorseland." Runa leaned against a nearby juniper tree, black braid over her shoulder, black eyebrows in a scowl.

"We know." The mother's voice was elegant, the Fremish accent silky on her tongue. "We're just passing through. Grandmother here is too sick to carry on. Will you help us?"

I looked the grandmother up and down, my gaze catching on the woman's much-mended wool dress, fraying at the hems and covered in patches. "Can you pay?"

"Yes," she said. "But not much."

"Good enough." I went to the older woman. She was petite, lean, her back bent and twisted from a life spent digging. She had thick hair to her waist, still a deep brown, though dull with age. Her eyes were sad, but shrewd. She wasn't feeble, not in her mind.

Juniper gathered the grandchildren together and began to whisper a prayer.

I looked at Runa, and she turned her head away. I looked at

Ovie, and she nodded. I would take this one. I reached for the flask in my side pocket and gave it to the woman. She took a long drink of the fiery *Vite*, and then handed the flask back with a nod of her sharp chin.

Dying makes you thirsty.

I slid my hand behind the mark's neck. Her skin was as dry and thin as an autumn leaf. "Just relax, lamb." I put my other hand over her mouth and nose, and pressed in.

I stole her breath, as Siggy had taught me. There would be no blood. I could spare the family this, at least. The woman was weak and would not struggle. Much.

When it was done, I laid her on the ground near the juniper tree. The father had tears in his eyes, but the mother shed none.

I wondered if the Fremish woman had been fierce when she was young. Something told me she had. Something told me she'd lived a full life . . . a life with many crossroads and dark paths. And now it was over. Everything she was, everything she'd done—it would soon be forgotten, lost to time, just as the name of the Vorseland hill we stood on had been lost to all living memory.

I dug into the soil, deep and deeper. From Mercy to grave robber, in two short days. Dirt pressed into my fingernails, and rocks scraped my knuckles. My clothing was sweat- and earth-stained. But I liked this work. It was hard and real. I liked feeling the ground between my fingers. Feeling my muscles move under my skin.

Maybe I would have made a good farm woman after all.

I shook my head.

Never.

I never would have been satisfied with farming, chained to one place and one experience year after year.

I flinched and looked up at the sky.

The gods liked to humble people who dream big dreams.

It was late afternoon by the time we were done with the graves, each of us Mercies standing over a deep hole, dripping sweat. We blinked in the slanting sun and stared down at the bones of four Green Women warriors, jade-colored shields covering their torsos.

Their axes were buried beside them, as the song foretold. I knelt again, belly in the dirt. I slipped my soil-black fingers over earth and bone until I felt metal. I pulled the weapon free.

The ax was lighter than a typical Vorse battle-ax. Shorter, slimmer.

The four of us gathered in the middle of the cemetery to compare our finds. All of the short, curved blades were similar, bearing an etching of the leafy Green Woman on the hilt. Rubbed with oil, they would be as good as new.

Trigve declined to dig up his own ax, and I honored his wish. We pushed the dirt back over the bones of the ancient women warriors.

"The 'Fire and Earth' ballad mentions twelve women by name," I said. "Three who lived and nine who died. I like to think we are holding the blades of four women from the song. The four bravest, perhaps. The four fiercest. The four—"

Runa groaned. "Enough, Frey." She glanced at me, and then went back to pushing dirt.

Afterward, Juniper said a prayer of forgiveness for disturbing the warriors' peace, and I said a prayer of my own to Valkree—a silent wish to follow in the footsteps of Green Women, to use their sleek, lithe hatchets as they were intended to be used. To fight. To battle.

We walked back to the road as the early-autumn sun set behind us.

Four Boneless Mercies stood at a crossroads near a hangman's tree.

It was like something from a Vorse saga.

In their hands they held four weapons, freshly ripped from the grave.

I smiled.

EIGHT

I*'d heard that Sea Witches will often cast shells and read them like* runes, but I'd never seen Juniper do this in the year she'd been with us.

Two mornings after we buried the hanged girl, we were eating a breakfast of apples underneath an old oak tree when Juniper pulled out a deck of worn green cards. She moved her witch-hair behind her ears, whispered a prayer under her breath—one about twists and turns and crossroads—then shuffled the deck. She cut it and flipped over eight cards, laying them out in a straight row across a scattering of copper oak leaves.

"Are we going to gamble?" Runa asked, eyes twinkling.

Juniper smiled. "No. These are Merrow Cards. Every proper Sea Witch has a deck. They help us."

"Help you do what?" Trigve, curious as always, had risen to his feet and gone to Juniper's side.

"Divine the truth."

"So you are going to tell us our fate." Runa threw her apple core into a nearby stream and looked bored.

Fate. I hated that word.

Juniper shook her head. "No. I'm going to read the truth. That is all."

We all drew near then, even Runa, and watched over Juniper's shoulder as she pointed to each card and spoke its name.

The Wanderer.

The Hanged Woman.

The Leaf Witch.

The Red Seer.

The Bone Man.

Death.

The High Priestess, reversed.

The Blue Moon.

"What do they mean?" Ovie leaned over and ran her finger down the Bone Man, touching his red eyes and skeletal frame.

Juniper pointed to the first card again. "We are the Wanderers, starting down a new path." Her finger moved to the second card. "The Hanged Woman can mean many things, but in this case it is literal—the dead girl at the crossroads. She was important to our journey." Juniper picked up the third card and held it gently between her thumb and second finger. "The Leaf Witch is a spirit of the forest, of nature. It says we will be given everything we need on our travels."

I nodded and put my hand to the hilt of my ax, pressing it into my hip bone. I'd made a sheath of leather strips and rabbit fur and tied it to my waist. My ax was now hidden under my cloak, hilt at my thigh, and it could be drawn quickly, if needed. It worked so well that the other Mercies had soon followed my example and made their own sheaths. I smiled to see the other girls walking ahead, weapons at their hips. It gave me a feeling like pride, but sharper, and more violent.

"What about this one?" Runa picked up the Red Seer card. It showed a green-haired woman standing on white sand, a black tree in the background. "It looks evil."

"It's not." Juniper reached up and gently plucked the card out of Runa's hand. "It's about the Sea Witches."

"And what does it portend?" Runa leaned against a crook in the tree and crossed her arms.

Juniper shrugged. "I suppose we'll find out when we get to the Merrows."

Trigve picked up the next card. "And this one?"

"The Bone Man." Juniper drew a circular symbol in the air, something I'd seen her do before to ward off dark spirits. "If you're looking for an evil card, Runa, this is it."

"Does the Bone Man signify the Blue Vee Beast?" I asked.

Juniper shook her head. "This reading is only about our journey to Blue Vee. It doesn't show what will happen when we get there. The Bone Man is something malevolent, something dangerous that will block our path, come between us and our destination." She put her fingers on the next card. "Death. It could be literal, or it could merely mean the end of something, a path or a choice."

"And the High Priestess?" I nodded at the card, which showed a woman in a black robe, upside down.

The Sea Witch drew another circle in the air. "The High Priestess, reversed . . . This is tricky. We will meet someone who appears to be a mystical leader, or visionary, but she is dangerous and should not be trusted. We will need to be on guard."

"What about the Blue Moon?" The Blue Moon card disturbed me more than the Bone Man. There was something about the shaggy Giantine Wolf howling at the great blue-white orb in the sky . . . It was ominous. Foreboding.

Juniper shrugged. "The Blue Moon indicates shadows and choices unmade. Our path will fork many times, and our choices will decide the outcome. Nothing is written in the stars—our journey is our own."

We followed Juniper as we walked now—only she knew the secret way into the Merrows. The sun was hot over our heads—one last swan song of autumn warmth before winter set in and buried the world in cold and dark and snow.

Around noon, the Sea Witch turned off the main road and took a narrow path that skirted a small woodland. The path was almost invisible, barely more than a deer trail.

We were getting closer, closer to the witches, closer to the sea.

I imagined what the Merrows would be like as we moved

down the narrow trail. I'd never met another Sea Witch, only seen a few in passing at Night Markets. The witches rarely left the Merrows. Some of the sagas told of them and of their famous Scorch Trees, and it had sparked my interest long ago.

I wondered if the witches would be like Juniper—sweet and gentle, with keen hearts. Or perhaps they would be wise and impassive, like Ovie, eyes deep and mournful, their speech crawling with prayers.

By early afternoon we found ourselves tramping along a broad pasture, nearby cows grazing lazily on the last of the season's grass. The meadow was bordered on one side by a wide, rushing river. The water misted as the river churned over rocks and formed tiny, perfect rainbows in the sunlight.

"I've read that rainbows bridge the world of Vorse to the realm of the gods." Trigve nodded at the ribbon of colors spreading across the water.

"What nonsense," Runa answered with a laugh.

"Quiet, both of you." Ovie pointed up ahead. "Look."

Two Boneless Mercies were crouched beside the river. One of them was blond, dimpled, apple-cheeked. She was bent over, washing her hands. The second Mercy wore her black hair braided tight to her head and was clothed only in her gray linen shift—she was cleaning her tunic in the water. She was older, thirty at least, with thin, drawn lips and a bold look to her brown eyes.

We came closer. They nodded to us, and we nodded to them.

Though Mercies had their own territories, we were not competitive. It was a sisterhood more than anything. How could we be at odds with women who'd been forced to deal in the same dark trade as ourselves? Besides, our lives were lonely, and it was pleasant to talk to other Mercies. Most travelers we met on the road, whether they were farmers or traders or fisherwomen, flinched at the sight of our Mercy-cloaks and refused to meet our gaze.

The river was deep and cold and clear, sparkling happily in the bright sun. It was flanked by rowan trees—clusters of bright orange-red berries danced on their branches each time the wind blew.

Juniper walked to one of the trees and touched the bark. She ran her fingertips over a cluster of berries, then put two fingers to her lips and tilted her chin to the sky. She made a sweeping crescent shape with her right arm and blew over her shoulder.

The blond Mercy looked at me and raised her eyebrows.

"Rowan trees are sacred," I explained. "She asked the trees to protect this river."

The blond Mercy regarded Juniper for a moment, then laughed, a soft chuckle under her breath. "So she's a Sea Witch, then. How did she end up with you, dealing out death?"

I shrugged, then knelt and began to refill my leather pouch in the now-blessed river. I pressed the sack into the water and then shrank back when I saw a streak of red cutting through the flow.

I looked to the left. Blood was leeching into the river from the dark-haired Mercy's tunic. She gave me a frown by way of an apology and pulled her garment from the water. I glanced at the dripping tunic and then back at the woman.

"He wanted a bloody death," she said.

I nodded. Runa nodded beside me. Then Juniper. Then Ovie.

The blond Mercy stood and dried her hands on her skirt. "I expect someday a foreigner will see us by a river and mistake us for banshees. They are supposed to haunt Elsh streams, washing the bloodstained clothes of the dead."

Trigve laughed. "I've read about banshees in books on Elsh folklore. They go about the countryside shrieking the names of people soon to die."

The blond Mercy smiled, her cheeks turning pink in the sun. "Maybe I should take to shrieking whenever anyone passes by. They'll call me Hag of the Mist and use the story to scare small children."

Trigve laughed again, and I joined him. I liked this Mercy.

Runa, always suspicious of merry people, crossed her arms and scowled. "I'd rather be taken for an Elsh demon than a Boneless Mercy. They at least bring fear to men's hearts."

"We do that, too," Juniper said, proud gray eyes meeting Runa's.

"The Sea Witch there is named Juniper," I said before a fight could break out between the two. "The girl with the scowl is Runa. The reader of folktales is Trigve, and the silent girl to my left is Ovie. My name is Frey."

The blond woman held out her hand. I took it and shook firmly.

"I'm Sasha," she said. She nodded at the dark-haired woman. "And that is Gunhild."

Gunhild looked us over, her gaze lingering on mine. "It's nice to see some other Mercies on the road. It's been some time since we met any of our kind."

In response, I pulled out my flask of *Vite* and passed it around. We all took sips, standing beside the river, in the shade of the protective rowans.

Gunhild tossed back a long swig of the fire liquor, and then smiled. "You're the youngest Mercies we've seen in some time. Most of the ones we come across now are crones."

I put my lips to the leather flask and sipped. Swallowed. "We've noticed it, too. Where are all the younger girls going?"

"We've heard they are fleeing to the Red Willow Marsh to follow the Cut-Queen." Sasha took the flask and drank deeply.

The Cut-Queen.

I felt the Mercies tense around me, felt it snap through the air like lightning.

Juniper put her hand in her pocket and fiddled with her seashells.

My eyes met Sasha's. "I hope you're wrong."

She shrugged and took another sip of *Vite*. "Ah, there he is at last."

I followed Sasha's gaze across the meadow. A long-legged boy ran lightly toward us, covering ground like a deer. He carried a bow in one hand and wore a wolf pelt over one shoulder and belted at the waist, like Trigve.

"My son, Aarne," Sasha said, pride making her chest swell. "He's twelve, but he shoots a bow better than any grown man."

"Your son travels with you?" Ovie stood near me, one hand resting on the hilt of the dagger at her ribs. These were the first words she'd spoken since meeting the other Mercies.

"And why not?" Sasha gazed at Ovie calmly, but there was a glint in her eyes. "Times are changing. I see all you Mercies carry hatchets at your waist—I won't ask you where you obtained these weapons." She paused. "It used to be that Mercies would send their sons into apprenticeships after their fifth winter. I've decided to keep mine, and I'll skin-fight anyone who thinks otherwise."

I held my hands up, palms out, a gesture of peace. "I see no reason you shouldn't keep your son with you. But what will he do when he's grown?"

"I'm going to join the Quicks." Aarne came to a stop in front of me and his mother, alert blue eyes and a wide smile. He was panting only slightly from his run.

"The Quicks?" This got Runa's attention. She turned and focused on the boy. "Can I see your bow?"

He laughed and sounded just like Sasha. "I coated the bowstring in wax to make it slide easier. It allows me to shoot at a greater distance."

He handed his bow to Runa, and she eyed it for a moment. "What feathers do you use for arrows?"

"Whatever I can find. Wild geese feathers are the best."

"Hmm. I've always heard the Yellow Cave Crow has the best feathers for fletching."

This sparked a heated discussion between the two, which I watched with interest.

Runa didn't carry a bow of her own, but I'd long suspected she was rather good with the weapon, based on her desire to join the Quicks. If the Quicks ever took in a woman, it was usually because she was a skilled archer.

Runa and Aarne soon began a shooting contest, the mark being a circular target drawn with charcoal on the side of a fallen oak tree several dozen yards away. The boy was excellent, hitting the mark again and again.

Runa was better.

Aarne handed her arrow after arrow from his quiver, and she never missed. Even when she stepped back another dozen yards. And then another.

We were all watching, laughing, and shouting out encouragement to the pair. Even Ovie was cheering. It made my heart beat faster. Beat redder. I couldn't remember when us Mercies had acted so . . . *merry*.

I held my breath as Runa stepped back another six paces and drew the bow. She hit her mark, and we all shouted *heltar, heltar.* It was an old Vorse term meaning "hero," but it was now used mostly as a cheer.

Runa swung her hair over her shoulder and loosed the last arrow. It sank deep into the wood, dead center.

Runa turned around, and I saw it.

Joy.

It radiated from her like heat from the summer sun. Her eyes shone with it. She smiled, and it was not cynical, but deep and real.

I knew then that Runa belonged with the Quicks. She was meant to move between the Seven Endless Forests, hunting, thinking only of the next sunrise, the next pursuit, the next arrow, the next night beside the fire.

We will join the Quicks, together. As soon as we've won enough gold to tempt them into taking us.

After the contest, Aarne offered his bow and quiver to Runa. "You deserve it more than me," he said simply.

Runa put her fist to her heart and shook her head. "Thank you, Aarne. Truly. But you will need it when you join the Quicks."

Aarne nodded and moved the bow back to his side. "Promise me you will find a bow of your own, then."

Runa paused, and then bowed her head. "I swear it."

. . . . .

We spent the rest of the day with Aarne and the two other Mercies, feasting that night on rabbit stew and fresh trout from the fast-flowing river. We finished off the last of my *Vite*. I wouldn't be able to replenish my flask until I got more coin, but at least I didn't need it for Mercy-killing. Not anymore.

We didn't speak of the Red Willow Marsh again. We didn't discuss where we were going or where we'd been. Aarne chattered away with Runa about the Quicks, and she told him stories she'd heard of their bravery and cunning. Trigve recounted a tale he'd read once, an obscure saga about a boy named Esca who was born with a snakelike mark in his right eye. He was only a young shepherd when he found a magical sword named Wrath and set out to change the world.

Recounting the legends of glory, of heroes, of war, of love, of monsters . . . it was Vorse. And it was far more pleasant than sharing stark, personal stories full of heartbreak.

Toward midnight the fire died down, and no one stopped it. Aarne had fallen asleep between his mother and Runa, and he looked as peaceful and wise as an Elver, the dying flames dancing shadows across his round cheeks.

Juniper watched him for a while, a soft look on her face, and then she glanced at Sasha. "All the death, all the Mercy-killing . . . Can it be good for him?"

Sasha looked down at her son. "I will not send him to live with strangers. With us, he is known and loved. This trumps everything."

Juniper thought for a moment, and then nodded. "It does."

A companionable silencc settled on us then, and everyone began to drift off to sleep. I lay awake in the dark under the bright stars, contemplating how our group had grown by three and how right it felt.

I didn't want to part the next morning. I didn't want to watch Sasha, Gunhild, and Aarne turn south on their way to the next town, the next death.

I'd been a wanderer for so long now. I should have been better at saying good-bye.

Aarne shifted in his sleep, and his blond hair fell across his forehead. I wondered how long it had been since I'd spent time with a child—a healthy child, not one on the verge of death. Years, maybe. I'd had no siblings, but my village had children of all ages. I'd forgotten how they could look shrewd one moment and innocent the next, switching between both as quickly as the flickering leaves of an aspen tree. Juniper still held a remnant of this, but it was long gone on the rest of us.

I hoped Aarne would grow up wild and free. I hoped he would kiss fierce girls under the midnight sun. I hoped he would join the Quicks, and we would meet him in one of the forests some quiet winter's eve.

I pressed my palms together and blew over my right shoulder, setting a wish out on the air in the way of the Sea Witches.

. . . . .

I woke to Ovie on her knees beside me, dagger drawn. "Men," she whispered. "On horseback."

I turned and began to shake Juniper awake. Trigve was already on his feet—he was almost as light a sleeper as Ovie. He leaned down and woke Runa.

"Get out your blades, Mercies. Quickly." I reached for my dagger at my calf.

Gunhild's eyes opened, then Sasha's. They jumped up and drew their daggers. Runa kicked the embers of the fire, dashing out the last of the light, and then woke Aarne.

Ovie took my arm and pointed. Five men on horses came into view at the top of a small hill near the woods, shadows outlined against the moonlit sky. They were less than fifty yards away.

"Mercies."

The tall man in the middle of the group waved a hand toward us, dismissive, almost lazy. His voice was commanding and deep, with a raspy edge. "Cowering together like mice in the middle of a field . . . How very fitting for a group of deathtraders."

Gunhild jerked, her head twisting back. "It's Osric Scathe."

Sasha tensed, elbows pulling into her ribs. "Are you sure?"

"Yes."

Gunhild turned to me. "He's Jarl Keld's man. Were you in Levin recently?"

I nodded.

"What did you do there?"

"Cut down a hanged girl from the crossroads and buried her."

"Hel."

Sasha and Gunhild dropped their small Mercy-daggers and unsheathed two mean-looking stilettos from leather straps under their cloaks.

Gunhild glanced at me over her shoulder. "Are you ready to die, Frey?"

I gave my dagger to Trigve and grabbed my ax. "I've no regrets about burying that girl, and I'd do it again."

Ovie drew her ax. Runa and Juniper gripped their knives. We crouched in the darkness, waiting to see what the men would do next.

"We're hunting a band of raven-cloaked girls." Scathe's voice cut across the field. He jumped down from his horse but stayed by its side. "They were seen cutting down a girl from the tree at the Levin crossroads. She was put there for a reason. Jarl Keld has decreed that someone must be punished for this crime, and I, frankly, don't care if you particular Mercies were the ones who did it. You're all the same to me, and you will serve the purpose."

"Why don't you come closer," Gunhild said, voice soft, almost a purr, but still strong enough to carry to the men. "Let's discuss this around the fire, like warriors."

Scathe tilted his head to the side. "Gunhild, is that you? Might have known you were behind this. You're a Boneless Mercy, not a warrior. And that Levin girl was a she-demon who tried to poison the owner of the Bliss House. She was lucky we didn't burn her. She was meant to hang at that crossroads until she rotted, as a warning to others."

Scathe began to move toward us, slowly, one foot in front of the other. "Put down your weapons, girls. Come with us quietly, and Keld's punishment will be fair—he'll take one of your ears, or a finger at most. Better than dying here tonight, unknown and unburned."

"He's lying." Gunhild moved into a fighting stance, legs apart, weapon held low.

Sasha's eyes met mine. "Scathe murdered our companion Embla six years ago. She performed a vengeance kill on a man after seeing him beat a stray dog to death. When Scathe found out, he slit her throat in the town square for breaking Vorse law. She was sixteen."

Gunhild passed her blade from one hand to the other, slowly, methodically. "He means to kill us all. Count on it."

"It's eight against five." Ovie moved to Gunhild's side, hatchet held high. "We can take them."

Sasha shook her head. "No. I will not let Aarne fight in this."

Aarne straightened his shoulders and drew his bow. "*Let me shoot.* I can kill three between one heartbeat and the next."

"*No.*" Sasha held up her left hand and pointed. "See that man on the far end with the broad shoulders? He is Keld's best archer. The only reason we're still alive is because Scathe likes to give his victims an intimate death. He will try to kill us by sword, if he can—he prefers the violence of the blade."

Scathe kept moving toward us, posture lazy and arrogant.

"That's right, Osric," Gunhild called out, "keep inching this way. Bring your men with you. Let's get this started."

Gunhild looked at Sasha, then me. "Get in the river and let it carry you west. Juniper blessed it. It will keep you safe. This is true, Sea Witch, yes?"

Juniper's hand went into her pocket with the seashells, and she gripped them in her fist. "Yes. I hope."

"Then I will stay here and buy you time."

"No, Gunhild." Sasha grabbed the Mercy's arm, fingers clenching tight. "I won't let you do it. There has to be another way."

"There isn't."

Ovie moved closer to Gunhild, until they were touching, shoulder to shoulder. "I'll stay as well."

"Ovie, no."

Gunhild turned and saw the fear in my eyes. She looked back at Ovie. "Go with your friends. They need you. This thing between Scathe and me . . . It's been coming for a long time. I swore vengeance on him the day he killed Embla. Let me finish it."

Sasha shook her head. "No. I won't leave you."

"You *will*. For Aarne's sake, if not your own."

"Say your farewells." Trigve's eyes had not left Scathe's since he'd dismounted from his Iber horse. "They will act soon. Hurry, Frey."

Sasha tilted her head back and howled, one low, deep wail, in the way of Vorse warriors.

Scathe began to run. The men behind him kicked their horses and charged.

Aarne jumped in the river.

Juniper went next, then Runa.

Sasha took one last look at Gunhild. *"I'll meet you in Holhalla, friend."*

"Be fierce," Ovie said to Gunhild. "Be Vorse." She jumped.

I stood on the bank, my eyes flickering between Scathe and Gunhild. Scathe drew his sword. He had almost reached us, his men at his heels . . .

Gunhild crouched low . . .

"Frey." Trigve took my arm. *"Now."*

I snatched my pack from the ground as Trigve pulled me into the water.

The river grabbed me. I was sucked down into the darkness.

I arched my spine and rose to the surface. I heard metal hitting metal. A man cried out, then a woman. Arrows fell beside me, stone tips ripping through the water, but none hit their mark.

I relaxed and let the river embrace me, nestling me in close until all I could hear was the hollow echo of its churning.

NINE

W*e floated on, until the river began to slow. I felt it ease* its grip on my body, and settle into a calm, gentle flow. We pulled ourselves onto the bank, huddling together in the long grass, gasping, shivering.

It had been easy to close off my mind when I was in the water, floating in the dark, my limbs going numb with cold. But now my heart began to pick up speed again.

I strained my ears, listening for the sounds of horses.

They would hunt us—Keld's men wouldn't be satisfied with Gunhild.

Ovie was the first to get to her feet. She shook off water, beads spraying outward, then straightened her shoulders and glanced at the horizon. "We need to run. Come. The men won't be far behind."

I looked at Juniper, who was curled under her wet Mercy-cloak, hair dripping. "How far away are we?"

She glanced around, marking where we were. "The river moves quickly—we've come almost two miles downstream. The path to the Sea Witches lies only a few miles from here. We will be safe once we reach the Thiss Brambles."

We all stood, except Sasha. Aarne took her arm and pulled her to her feet. He adjusted his wet quiver and bow and then lifted his chin. "We can keep up. Let's go."

Ovie cocked her head.

Trigve did the same.

A moment passed.

"Horses," Trigve said. *"Run."*

We were Boneless Mercies. We had grave-dug weapons and the courage of the Vorse, but we ran.

I heard hooves pounding into dirt, close behind.

We ran.

My legs felt thick, slow. I stuck my chest out, *willed* my heart forward. My thoughts tightened, *lift leg, lift foot, hit ground, again, again* . . .

Finally, Juniper raised a pale, moonlit arm and pointed. A dark line of nine-foot-tall Thiss Brambles ran along the edge of the meadow in front of us.

We came to a stop in front of them, panting, staring into the thorns.

"Come." Juniper pointed again. "This is the way."

Aarne stepped forward.

Runa thrust her arm out in front of Aarne. "No. He'll be pierced to pieces."

"Not if he follows the path." Juniper hovered, half her body already in the brambles. "Look down. See the line of small white stones? They mark the route . . . except when they don't."

I saw the stones, hardly more than pebbles. They led into the dark thicket, then disappeared.

Runa, Ovie, and Trigve looked at me, unsure what to do. I peered into the twisting branches. Each Thiss Bramble bore thousands of tiny spikes, the soft white color of bone.

Juniper pulled the wet hood of her cloak up over her curls. "Follow me, do not veer off the path. All will be well."

Runa crossed her arms. "I'm not going in there. And I won't let Aarne go in, either."

"Frey." Ovie caught my eye, and then nodded at the horizon. Four horses, four men, dark shadows against a midnight-blue sky.

Scathe wasn't with them. Gunhild had gotten her revenge.

The archer with the broad shoulders spotted us first. He gave a short, deep yell—

The arrows began to fall. They thrummed into the thick brush and disappeared, lost among the dark thorns. I felt the air stir as one sank into a spiny trunk two feet from my head.

Runa threw herself in front of Sasha and Aarne.

"Thorns are better than arrows." Ovie grabbed my arm and dragged me into the brambles.

Another round of arrows hit into the ground, inches from Runa and Aarne. They backed into the briar, Trigve and Sasha right behind them.

"*Come.* I will keep you safe." Juniper turned and began to move down the path in a slow, careful trot.

I followed her, and the rest followed me.

We wove through the dark branches, dodging and twisting, sliding between thorns.

I looked back over my shoulder. Trigve, Aarne, and Runa followed Ovie, with Sasha at the end. She was moving quickly and smoothly, despite her grief.

I felt Ovie's fingers on my elbow and stopped.

"Listen," she whispered.

Men, their voices creeping through the brambles. They were arguing about whether to follow us into the thorns.

I looked up, but the stars were gone, blocked out by thick, waxy Thiss leaves. The men's voices grew louder.

I heard their swords, hacking at the brambles as they tried to reach us.

Juniper glanced at me over her shoulder. "Don't worry. Only a Sea Witch, born and bred, can survive the Thiss."

"Would you stake your life on it?" Ovie put her hand on her ax, her head turned back the way we'd come.

Juniper picked up her pace. We were now going as fast as we dared, one careful step after another, the white thorns glowing faintly in the dark.

I kept my feet on the winding white pebbles, afraid to step even a few inches to the left or right. I reached up to push back the hood of my cloak, and a thorn tore my right arm, opening the sleeve of my wool tunic at the seam. Beads of blood broke across my skin.

We loped on and on. The sounds of the men began to fade. I breathed easier. I looked up again and saw tiny Thorn Doves darting in and out among brambles, chirping their melancholy midnight songs and grabbing the small Thiss berries in their beaks.

There was beauty even in this bleak forest of spikes.

In front of me, Juniper raised her chin and sniffed the air.

I smelled it, too. Salt.

And then suddenly I could hear the sea, waves crashing on sand.

The brambles began to thin slightly, allowing the moonlight to come through. Juniper was now several feet ahead, darting between thorns as quick as the birds. She still feared Scathe's men. Or was simply eager to get home. Both, perhaps.

The rest of our company piled up behind me, hissing curses as thorns tore through their cloaks and tunics and skin and hair. I tried moving as Juniper did, dodging instinctively like the doves, but I was clumsy and slow. My wet hair hung limply down my back, making me shiver.

Another thorn cut across my face, temple to ear.

"Juniper?"

"Yes?"

"Are these thorns poisonous?"

She slowed and looked back at me. "Yes, but only if several prick you all at once."

"That's comforting."

I heard Trigve laugh behind me. I shuddered, feeling something shift inside me, as if my heart were shaking off ice.

I felt Ovie's fingers touch my arm. *"On your left, Frey. Look."*

I turned. A small animal skull hung from one of the branches, swinging lightly though there was no breeze.

We spotted many more skulls after that, squirrel and rabbit, mostly, until . . .

"Juniper?"

"Yes?"

"Are you sure the Sea Witches will welcome us? These bones say otherwise."

Juniper came to a halt and turned around. "The Thiss bones aren't prayer-cast. They can do us no harm. They're simply here to keep people away."

"The thorns aren't enough?" Behind me, Ovie ran her thumb down a rip in her sleeve, and it came away with blood.

Juniper put out a small finger and touched a bramble near her cheek. "The witches call this the Prickly Path. Or sometimes the Barbed Briar. Mother Hush refers to it as the Ticklish Trail, but that's just her little joke." She twisted at the waist and caught my eye. "Can you taste the salt in the air? We are in the Merrows. *I am home.*"

I envied her suddenly. Juniper had a home.

It was something.

It was everything.

We walked on, another few dozen yards. A sea breeze swept down the path and rattled two nearby skulls. I turned—

A body in the thorns. Tangled dress and hair and pale limbs, dead fingers almost touching my hip.

"*Juniper*," I whispered.

She followed my gaze. *"Oh."*

The rest of our company piled up behind me on the path again. We stood frozen in place, eyes on the girl.

"Dead a few days," Ovie said. "Maybe longer."

Her clothing hung in shreds, dried blood on pale skin. I leaned forward to get a better look at her face, and a bramble slit the front of my tunic. A line of blood shot across my abdomen.

"Careful," Juniper warned.

I nodded and fought the urge to straighten the girl's skirt and touch her dead-white cheek.

Dying in these brambles alone . . . It was a sad end.

Juniper began a death prayer. It was a familiar invocation, asking the sea to bring the peace of deepest sleep, and the wind to whisper the girl's name in its travels. I'd heard Juniper murmur the same chant many times after a Mercy-kill.

She finished the prayer, and Runa tossed her the flint box. Juniper lit the stick of Heart Ash and swept the smoke over the body. A thorn cut her across the forehead as she moved, dripping blood into her eyes.

"Another dead girl," Ovie whispered. "Death tracks us, unwilling to let us go."

"We're cursed." Runa brushed a thorn away from her shoulder, and it sliced open the top of her hand.

"What would cause a girl to run into these thorns if she didn't know the way through?" Trigve's black hair was loose and wet, clinging to his shoulders like ivy. "Nothing good brought her into the Thiss."

Juniper sighed and put her hand on her heart. "Girls come here hoping to join the Sea Witches. We couldn't take them in, even if they did get through the thorns, but they don't know this. Mother Hush sends armored witches into the brambles a few times a year to clean up the bodies. This one is too new. I . . . I will tell her about it when we arrive."

Juniper began another prayer, one of long sadness and quiet forgiveness.

"What a *waste*." Runa swatted at another bramble, and then swore when it cut her palm. "Who are you Sea Witches to deny girls who are willing?"

Juniper simply shook her head. "It's not as I would wish, Runa. But these girls are always running from something. They bring demons with them. And Mother Hush says a witch needs to be born in the Merrows to understand the magic that lives here."

Runa threw back her head and swore. Another thorn sliced her cheek. She wiped away the blood with her forearm.

We walked on.

I figured it was near dawn, but the darkness of the Thiss path was disorienting. Exhaustion was closing in, making my mind drift.

When we finally stumbled out onto the white sand of the Merrows, the sun was scratching at the horizon. I closed my eyes and angled my face toward it, soaking up the first pink rays of light.

I felt Trigve at my side, shoulder touching mine. "Look up, Frey."

I turned. My eyes followed the white sand inland, some fifty yards, until it ended in a pile of leaves and a line of black trunks. I tilted my head back . . .

The witch trees.

They were as thick across as I was tall, and they towered over the landscape, the shortest forty feet high, the tallest, over a hundred. Their dark trunks stood straight and proud, but their branches wove together overhead, like entwined fingers—forming a loose, twisted sort of ceiling. The roots of the trees were so thick they arched up out of the ground like the tail of an ancient sea serpent, and the forest gave off a scent of ash and burning that cut through the sharp scent of the sea.

I'd been to the Quell Sea only a handful of times—twice when I was a child, and three times with Siggy, for a Mercy-kill. The rugged coastline belonged to another Mercy group—Allis and her three companions—but Siggy was older and well-known, and she was occasionally requested outside our territory.

My visits had been to simple fishing villages much farther south, ones that had been easy to reach via the main coastal roads. This was something else entirely. Few people had been to the Merrows, protected as they were by towering rock cliffs on two sides and brambles on the other.

The Scorch Trees formed a crescent-shaped forest, framed by the cliffs, with the white sand in front leading to the sea. The core of live Scorch Trees burned like fire and gave off heat all year long—the witch huts were warm as a summer's day even in winter. I knew this from Juniper's tales, of course, but there was also an old nursery song called "The Merrow Tree" that every Vorse mother sang to her child.

Narrow grow the Merrows,
Women straight as arrows,
Scorch Trees, torch trees,
Black bark burn.
Narrow grow the Merrows,
Women straight as arrows,
Tree Witch, Sea Witch
Seasons never turn.

I shaded my eyes from the sunrise and spotted dozens of witch huts in the strong top branches of the trees, wooden bridges connecting one to another, conical tops like the funnel-shaped hat of a Potion Peddler.

"Home." Juniper spun in a circle, whispering a prayer of thanks to the wind and the sea.

We moved inland, feet shifting the soft white sand as we walked. The sand ended as we reached the first line of trees, giving way to dirt and leaves. We stopped, blinking in the deep, sudden shade.

Ovie reached forward and put her hand on a trunk. She smiled as it warmed her palm.

"I wish Gunhild could have seen this." Sasha leaned back against one of the trees and sighed. They were the first words she'd spoken since we jumped into the river.

A moment later we collapsed onto a heap of black leaves and slept like the dead.

It was near noon when I woke again. I lay still for a while, tucked between Ovie and Juniper, and listened to the sound of the sea and the rustle of leaves high above.

I felt Ovie tense beside me, a small jerk of her right hand as she reached for the dagger at her ribs.

They appeared suddenly out of thin air, floating in like mist.

Seven Sea Witches.

Seven of them, seven of us.

Not even Ovie had sensed them closing in, and she had the instincts of a snow cat.

"Rise, Mercies," I said. "The witches are here."

Each was tall and straight as an arrow, like in "The Merrow Tree" song, and dressed in layers of green. Green hair, green tunics, sea and grass and moss. Earth colors. Witch colors.

They held long, gnarled pieces of driftwood. As one, they lifted the sea-worn branches and pressed them to our throats.

"Did you know they were coming?" I whispered in Juniper's ear.

"Yes," she said.

The witch wands smelled of salt and wood smoke and the toasted sweet smell of pine resin.

"Watchers." Juniper lifted her chin as the wand pressed into her skin. "Lookouts. There's no need to fear them. They knew we were here, and yet let us sleep."

The witches turned to Juniper when she spoke, eyes taking in the pale green luster of her hair.

"Juniper?" The tallest of the witches lowered her wand. She had high cheekbones and bright green eyes. Her feet were bare, and she wore a green wool skirt over green wool leggings, same as the others.

"Sage." Juniper lunged forward and threw her arms around the tall Sea Witch.

The other six witches lowered the driftwood wands but still watched us closely. I rubbed my neck where the point had been.

My skin tingled in an odd way, something between pleasure and pain.

Juniper turned to us. "This is Sage, my witch-sister."

Sage lifted her hand and ran a thumb over the cut on Juniper's forehead. "How was the Thiss?"

"Prickly," Juniper said, and smiled.

"I reached out to you in your dreams, soon after you left." Sage slid her arm around Juniper's waist and pulled the girl to her again.

"I know." Juniper put her fist to her heart. "It saved me, those first hard nights. I would have been lost if you hadn't sought me on the other side of sleep. It kept me from turning back."

The sisters were quiet then, just for three or four heartbeats, but it spoke oceans.

I wished I had a sister.

Siggy would have said the Mercies were my true sisters. And she would have been right. I didn't share blood with the other Mercies, but that matters little, in the end.

Runa stepped forward, toward the witch nearest her, a girl with brown eyes and a muscular frame. "What's your name, then?"

The witch just shook her head. "Come. We'll take you to Mother Hush."

They led us a dozen yards deeper into the forest, our feet stirring up a blanket of fallen Scorch leaves as we walked. Juniper pointed to a ladder that stretched up the side of one of the trees—it was painted black to blend in with the Scorch bark and hard to see unless you were looking for it.

"We climb." Juniper reached for the ladder and pulled herself up, quick and easy, as though she'd done it a hundred times before, which I supposed she had.

Next went Runa and Ovie, Aarne and Sasha, then the seven Sea Witches, one after another, green hair and bare feet, up and up.

Trigve waited with me while everyone else climbed. I'd never been easy with heights, and he knew this.

"Go on," Trigve said. "Close your eyes and start moving, Frey."

I took a deep breath and clamped my hands on a rung. He nodded at me again. I shook off my fear and began to climb.

TEN

Siggy had always wanted to meet the Sea Witches.

She'd been on her own for about a year after her companion died. If there's one thing people hate more than a pack of Mercies, it's a Mercy who walks alone. So Siggy sought out the four of us, starting with me.

There are three ways to keep warm during a Vorse winter. One is fire, one is *Vite*, and one is storytelling.

On a frigid winter night when it was too cold to sleep, Siggy unbraided her long white hair, shook it down over her shoulders, and told me a story from her past.

"I was married at eighteen to a blond-haired man named Rol. He lived at the other end of my childhood village, and we grew up together. We were married for three months before he went off with the other village men to raid an Elsh monastery across the Quell Sea—they still raided back then, for there was still gold in those stone abbeys."

Siggy had a clear, striking voice and an elegant, tall way of sitting that drew your eyes right to her. I would have been captivated even if this weren't a rare personal tale.

"Rol's blue eyes danced when he kissed me good-bye, his hand on my belly. He swore to bring me back a gold cross, one he could melt down into a brooch for my cloak.

"He never came home. I gave birth, and the child died. I set off west, determined to find something, anything, that would bring meaning back into my life. I imagined bribing the Sea Witches to take me in. I dreamed of crossing the Quell and wandering Elshland and finding the lost city of the Green Women. I dreamed many things.

"But then I met Iona one summer during a Night Market in the town of Leer. Her black hair was the same shade as her dazzling Mercy-cloak. She was gentle and fearless. I was half-wild from months of wandering Vorseland alone with no purpose. We would spend the next several decades roaming together, eating together, killing together, living coin to coin, death to death.

"One winter night, Iona went for a walk when she couldn't sleep. She was attacked by a pack of starving wolves at the edge of Lake Gead. I tried to save her, but she was bleeding on the inside and beyond help. She begged me to kill her. I gave her Blue Seed and held her as she slipped away."

I turned to the fire, away from Siggy's gaze. Her voice had gone hoarse with emotion. I gave her privacy until she overcame her sorrow. "How did you bear it?"

"I did what I had to do." She paused. "When I die, Iona will pass out of living memory. I wanted to take on a young apprentice back then, but she was content with it just being the two of us."

I glanced toward her and saw that she was calm and composed. "Are you glad you met Iona?"

Siggy shrugged, strong, slender shoulders lifting to her ears. "Together we met life head-on. And later, death. We had a good run of it."

I thought about this conversation many times after Siggy died.

She'd slipped on ice and broken her hip the previous fall. She couldn't walk, and she was in pain. Runa held her tight while I cut her wrists just as she'd taught us in those long, dark nights by the fire. Two swift, clean cuts through delicate skin, blue veins opening to red.

I gave her a drink of fresh, clean water while Juniper whispered a dying poem in her ear.

We were Mercies.

Siggy, never sentimental in life, became sentimental in death. That was the way of it, sometimes.

"I wish Rol had come back," she said to me, one hand on her heart, one hand on my arm.

"Yes," I whispered.

"I wish I could have gazed upon one of the trolls that live in the far north. I wish I could have seen a giant snow bear, fresh from a kill. I wish Iona and I could have spent our last years in a warm stone hut by the sea. I wish I could have met the Sea Witches and seen the Scorch Trees."

"Yes."

Our Mercy mentor took her last breath.

We set her on a hastily made pyre of pine branches and watched as her soul was swept up to Holhalla on the flames.

I shook as I climbed the Scorch Tree, Trigve's voice urging me higher and higher. I looked over my shoulder only once. I saw black trees, white sand, and blue water.

I grabbed the last rung, fingers closing around the wood, and pulled myself up onto a bridge. I waited for my legs to stop shaking, and then took a deep breath and looked around. The bridge connected to a series of other wooden bridges, dozens of huts scattered between. An entire village in the sky.

I heard Trigve climb up behind me, his feet landing lightly on the wooden planks. The others had crossed the bridge and were entering a large, circular wooden building at the end, its conical roof twisting up toward the clouds.

I began to walk slowly toward it, one foot in front of the other, my hands gripping the rope railing. I flinched each time the wood creaked beneath me. The wind was stronger up in the trees, and the black leaves of the Scorch Trees twitched against me as I moved.

Sage exited the large hut and smiled when she spotted me creeping slowly toward her, Trigve a step behind. She ran down the bridge, took my hand in hers, and started chanting a prayer. She called to the wind, the birds, and the clouds, and then she brushed one finger down each side of my face.

My fear left, snap, like a twig breaking underfoot.

I let go of the rope, straightened, and smiled. I could stare down now without terror, and I gasped at the beauty of the trees and the sea.

"*Grew black wings and soared up high*," I said.

"Sailed through the clouds, and scraped the sky." Trigve, voice deep and clear.

Sage laughed. *"Witch on the fly, witch on the fly . . ."*

Mother Hush's hut, despite the name, was a cavernous, circular space, almost as large as a Great Hall. I followed Sage through several sections, separated only by long strands of tiny seashells—they clattered softly as we moved through them.

Sea witches were everywhere, young and old, ranging in age from tottering infants to white-haired women like Siggy. Some wove wool thread on large wooden looms, some baked bread near a giant hearth, some stained wool the color of sea foam, some prayed near an open window. They all wore green wool skirts and let their hair fall loosely down their backs.

The thick branch of a Scorch Tree rose up through a hole cut in the center of the floor and stretched out through another opening in the roof. It gave the hut a living feel, as if we were North-Fairies, building our homes inside ancient oaks. I felt the heat emanating from the tree, a soft wave of warmth. I held my hands up, palms out, and soaked it in like sunshine.

Runa, Ovie, and Juniper joined me at the tree, joy pouring off Juniper like perfume. Aarne and Sasha appeared from behind a curtain of seashells, Aarne's eyes wide and excited. Sasha had shed some of her quiet sadness as well and she looked around the hut with interest.

A few witches recognized Juniper and nodded to her. Sage and the other Watchers had gone to fetch Mother Hush, so we stood near the tree, waiting. Some of the witches smiled at us, and some looked at us curiously, and some tranquilly went about their work.

After a few moments, a middle-aged witch approached us and gestured at our shredded clothing. "I will wash and mend those for you if you remove them."

She motioned to another witch, a younger girl of about twelve. The girl left the hut and returned shortly, holding out several folded garments on smooth, freckled arms and smiling shyly.

I took off my boots, dropped my cloak, then my ax, and started to strip down to my leggings. When I was done, I tossed aside my bloodstained Mercy-clothing and gave my tunic a kick, glad to be rid of it. I slipped into the clean Sea Witch tunic, and the wool smelled like apples and fresh air.

I turned and caught a flash of Ovie's scar before she pulled the witch tunic over her head—it was thin and pink, stretching from her lower ribs to her navel. Juniper had once speculated that Ovie had gotten it in the same battle that took her eye.

Trigve and Aarne were given new tunics as well. Trigve's thick linen trousers were finely woven and had escaped the wrath of the Thiss thorns, but his tunic was ripped in four places. He dropped his fur and stripped to the waist. Aarne did the same.

I bent down and gathered our tunics into a pile. "There's no need to mend our old clothing," I said to the witch. I walked over to the large hearth and threw them in.

I watched our plain, bloodstained Mercy-tunics go up in flames, and smiled.

All the death we'd dealt in that clothing, all the bloodstains . . . gone. I wished I could burn our cloaks as well, but we couldn't afford new ones, and we'd need something to cover us with winter coming on.

I felt a shift in the air, a quiet buzz. The witches looked up, their eyes on the doorway.

Mother Hush.

She was tall, taller than Runa even, at least six feet. Her skin was as smooth as porcelain, despite her years. Her nose was long and straight, and her blond-green hair was loose, flowing in waves around a pointed chin. In her right hand, she held a thick walking stick made of driftwood, like the Watchers' wands.

Mother Hush was regal and beautiful. I'd expected this. But something about her also felt . . . timeless, like sea and sun and stars.

She walked toward us and came to a stop in front of me. She bent her head, and I bent mine. She straightened, and so did I.

"Do you believe in the sea goddess, Jute?" she asked. Her expression was serene, but her gaze was bright and sharp.

"I do."

"Do you believe that sea magic is the only good and pure magic and that all other magic is false and corrupt?"

I paused.

Magic.

Siggy had taught me to pray to Valkree . . . but she also used to say that prayers were as intangible as air.

On sorcery, she had nothing to say at all.

I echoed her sentiments on prayer, but I did believe there was something more in the world, something greater than us Vorse and what we understood. Call it what you will.

"I believe in sea magic," I said. "And *all* magic."

"Good." She smiled then, and her eyes crinkled at the corners. "Then you are free to stay as long as you like."

She turned and embraced Juniper and whispered something in her ear. Whatever it was, it made Juniper smile and the tip of her nose turn pink.

We held a death service that evening for Gunhild. It was short and simple, with Mother Hush presiding. Sasha sang an old song, one of bravery and loyalty, and Juniper said a special prayer reserved for those who fall in battle and remain unburned.

Sasha did not cry. She was a Mercy. She was Vorse.

Afterward, we feasted on a wooden platform built off the side of Mother Hush's hut. I sat on a bench, elbows on the table, surrounded by witches and Mercies, and listened to the sound of the sea far below, waves hitting sand. The night air smelled of salt and the slightly burnt scent of the Scorch Trees.

Mother Hush sat at the far end of the long wooden table. Sage was with us, between Juniper and Ovie. In the distance, I could see other women and children eating at smaller tables outside smaller huts, candles burning across the treetops like stars. Black Scorch leaves brushed my limbs when the wind blew and left warm traces down my skin.

Sage lifted a pitcher and poured rosy wine into wooden mugs, and then ladled cool white almond soup into black wooden bowls. A younger witch, dimpled and graceful, set a large, covered clamshell in front of me—it held a whole cooked fish, spiced with salt and pepper and thyme.

"Here." Juniper picked up a small, corked bottle. She removed the cork and dripped golden-green oil onto my soup, and then my fish. "It's pressed from olives."

"Olives?"

"Small green fruits that grow in Iber." Juniper smiled, and her whole face shone.

She was home. She was happy.

I sipped the wine, and it was tart, clean, and refreshing. It warmed my throat as it slipped down, just as the Scorch leaves warmed my skin.

I'd had wine once before. A year before, we had Mercy-killed a jarl's sickly wife. She screamed and scolded right up until her last breath. Afterward, the sad-eyed jarl took us into his Great Hall, poured a honey-colored wine into a silver goblet, and handed it to me. He poured another for himself and drank it in one long gulp. "To her death," he'd said. "May she never rise again."

I tried the witch soup, and then the fish. They tasted of sun and sand, instead of snow and cold. I ate cheerfully and heartily. We all did. After I'd licked my plates clean, I heaved a deep sigh of contentment. I began to lazily look around at the witch huts scattered through the leaves, candles twinkling, green-clad women talking in low voices, children laughing.

So this was life in the Merrows.

Juniper picked up the bottle of olive oil and dribbled it onto her second helping of the soup. Next to her, Aarne reached over and stole something from Sasha's plate, and she smiled. The service for Gunhild had lifted her spirits. It was done, her friend was gone, and she and her son were safe again. Now she could heal.

I'd begged for her forgiveness earlier in the day, while Aarne and the Mercies explored the treetop huts with Trigve. I went down on one knee before her, bent my head, and put my fist on my heart. It was our fault that her friend had died, even if Gunhild had a score to settle with Scathe from long before.

Sasha had embraced me, kissed my cheek, and called me her Death Sister.

Because of us, she was now a Mercy on the run. She couldn't return to the death trade, not with Jarl Keld out for blood. And she couldn't follow us into the Red Willow Marsh, either—she'd never risk putting Aarne in the Cut-Queen's path.

I hoped I could find a place for her and her son before we moved on—somewhere that would see them through the winter and keep them safe for as long as they required it.

Trigve reached across me for more wine and drank his third cupful in one long, thirsty swallow. Ovie winked at Trigve and poured another mug for herself as well.

"This isn't Vorse wine," she said. "It's far too delicate."

Sage smiled, and it made her look so much like Juniper that my heart skipped a beat. "We trade with passing ships," she said. "There are several Iber captains who know of the Merrows." Juniper nodded. "They stop here on their way to Elshland, and we take them in for a few nights. We give them our prayers in trade for olive oil and perfumes and nuts and spices."

"Prayers." Runa laughed. "Anyone can say a prayer. I think the sailors are making a bad bargain of it."

Juniper put down her wooden spoon and met Runa's gaze. "Our prayers guard the ships from storms. They never sink, not when they are under our protection."

Sage nodded at this, as did all the other witches near us, and Runa wisely kept her mouth shut.

I didn't know why Runa liked to goad Juniper. Something about Juniper's sincerity and sweetness rubbed her the wrong way. Perhaps she envied the Sea Witch, especially now, when we'd seen all that Juniper had left behind to take up with us.

Juniper leaned over the table and poured some more wine for Runa. Always the peacemaker. "My father was an Iber sailor," she said. "The witches take lovers when the mood strikes them. The men come, share a witch's bed, and then sail away a few days later. We usually give birth to girls here in the Merrows, but there have been a few witch-boys. They take to the sea as soon as they are old enough—it's in their blood, I suppose."

She looked at Trigve. "You are the only man here at the moment."

Aarne pounded a fist on the table, and Juniper turned to him and smiled. "Sorry, Aarne. You and Trigve are the only men here."

Trigve just laughed at this, a deep rumble in the back of his throat. He glanced left, then right, and eyed up the nearby witches. "Where is your mother, Juniper? Can we meet her?"

Juniper flinched.

Sage turned to her sister, whispered something in her ear, and then kissed her temple.

"My mother died." Juniper's wispy voice drifted down the table, and several other witches turned our way. "Over two years ago. The Sea Witches never get ill, and the snow sickness doesn't touch the Merrows. She died from a broken heart."

Juniper paused. "My mother brought an Iber sailor to her bed that summer. His name was Sebastian, and she fell in love with him. He left at dawn on the third day, back to his ship . . . and her joy went with him. She withered slowly, day by day, like a bowl of fruit left to rot."

Juniper's cheeks were flushed, and her gray eyes glossy. "This is why I left. I couldn't get past my grief. Mother Hush told me to wander the world until I made peace with death. She said I was at risk of dying of heartache, just as my mother had."

"So this is why you became a Boneless Mercy?" Runa asked.

Juniper nodded. "I set off alone and expected to stay alone. But the gods sent me you."

Our end of the table was quiet for a while after Juniper's tale. It had been her choice to tell us this story from her past, and we treated it like the gift it was.

The moon rose higher in the sky, fat and full and bright, and a wave of peace spread over us. Juniper seemed relieved after sharing her tale, and when her sister whispered to her again, she let out a quiet, silvery laugh.

The good food, the wine, the sea breeze, the gentle voices of the other witches . . . It soothed me.

A feeling of serenity came from being up in the treetops. We were living in the clouds. I wondered if this was how the dead felt, when their spirits floated up to Holhalla as their bodies burned to ash.

I'd experienced joy before. Not often, but enough to know what it was, enough to ache for it late at night when I sat quietly beside the fire. Joy was different from peace, though. Peace was slower, calmer, and lasted longer. I hadn't known this kind of tranquility could exist.

I wished Siggy could have visited these witches. I wished she and Iona could have spent their last years here together.

Trigve leaned his shoulder into mine. I turned to him, and his hair brushed my cheek. It flowed loose around his shoulders, soft and dark. I undid my own braid, shook my hair down, and sighed.

I felt Trigve's contentment, felt it emanating from his skin, muscle, blood, bone, and it relaxed me even more.

The wind picked up, and the voices died down. The youngest of the witch-girls slid sleepily off the benches and curled up next to the wiry, sweet-looking witch-hounds that were sleeping under the table.

Trigve filled my mug with more wine. I drank deeply—deeply enough to lose my sense of place and time. At some point we all moved down to the wooden floor of the platform, backs against the black wooden railing, faces toward the stars. I reached forward, wrapped my arms around Runa, and pulled her into me. She stiffened, and then relaxed. I pressed my face into her hair.

Aarne stretched out and rested his head on Runa's legs. Ovie and Trigve leaned against each other, sharing another cup of wine. Sasha whispered with Juniper and Sage, and then laughed.

I thought of the dead girl at the crossroads and the dead girl in the Thiss Brambles. I thought of Gunhild. I wondered about their childhoods and their families. I wondered if they'd known love. Or joy. I wondered if they'd picked cloudberries on green-grassed hills, under the midnight sun. I wondered if they'd dreamed of great adventures, of crossing seas and mountains, in search of whatever lay on the other side.

We all have dreams. All of us. Gunhild, those dead girls, me, the other Mercies . . . all of us.

A raspy caw echoed somewhere above. Runa swore quietly. She shifted in my arms, and then fell back asleep. A raven flew down and landed on Mother Hush's shoulder. She turned to it and whispered. It cawed again, and then flew off, up beyond the Scorch Trees, into the black night sky.

ELEVEN

Mother Hush found me at dawn.

We'd moved back inside her hut sometime around midnight, after a cold sea-wind blew in. The other witches had retreated from the platform hours before, except Sage, who had fallen asleep with her arms wrapped around her sister.

We slept near the large Scorch Tree branch, as if it were our usual fire. It gave off a steady, soft, sensuous heat.

The bliss of bedding down next to such a tree every winter evening . . .

I dreamed soft, warm dreams.

Mother Hush put a finger on my cheek to wake me. When I opened my eyes, she motioned for me to follow her with a flick of her pointed chin.

I stood and tried to shake off sleep. I hadn't slept so deeply in months. Years.

Ovie reached up and grabbed my hand as I stepped over her. "Careful, Frey. The sagas speak of the slyness of witches. Don't let this witch-mother put a spell on you like she did that raven."

I glanced over at Mother Hush, standing near a doorway by the looms, and then back down at Ovie.

"I trust her."

Ovie nodded and let me go.

Mother Hush took me outside, her driftwood walking stick thumping with each step. We crossed several walkways and a long bridge, finally coming to a large, circular platform. This one had a series of ropes and pulleys that stretched out over the treetops. The ropes led to a thin, silvery waterfall, which slipped down the side of the great rock cliff that rose grandly to the south. I saw buckets fastened to the ropes, hanging solidly from great wooden hooks.

So this was how the witches got fresh water. It was very clever.

As I watched, Mother Hush tugged on the top rope, hand over hand, until a bucket came floating toward us, filled with cold, clear water.

I reached up to unhook it, glancing quickly down to the shore below. I prepared myself for the fear to return, but there was no trace of it. Sage's prayer held.

I began to enjoy the view. Mother Hush and I weren't the only women awake. I saw four witches on the shore digging for clams. Two more tended a garden around a Scorch Tree at the far end of the woods. I turned and saw the Thiss Brambles stretching east, on and on forever, and after them, the white-tipped Skal Mountains.

I felt Mother Hush watching me and met her gaze.

"So you are the girl who will try to defeat the Blue Vee Beast." Her green eyes were sharp and shrewd. They reminded me of Siggy's. "My witches dreamed it years ago. They had a vision of a girl who would try to slay a monster. Trust Juniper to track down a glory-seeker among the Boneless Mercies, of all people. She's like her mother."

This is what Juniper had meant when she said the Sea Witches would want to meet me, too. She'd known about the vision. I wondered when she'd first connected it to me—when I mentioned fighting the Blue Vee Beast in the Hail Inn?

Or had she known from the first moment we'd met?

I ran a hand through my hair, which was still loose around my shoulders. "Well, did the dream say I would succeed?"

"It did not." Mother Hush spoke softly, so softly that I leaned in toward her without thinking.

The Sea Witches loved to whisper, I'd noticed.

"I wasn't even certain it would come to pass," she said. "Dreams show only one path. You might have made a different choice, gone down a different road. You still might."

"But I'm here now."

She smiled. "True. You've come this far. It bodes well."

"Will your sea goddess help us defeat this beast?" I asked. "Will you pray for us?"

Hush shook her head. "Jute won't help you."

I laughed. "Then tell her to stay out of my way."

Mother Hush smiled again. "There's an old Sea Witch saying

that goes: *If we kill all the monsters, mankind will take their place.* Do you think that's true, Frey?"

"It has the ring of truth," I said. "But it won't stop me from trying."

Mother Hush reached forward and took the bucket of water from my hand. She began to pour the contents into a large wooden bowl on a table off to her right. When she finished, she gestured to the bowl with one long, slender finger.

"Gaze into the water. Tell me what you see."

I bent over the bowl. The water was sleek and black, like the Iber woman's silk. I could see nothing, not even my reflection, as if I were staring up at the sky on a starless night.

"Keep looking," Mother Hush whispered when I started to fidget.

I stared . . .

Stared . . .

Nothing.

Mother Hush took the rope again and pulled in a fresh bucket. She fetched a scallop shell from another small table, slipped it into the water, and offered me a cool sip. It spilled down my throat, clean and pure.

"Now look into the water again."

I looked and saw nothing.

"You have no natural magic in you," she said finally. Mother Hush waved her hand toward the sea. "I see we must do this the hard way. Let's go down to the shore."

Mother Hush walked to the far end of the platform, reached out, and grabbed a black rope ladder that swung from the nearby tree. She began to climb down, gracefully, easily. I followed.

Hush and I walked side by side through the witch woods in the early-morning light. She was barefoot and strode as lightly and quietly as a deer. I trailed my fingers across the Scorch Trees' bark as we passed and sighed at the warmth.

When we reached the shore, we both paused on the white sand for a moment, letting the sea mist settle on our skin, the wind rush through our hair, the taste of salt tickle our tongues.

Finally, Mother Hush turned to me and gestured with a flick of her hand. "Undress. Down to the skin."

The morning air was cold and full of teeth, and I had little desire to let it whip across my bare body. Yet I did as she asked. I was curious to see where this would go.

I dropped my Mercy-cloak on the sand, then my tunic, then boots, wool leggings, shift. I stood at the foot of the waves, naked, my silver hair loose and wild, the cuts from the Thiss thorns marking red lines across my skin. I pushed my shoulders back and stood straight. Being naked like this, as cold as I was . . .

I didn't feel vulnerable.

I felt *free*.

Mother Hush pushed me forward, one hard hand on my back. "Walk into the waves until the water reaches your thighs. Then kneel."

I didn't move. I eyed her over my shoulder and fought the urge to push her back. I'd never enjoyed taking orders. She stared me down. I let my curiosity quash my pride and put one foot into the sea. The cold seared my skin like fire, but I kept walking, feet, ankles, calves. When the waves hit my thighs, I sank down, my knees melting into the shifting sand.

The sea lapped at my shoulders, lifting me softly a few inches, and then dropping me back down again. I kept my breathing even and my eyes on the horizon.

Was this the Sea Witch's plan? To drown me at sunrise?

Hush waded in, coming to stand beside me. Her green tunic turned black where it soaked up the sea.

There was an edge to her now, a sharpness. A steel. Her expression was still serene, but underneath it, I sensed something simmering . . . something raw and wild, like desire.

Or fury.

Or vengeance.

Mother Hush held up her driftwood staff in one hand. She gripped the back of my neck with the other and shoved me underwater.

I flailed, limbs slicing through frigid sea. I jerked, kicked, fought the water, arms out, muscles tight, lungs seizing up. The witch's grasp didn't lessen.

So this is how I will die. It was all for nothing. I'm just like the girl at the crossroads and the girl in the brambles. A sad end to a short, meaningless life.

No.

No.

If death was coming for me, then I wouldn't meet it like a coward.

I would die with dignity.

I gave in to the drowning. I relaxed, arms out, my hair floating around me like wisps of seaweed.

The moment my muscles softened, I felt the cold recede. I was warm suddenly, as if I were touching a Scorch Tree.

Lukewarm.

Blood-warm.

Tree-warm.

My mind began to drift.

I began to imagine I was an Arctic Syren, swimming in the sea, on and on, endless darkness and smooth, briny swells. I could still feel my body yearning for air, my lungs struggling, heaving, shaking . . . But my mind was at peace.

I opened my eyes.

Through the icy haze of the sea, I saw a black spot emerge in front of me. It was darker than the water, drippy and heavy, like ink dropped in oil. I reached out to touch it, and the black spot began to spread, coiling out, tendrils reaching toward me.

"Look."

I heard Mother Hush shouting above me, over the sound of the waves.

"Look, and learn."

I stared at the spot.

I expected it to turn into the Blue Vee Beast.

Instead, I saw a girl.

She was young. Younger than Juniper . . . eleven, twelve at most. She knelt on a red rug beside a straw bed, her back to me. Her long, honey-gold hair was gathered together and hung over her thin shoulder.

The nearby candle flickered. I heard the distant sound of drums. I smelled stagnant water and mud.

A breeze blew in through a square window, the canvas flap whipping to the side. The candle flame swelled, and its light fell across the girl's back, which was now bare. Her skin was a mass of long red welts.

The girl picked up a slender willow branch from the bed and began to strike herself with it. Again. And again, and again. The branch hissed as it sliced the air. The girl flinched as an older welt reopened and began to leak blood.

She hit herself again. Harder.

She began to scream.

It wasn't a scream of pain.

It was scream of . . .

Victory.

The girl lowered her arm . . .

One quick turn of her head . . .

She looked at me, right at me, green eyes bright as stars.

My body began to shake from lack of air. My lungs stretched, strained . . .

The vision went dark. Everything went dark.

I was drowning. The sea was stealing my life.

Everything . . .

Dark.

Strong fingers gripped my shoulders and pulled me out of the water.

Mother Hush dragged me back to the sand. I heaved up water as she rubbed life back into my body, heat back into my skin. She chanted a prayer under her breath, one of water, steam, boil, singe, sear.

Blood returned to my limbs slowly, the sting of it making me gasp. Hush pulled my Mercy-cloak over my shoulders, and I huddled under it, breathing in the familiar smells of wool, and Mercy, and *me*.

The girl's eyes had been bright green, like Trigve's, but cold. Dead cold.

Mother Hush knelt beside me and took my arm, fingertips pressing into my flesh. "Frey, what did you see under the water? Tell me."

"I saw a girl in the marsh. A girl with green eyes and a willow branch in her hand. She whipped her back until it ran red."

"*Yes.* It is as I thought. You are the one." Mother Hush pulled me to her. She smelled of salt and sand and frankincense. She smelled like Juniper. "Frey, I need you to enter the Red Willow Marsh, find the village in the reeds, and kill the Cut-Queen."

"What?"

"I need you to do this for the Sea Witches. I need you to do this for Vorseland."

I moved backward a few inches, my hands sinking into cold sand. "So you're telling me the Cut-Queen is nothing but a child . . . and you want me to kill her."

"Yes."

I tugged my cloak tighter around my naked body. "Dying at the hands of the Blue Vee Beast . . . It is a worthy death. It is *Vorse.* But the Cut-Queen? There is no honor in killing a child. And I would know."

"Do you still plan to cross the Red Willow Marsh?"

I nodded. "We are headed to Blue Vee, and we have no ship. It's the only way, unless we want to take the mountains, and then we face the Jade Fells along the Ribbon Pass."

"If you go through the marsh, then you might be captured anyway. If you are captured, you will be tortured or forced to convert."

"True," I said.

I'd heard the rumors. We'd be cut and beaten, and then drowned in the bog mud like a Skyye criminal. Our souls wouldn't drift up to Holhalla; we wouldn't even be buried in the earth like the Elsh. We would become ghosts, forced to haunt the Red Willow Marsh for all eternity.

It was a horrible fate. Unthinkable.

"Then isn't it better to go in with a fighting chance?" Hush turned away from me, eyes on the sea. "The Cut-Queen is taking in former Boneless Mercies. Declare your intention to join her. Convert, if she demands it. Get close to her, and then kill her."

"No. It's too risky. I won't ask this of the Mercies. At least if we stay hidden, we have a chance of sneaking by her. To march right in . . . That is certain death."

Mother Hush picked up her driftwood staff and set it across her knees. "The Cut-Queen is spreading evil with her marsh magic. All magic costs something—happiness, love, land, *blood*. A change is coming, and this Cut-Queen will be at the heart of it if she can. Her path is darkness. The Sea Witches seek light. She must die, Frey."

"Not by my hands, or the hands of my companions."

Mother Hush made a witch sign with her right hand, one I didn't recognize. "You were born during the Lion Star, no? I can see it all over you. The Blue Vee Beast—that is one quest. I ask you to take on another. Kill the Cut-Queen for us. Do this, and we will consider you a friend. You will be welcome here always."

"Why don't you task your own witches with this?"

"Because they are harmony. They are serenity. It's all they've known. They say prayers to the sea when they catch fish, and prayers to the earth when they dig up onions. It's their way. It's my way."

"And I suppose I'm nothing but a butcher."

"You are not a butcher. You are a warrior."

My blood buzzed when she said this.

"Do this," she said, "and I will tell you how to defeat the Blue Vee Beast."

I narrowed my eyes, then laughed. "Don't tell me you're going to offer me a prayer."

"No. I'm going to give you something more practical." The witch gave me a cunning look. *"Information."*

"Ah." I held her gaze. "If you want me to ask this of the Mercies, then I have two requests."

Mother Hush nodded. "Of course. Tell me."

"I want you to let Sasha and Aarne stay here for as long as they wish. I brought danger on them, and it ended with the death of their friend. They can't go back to Mercy-killing in their old territory, and they can't go with us to Blue Vee."

Hush nodded. "Fair enough. We will take them in. What is your second request?"

"I want you to allow other girls to become Sea Witches, not just the ones born on the banks of the Merrows. I want you to cut a path through the Thiss Brambles and let the girls in need come to you. Will you do this?"

The wind whipped Mother Hush's pearl-green hair around her beautiful face. She pushed it back behind her shoulders with her palms, impatiently, like a child. "No, Frey. We've never taken in outsiders. Not since the very first High Sea Witch brought a hundred witches north to escape persecution in Frem a thousand winters past. She established a settlement here among the Scorch Trees, and we've kept to ourselves ever since." Hush spread her arms wide, palms up. "Those girls bring demons with them, Frey."

"Yes, that's what Juniper said. But you are the famous Sea Witches of the Vorse Merrows by the Quell Sea. How much harm could they do you? Help them. Don't leave them to the thorns. These are my terms."

She was silent for a while. We sat side by side, watching the waves crest on the sea, white tips rolling across the horizon. The clam-digging witches walked by behind us as we sat, chatting cheerfully, wooden buckets thumping against their sides. They nodded at Mother Hush and ignored me, still naked and dripping under my Mercy-cloak.

"Done." Hush held out her hand, and I gave her mine. "Kill the Cut-Queen, and we will open a way through the Ticklish Trail."

Hush released my palm. I reached for my clothes and began to dress. "Tell me how to defeat this beast, then."

"We believe this creature is a remnant of the giants who used to live in the far north on the Wild Ice Plains."

"Do you mean a Jotun? I've heard of them, from the *Blood Frost Saga*."

"Then you know that they can't be slain by ax or sword, for their skin is like hardened leather. But my witches dreamed of this Blue Vee creature—they dreamed of a small weak spot on the back of its head. It is only through this spot that the creature can be killed. Have you heard the saga of Ergill?"

"Of course. The young boy Ergill spies a chink in the dragon's armor and pierces it with his arrow. The dragon dies."

"Yes. Exactly."

"Thank you," I said, and meant it.

She stared at me for a long moment, and then gazed off in the direction of Blue Vee. "Jarl Roth's mother was a Sea Witch, you know."

I raised my eyebrows. "How did a Merrow witch end up marrying a jarl?"

Mother Hush shrugged. "That's a story for a different time. You need to eat and then be on your way. Snow is coming—this week or the week after. You will need to hurry."

I looked up into the Scorch Trees. More people were beginning to rise. I saw green shapes moving across the walkways. I saw sun glinting off green hair.

We would share a quick breakfast with the witches, and then we would leave.

More good-byes. How I hated them.

I went looking for Juniper after I returned from the shore with Mother Hush. I found her and Sage standing on one of the walkways, whispering to each other.

Sage smiled as I drew near. "I'll go check on your provisions." She kissed Juniper on the cheek, and then headed off toward Mother Hush's hut.

"Where have you been?" Juniper's eyes scanned my wet hair and damp tunic.

"Mother Hush made me undress and wade into the sea so I could have a vision. I'll tell you about it later."

She laughed. "Fair enough. Are we leaving right away, then?"

"Yes." I paused. "But Juniper, I will understand if you decide to stay here in the Merrows. Just say the word. I will tell the others."

The Sea Witch lifted her small hand and pressed her palm to my heart. "No. I will not be left behind. We will fight this beast together."

And Hel, but I was relieved when she said this. My heart beat stronger when Juniper was nearby. My life burned brighter with her in it.

Perhaps I should have insisted she stay, even fought her on it, but I let her choose her own path. This was a sign of respect in Vorseland, according to the old ways. It was a sign of love.

Trigve once said everything had a price, and love meant letting fear into your life.

Juniper and I went together to seek out Sasha and Aarne, who were helping prepare food in Hush's hut. Sasha laughed when I pulled her aside and told her the Sea Witch had consented to let them stay. She laughed and embraced me. Her son would be safe, and she would be able to relinquish the death trade. They would spend a warm winter in the witch huts, eating well and sleeping soundly, their peace interrupted only by the exciting arrival of ships and Iber sailors.

We ate our breakfast outside among the treetops, as we'd eaten our dinner the night before: barley porridge with olive oil, warm flatbread, honey-drizzled nuts, and green tea served in hand-carved wooden cups.

A part of me envied Sasha and Aarne for staying with the witches.

I told the Mercies about my sea vision as we ate, and about Mother Hush's advice on slaying the giant, and about the pact I'd made.

They listened quietly, wooden spoons lifting in and out of porridge, lips sipping from steaming cups.

"You don't have to follow me in this," I said. "The promise I made with Hush was for myself alone."

Runa pushed back her bowl and met my gaze. "So if we seek out this queen of the reeds and kill her, Aarne can stay with the witches."

I swallowed a piece of warm, sweet flatbread. "Yes."

"And if we succeed, then Mother Hush will open up the Thiss Brambles and let the outsider girls come to her?"

"Yes."

"And you believe her?"

Juniper tensed, slim shoulders pulling up into green curls. "Sea Witches don't lie. We have no need. Mother Hush will keep her promises." She turned to me. "This won't be an easy thing, Frey. The Cut-Queen has fierce magic. It's said to be ancient, older than the Merrows, older than the sea itself."

I set my knife down and looked off toward the Quell. A few moments passed.

Ovie drained her mug of green tea and reached for a pitcher of chilled wine. "I say we find this marsh-queen and see about this so-called marsh magic. We can make our decision after we've assessed the situation. Then we decide for ourselves if Mother Hush is right and this girl-queen is truly evil."

"Sound logic," Trigve said.

"I agree." I turned to Runa. "Any other thoughts?"

Runa rubbed her cheek with her palm. "Siggy never would have made a bargain with a witch."

"I'm not Siggy."

"What is your plan, Frey, when we find the village?" Runa finished her tea in one steaming gulp and crossed her arms. "Do we simply sneak up and kill every girl we see, hoping we slay the queen?"

"No. We will ask to join them. They are taking in young Mercies—Sasha confirmed as much. We will convert to their Fen religion and get the lay of the land. Then, when the moment is right, we strike."

"I don't like it."

"Then stay here with Sasha, Aarne, and the witches. I would welcome it. It would be a relief to know you're safe."

Runa paused for a moment and then smiled. "As if I'd ever let you leave me behind. Nice try."

I laughed. "There's no winning with you, Runa."

"What about Trigve?" Juniper poured him another cup of tea, eyes lowered.

"He'll have to stay behind." Ovie tossed back a mug of the Iber wine. "The Cut-Queen only converts women."

Runa nodded. "She will drown him on sight."

It was true. All the Red Willow rumors said the same.

"I'm coming with," Trigve replied, voice low.

Trigve and I looked at each other. "Stay until we find the marsh village," I said, "and then you can head on, toward Blue Vee. We will meet up later, after the deed is done. It will still be risky, but I have a feeling you won't care."

He nodded. "You are right. I don't care."

I poured myself a cup of the cool, rose-hued breakfast wine and got to my feet.

"It's decided, then. Are you with me, Mercies?" I raised my mug into the air.

Ovie refilled her cup and stood. Then Juniper. Then Runa.

"We are with you to the end," Ovie said.

"To the end," Trigve added.

We smashed our mugs together, hard, and wine splashed over the sides.

"*Heltar*," I cheered.

"*Heltar*," they echoed.

. . . . .

Mother Hush gave us new clothing before we left—we couldn't march into the Cut-Queen's territory wearing green Sea Witch tunics. We changed into undyed shifts, brown wool tunics, and gray leggings, and then pulled our Mercy-cloaks over our shoulders.

It was a good thing Runa hadn't burned her cloak the night we'd decided to go after the beast. We needed them now to get into the Cut-Queen's village.

"She will ask you about your Elsh hatchets," Hush said when we'd finished.

I nodded. I'd already prepared for this.

Aarne threw his arms around Runa before we left. "Promise me you'll come back," he said, looking all of his twelve years, eyes round and somber.

Runa nodded. "I promise. We will kill this beast, and then we will return to the Merrows and join the Quicks together. We will spend our lives wandering the Seven Endless Forests, free as birds."

Siggy used to say that Mercies should never make promises. I should have stopped Runa when she gave her word to Aarne, but I didn't have the heart for it.

TWELVE

T*rees rose out of blue mist, their crimson trunks twisting upward.* Dark pools of water stretched on and on, dotted with white reeds that whistled in the wind with an eerie, sorrowful sound, like a mother cooing to a dead infant.

The blue mist clung to our skin and clothing, ghostly fingers that left wet trails down our arms. The water teemed with plump black leeches, and strange green snails that glistened with an oily sheen.

The air was cold and fetid, like the melting of muddy snow on an old battlefield.

After the warm hospitality of the Sea Witches, after the balmy Scorch Trees and the delicious food and the peace and safety of the treetop huts . . .

The Red Willow Marsh was desolate, and melancholy.

The marsh stretched from the Quell Sea, north of the Merrows, to the Destin Lush Valley of Blue Vee. We'd taken another path through the Thiss Brambles to reach the bog, but our second trip into the thorns was far more pleasant—we left in broad daylight, with the gentle farewells of the Sea Witches singing in our ears, rather than the sounds of horse hooves on dirt and raised male voices.

The brambles began to thin around midday, and the air grew colder.

When we reached the edge of the reeds a few hours later, it was Trigve who spotted the thin, ancient footpath that wove between the worst patches of water.

Every sound in the marsh made us jump, hands to our daggers, dark images of wild-eyed marsh-girls filling our thoughts.

The path ran narrow, widening around the willow trees, and then narrowing again. A moment's distraction and one wrong step meant a dunking on either side.

We saw no game. No hares, no grouse. Ovie tried catching a few fish for our lunch, but they had an odd color and smell, and we did not eat them. The Sea Witches had given us a supply of dried fruit, hard cheese, and nuts, and this was all we would have until we reached Blue Vee.

The water was too salty to drink, and we wouldn't have wanted to in any case—we carried large flasks filled with the crystal-clear water from the Merrows, and it would have to last.

We were quiet as we trudged through the bog. Especially Juniper. Parting with the Sea Witches had been difficult.

I ducked under a drooping Red Willow Tree and swatted at one of the skeletal black-and-white marsh bugs. I reached up and plucked a gray leaf from the tree. It had a leathery feel, like the hide of a deer, and I shuddered at the touch.

I stepped backward, and my foot slipped off the path. I sank knee-deep into the marsh. Trigve held out his hand and pulled me to my feet. The water made a thick sucking sound as I dragged my leg free.

"Careful, Frey." He pointed at a green viper as it slithered past.

Trigve had been uncharacteristically jittery since we'd entered the Red Willow. He was uneasy, and that made me uneasy.

He knelt, plucked a leech from the tip of my boot, and flicked it back into the dark water.

I hated leeches. They lived in dark places, feeding off blood, like creatures from Hel.

"Can you hear that?" Juniper came up beside us, putting her hand on my arm.

I went still, listening. Trigve did the same.

Nothing.

Nothing but the sound of water lapping against reeds, and leaves rustling on willow branches.

"It's a sort of . . . whispering." Juniper cocked her head and frowned. "I can hear screams sometimes, howling on the other side of the wind." She drew a circular symbol in the air, the one used to ward off demons.

I slid my arm around the Sea Witch's waist and pulled her to me. Ovie stood silently in front of us, legs among the white reeds, her hand on her dagger. Next to her, Runa glared off into the distance, arms tense at her sides.

We didn't know how to find the Cut-Queen's village or how far ahead it lay. I'd asked Mother Hush about it before we left, but she'd merely shrugged.

"I can't give you specific directions. The village seems to . . . move. It's sometimes deep within the marsh and sometimes more on the outskirts, near Blue Vee land." Mother Hush lifted her driftwood staff and tapped it on the Merrows sand, one, two, three times. She whispered something under her breath, but the sea-wind ate the words.

"The Cut-Queen's magic is strong," she added, leaning in so I could hear. "But you are stronger. Rely on Juniper. She will help you. Sleep at the feet of the willows—their roots will support your weight. And don't light a fire. You will just have to shiver through your dreams."

This was all the information we had received.

Trigve reached out and touched a nearby Red Willow Tree, dragging his fingers through the slender gray leaves, down the red trunk. "I suppose we should stop here for the night."

I nodded, and then motioned for Runa and Ovie to join us. We sat down on the wet earth, wrapping our cloaks around us. I handed out the Sea Witch provisions, and we ate in silence.

The first sunset in the marsh was beautiful, in its way. The deep orange racing across the sky, the water reflecting the light in bright, rippling streaks. But it failed to lift my spirits. A sharp scent was on the air—a smell of mold, and rot, and blood.

I didn't look forward to tossing and turning all night, fearing what was out there in the marsh.

"I dread the coming of dark," Juniper said, as if reading my mind.

"So do I." Ovie looked over her shoulder, scanning the horizon.

Runa pulled her cloak tighter about her shoulders and shivered. I moved closer to her and nestled into her side, blocking the wind. The cold often bothered Runa more than it did the rest of us.

Trigve took another bite of the nutty Sea Witch cheese and sighed. "We need something to take our minds off this place."

Juniper made a quick witch sign for hope. "Yes, we need a distraction."

Ovie got to her feet. She brushed crumbs off her leggings, and then reached for her ax. "I could teach you all how to use your blade. Properly, like a Vorse warrior."

Runa raised her eyebrows. "You know the steps of the Seventh Degree?"

The Seventh Degree was an ax-training sequence that involved a series of steps timed with deadly spins, twirls, and weapon swings. It was practiced by Vorse warriors and was not taught to women.

Ovie swung her ax through the air with one hand. "These

grave-dug Elsh hatchets are a gift from the gods. They deserve our respect. There is a subtlety to learning how to use such a blade. A poetry. The men of Blue Vee will know this. We should, too."

"Where in Hel did you learn the Seventh Degree?" Runa asked again.

Ovie held her ax in her right fist and made another graceful, expert swoop through the air. "I've lived many lives before this one, Runa. One of those lives was as a poison taster and whipping boy in the jarldom of Snow-Deep." She paused. "My mother died when I was nine. By the age of twelve, I was just another dirty, half-starved orphan running about the village. I was wiry and had passed as a boy for years. When the local jarl desired a companion for his only son, his men went into the village and grabbed the first boy they saw, which happened to be me."

If Trigve wanted a distraction, he couldn't have asked for a better one. It was rare enough for Ovie to talk, but to also tell us about her past . . .

This from the girl who protected all our secrets, as well as her own.

It was a great honor and a show of trust. We showed our gratitude for Ovie's story by sitting *savalikk*, still as if dead. *Savalikk* was an old Vorse word that meant "like a corpse." It was the traditional pose listeners took when a saga was told around the fire.

"The jarl's son was named Rafe," Ovie continued. "I was

educated alongside him and taught how to use a sword and a hatchet and a double-bladed battle-ax. He and I wore the same tunics, kept our hair the same length, ate at the same table. If any servants in the Great Hall guessed I was a girl, they said nothing. As long as the jarl didn't know, they figured it was best to leave the subject alone." Ovie paused. "Rafe was headstrong, curious, and reckless. He was not made for obedience or for rules. I took his beatings for him, and there were many. Usually it was a switch across the back until I bled. But Rafe was as compassionate as he was stubborn, and the whippings made him miserable. He was ashamed to have a whipping boy, as well he should have been.

"I lived at Jarl Frigg's Great Hall through two winters. Looking back, I think Rafe suspected the truth about me long before I realized, but it all came to a head soon enough, regardless. Rafe and I were sparring—he was good at swordplay and knew it. We were in the stables, doors open wide. It was a beautiful autumn day, with a gentle breeze. Rafe was excited about an upcoming journey to the Gothi temple, and distracted. He swung his blade toward me, as he had so many times before, but this time it hit home. He sliced my tunic open to the waist, my skin as well.

"He dropped his sword when I fell to my knees. He tore open my tunic to see the extent of the wound . . . and he learned what I was. I had developed a little in the last few months and had been taking great pains to hide it, even praying to Valkree that Rafe wouldn't get me a whipping. Stripping down to my waist was no longer an option.

"Rafe saw the wrappings around my upper chest and was astute enough to know what they meant and what they hid. There was no going back. He helped me treat my wound in secret. Rafe and I had been as close as brothers, and after that day in the stables, we grew only closer. When Jarl Frigg found us in bed together five months later, he took my eye. It was to serve as both my own punishment for disguising myself as a boy and Rafe's, as well, for not telling his father after he found out the truth. Jarl Frigg said I should be grateful, for losing an eye was better than losing a life. And perhaps he was right, though it didn't make me feel better at the time.

"Two of the jarl's men dragged me half-naked into the Great Hall that night and dropped me in front of the huge stone hearth, so all could watch. I swore I wouldn't scream, but they hit me until I did. Jarl Frigg took my eye himself—he bashed it in with the hilt of his sword. Rafe howled when the blood poured down my face. I think he would have killed his father if Frigg hadn't ordered three of his warriors to hold him back.

"I was handed over to the jarl's healer. Fitela was a kind man, gentle and wise—he'd been trained by the Orate Healers. He cared for me over the next six days, until any threat of infection had passed. It was Fitela who told me that Frigg had threatened to hang me at the crossroads if Rafe went near me again."

Ovie kept her eye on the fire, hand on the hilt of her blade. "I left on a cold spring day and walked north, the wind behind me and a dagger strapped to my ribs. I didn't look back."

"So that's how you lost your eye," I said quietly.

"And how you got that scar," Juniper added.

She nodded, once.

"Did you ever see Rafe again?" Trigve handed her another dried fig from our stash.

Ovie shook her head, then popped the fruit into her mouth.

"So you were educated with this jarl's son." Runa was eyeing Ovie with something between awe and annoyance. "You can read letters like Trigve."

"Yes, I can."

Juniper reached across me and touched her palm to Ovie's cheek. "The goddess Howl lost one of her eyes when she dove into the Well of Wisdom."

Ovie took another fig and nodded. "I've heard the saga."

I leaned forward and pulled Ovie to me. Unlike Runa, she didn't stiffen, but melted into my arms like snow in the sun. "Thank you for telling us your story, Ovie."

I felt her nod against my neck, blue-tipped hair sliding across my cheek.

And with that, Ovie began to teach us the Seventh Degree.

The following days in the marsh blurred together. Black water and cold mud. Bugs and snakes and reeds. Sunrises and sunsets and long, dark nights. We covered ground slowly, reaching ten miles a day at most. The land never varied, mile after mile, just more of the same. I would have feared we were walking in circles except . . .

Except I could *feel* her.

The Cut-Queen.

It started with an eerie, oily sensation that came upon me whenever I stared into the dark marsh water too long. Then came a queasy feeling in the pit of my stomach whenever a dank wind blew by.

Every night we were drawing closer to her, and something told me she knew we were coming.

I began to see her in my dreams. The child-queen was in a hut, whipping the reed into her flesh. At the end, she'd turn over her shoulder and look right at me, cold green eyes, just as she had in the sea vision. I would jerk awake then, startling Ovie and Juniper.

Trigve would reach out and take my hand, but the dream lingered.

The Seventh Degree helped. The four of us in a line along the path, following Ovie, moving through the *edge dance*, as she called it. Trigve joined us as well, though he had no weapon.

I enjoyed it, the series of poses and steps. We lunged right, then left, spun, jumped, crouched, and swung. Again and again and again, as Ovie called out the positions. It was a dance, but not a dance of fire and freedom, like the wild hilltop revels during the Ostara festivals.

This was a dance of blades. A dance of battle.

I woke up sore, and I went to bed sore, and it felt right and good. My shoulders ached, and my thighs burned. My palms grew blisters. But it was easier not to think about the Cut-Queen when I was holding the ax and following the steps. Juniper said she stopped hearing the screaming on the other side of the wind, and Runa stopped complaining about the cold.

Meanwhile, we were running out of the Sea Witches' food.

Runa enjoyed pointing out that we could end up wandering the marsh, lost, until winter settled in and we starved to death in the mist. And even I was starting to believe her.

But then, on the eighth night, we heard drums.

THIRTEEN

W*e'd practiced the Seventh Degree that night, like every* other.

We were already mastering the basic steps—the beginning movements looked tricky but were actually quick to master. The hardest element was learning to react instantly, and instinctively, while also closing off your mind to all thought. It was a unique balance, one that got easier with practice. It was rather like the Two-Pronged Path, which Trigve had tried to teach me last spring.

We were hungry when we went to sleep, and cold, but a core of peace thrummed inside us, a glow left over from the *edge dance*. We huddled under a willow tree, gray leaves dripping down, cloaks pulled in tight. The day had been crisp and bitter, with a bright blue sky. Winter was on the way. A heavy wind blew—it seemed to move up from the marsh, rather than across it.

I thought I was dreaming at first.

Drums.

Deep.

Hollow.

Close.

I felt Ovie go rigid beside me. We both sat up, eyes turned north.

Clusters of bright orange light, reflecting in the dark water of the marsh . . .

Fire.

Trigve was up now, too. He woke Runa. I woke Juniper. We all sat in the dark, watching, listening.

"There is a town called Mista," Trigve said after a few moments of silence. "It lies on the Blue Vee border, at the edge of the marsh. I've seen it on a map. I will wait for you there at the inn."

I'd known this farewell was coming, and yet the sting of it still took me by surprise.

I grabbed Trigve and held him. "We will be gone a day. Two at most. When it's done, and the Cut-Queen is dead, we will find you at the inn."

"See that you do, Frey. I'll give you two days. After that, I'll come looking for you."

The drums began again. I pulled Trigve tighter to me, until I could feel his bones. I whispered in his ear like a Sea Witch. Then I let him go.

He turned off the path and headed into the bog, toward the bright Elver star that would lead him out of the Red Willow Marsh.

I watched him wade through the murky water, growing smaller and smaller.

I leaned my head back and sent a prayer up to the Gothi god Obin. Trigve had turned from the Gothi path, but I figured Obin wouldn't care. If he did, then I didn't want his help anyway.

I straightened and felt the hilt of my ax against my hip bone. "Are you ready, Mercies?"

"Yes," they said as one.

And Hel, but my heart beat faster when they said it.

We crept forward slowly, heading toward the sound of the drums. I glanced over my shoulder again, but Trigve had turned into shadow, blending into the vast, marsh-mist dark.

The drums grew louder.

Our footpath widened, and we soon reached a wooden walkway. The walkway led into a dark grove of willows—we slipped between the trees and stepped right into the outskirts of the village.

The four of us hovered there, unsure of what to do next. No fence surrounded the hamlet, no guards, no defenses of any kind.

Ovie caught my eye and frowned. It worried her, too. Why wouldn't they need to defend themselves?

The reed-village consisted of a few dozen round huts, like the Sea Witches' homes, but with thatched roofs instead of shingled cones. I squinted. I could see gardens, abandoned wheelbarrows, clothing drying on lines. If not for the white reeds waving nearby, we could have been anywhere in Vorseland.

Except . . .

Except in a regular village, even in the middle of the night, dogs would bark, pigs would grunt, an infant would cry . . .

But there was nothing, nothing but the rustling of the reeds, and the *thump*, *thump*, *thump* of the drums.

Juniper began to fiddle with the seashells in her pocket.

My mind drifted back to the comment Mother Hush had made about the Cut-Queen spreading evil with her marsh magic. I'd thought this reed queen was just another Vorse cult leader, performing esoteric rituals, torturing outsiders, and leading Mercies into darkness. But if there was magic here . . .

True magic . . .

Witch magic . . .

Hel.

Runa turned to me, eyebrows raised. *What now?*

"Come." I gestured for them to follow.

There was a clearing in the center of the circle of homes. Several fires burned in tall iron braziers—this was the orange glow we'd seen earlier. A crowd of girls milled around, long hair tied in thick braids that swung over slight shoulders, dark tunics worn tight to the skin, quiet feet on shadowed ground. None looked younger than twelve, or older than twenty.

A handful of girls knelt in the center, beating on five large wooden drums, *thump*, *thump*, *thump*.

We walked toward the clearing, hugging the shadows, timing our footsteps to the beat. The nights we'd spent learning the Seventh Degree on the boggy marsh had improved our stealth. We were lighter on our feet, more graceful, more silent.

A lone girl stood outside the fire circle, a tiny thing with black curly hair. I crept toward her . . . *slowly* . . . *slowly* . . . until I was close enough to kiss the back of her neck.

I covered her mouth with one hand and yanked her backward into the dark.

"*Where is the Cut-Queen?*" I whispered, lips by her ear. "*Take us to her.*"

I moved my hand away from her lips. The girl shook her head and said nothing.

Runa leapt forward and put her dagger to the girl's slender throat. "Tell us where she is, marsh rat, or—"

The drums stopped midbeat.

My heart stopped with them.

The air felt heavy. Thick. Choking. The sudden quiet was worse than the drums.

The throng of girls in the clearing shifted, separated . . .

The Cut-Queen.

She was small, like Juniper. Smaller, even. She wore a snow-white tunic over brown leather leggings. Her honey-gold hair was loose, hanging in soft waves to her waist, and her bright green eyes were sharp and shrewd and lovely.

I heard a noise, and my gaze moved past her, down to a

young man at her side. He was on his knees, head bowed, his hands tied behind him. His dark hair fell across his forehead, hiding his face . . .

Trigve.

I tensed, muscles snapping to bone. I readied myself to scream, to charge, to attack, *to kill* . . .

Ovie grabbed my arm and shook me, hard. "It's not him. *Look.*"

She was right. He was too thin. Too young.

I put my hand to my heart, as Juniper would have done, and gave thanks to any god listening that it was not Trigve at the Cut-Queen's feet.

The child-queen didn't convert men. This tied-up stranger wouldn't live through the night.

The drums began again. Five beats from five girls kneeling next to five drums, mallets in hand, arms raised, their eyes on the queen.

We stepped forward, toward the firelight, out of the shadows.

The Cut-Queen didn't smile at us or nod in a false, welcoming way. Her cheeks were flushed, and her plump child-lips were pressed together sweetly. She could have been any young Vorse girl, off to milk a cow or fetch water from the stream . . . Except the expression on her face was not one of childlike wonder and energy and spirit, as in Aarne's. It was aloof. Distant.

And dangerously righteous.

"You're here," she said, simply. She nodded at me, a small

flick of her delicate chin. "The reeds told me you'd entered my marsh. You're late. I expected you sooner."

"Did you, then?" I replied, calm and easy, as if the thought hadn't made me go cold.

"Yes. You took your time."

The Cut-Queen's voice was firm and husky, more like that of a grown woman's than a girl's.

I took a step toward her, my hand on the hilt of my ax. I felt Ovie press herself to my right side, and Runa to the left. Juniper stood slightly behind, whispering a prayer of protection.

Whatever I did next, the Mercies had my back. To the end.

Loyalty like this was a rare thing, beautiful and pure.

If the Cut-Queen took my life when I tried to take hers, would it matter? I'd earned the trust of the three women beside me, and their love as well. I'd tasted freedom, however short-lived. What else was there in life?

I took another step forward, and the Cut-Queen gave me a quick, shrewd smile. "They call me the Cut-Queen out there in the world beyond the willows and reeds, do they not?"

I nodded. "They do."

"Here they call me Elan Wulf."

The queen moved toward me now, slowly, one small, boot-clad foot in front of the other.

My eyes scanned the marsh-girls who had gathered in a pack behind her.

Some of them looked like girls anywhere, sweet, shy, bold, indifferent, sad, eager, nervous. But others had a *raw* look in their eyes, a look that made me want to creep backward into the dark and *run*.

The Cut-Queen reached me. I stood my ground, Mercies beside me.

She put her hands on my shoulders, then stood on tiptoe to reach my ear. "I felt your coming," she whispered. "I felt it in the way the reeds moved in the breeze. I felt it in the way the water lapped against the edges of my village. I felt it in the curve of the moon and the shimmering line of the horizon."

I wanted to feel disgust at the closeness. Even fear. But when the Cut-Queen breathed into my ear, I felt . . . *strength*.

This marsh-queen was *alive*. More than most.

Elan Wulf pulled away from me and took a step back. "What is your name?"

"Frey."

"Frey, are you here to join us? To become a Willow, like these other girls? Are you ready to leave your old life behind, to obey my command, to follow your reed-sisters wherever our path of vengeance may lead?"

"Yes," I lied. "Willingly. With my whole heart."

"Do you believe in the goddess Fen?" Her voice was louder now, echoing across the hamlet.

Out of the corners of my eyes I saw the brazier flames rise higher, as if in answer to her question. "Yes," I said.

"Do you believe that marsh magic is the only good and pure magic and that all other magic is shadowed and evil?"

The reed-girls tensed behind her, awaiting my answer.

I hesitated.

Elan's question was eerily similar to the one Mother Hush had asked when we'd first met in her Scorch Tree hut.

I'd missed something. Something important.

This was not about simply killing the Cut-Queen, of ridding the marsh of danger, of marching into Blue Vee a proven warrior.

Sea magic.

Marsh magic.

It became clear, a burst of sun through a dark cloud.

This was a battle between witches.

Mother Hush had said this task was about darkness and light, and maybe it was.

But it was also the beginning of a Witch War, and I had just walked right into the middle of it.

There were ancient songs and sagas that told of the great Witch Wars during the Lost Years, of the tragedy of the Maidens in the Tower, and the Battle of the Red and White, and the Moss Witch Massacre of the Western Hills. The wars raged season after season, until one witch finally bested the other. People slain, villages burned, ceaseless storms, thundering seas, bloodred skies, resurrections . . . It made for beautiful, terrible stories.

There hadn't been a battle between witches in centuries, not since the Sun Age, when Vorseland was ruled by a series of fierce female jarls.

Was this how a Witch War began? One witch trying to

quietly kill the other, back and forth, back and forth, until it dissolved into an endless battle, with all of Vorseland on its knees?

"I know nothing of marsh magic," I answered the Cut-Queen finally, ignoring the rush of blood to my heart. "But we came here to learn."

Elan Wulf gave a curt nod and shifted her gaze to our black Mercy-cloaks. "We have many of your kind here. They grew tired of wandering, of being treated like vermin. Here, they are treated like Vorse. Here, they matter."

The Cut-Queen raised a hand and gestured toward the fires. "Follow me into the light, Mercies."

What else could we do?

We followed Elan farther into the clearing, into the ring of fire. The dark-haired prisoner looked up at me as I walked past. His eyes were dark brown, and afraid. A girl stood to each side of him, daggers drawn.

"Please," he whispered. "Please."

This was all he said, and it was enough.

I would have risked it all right then to free him. I would have taken on the queen and all her reed-girls.

I closed my eyes . . .

I could do it. I could rush the Cut-Queen, knife forward, slice open her neck ear to ear before she took her next breath. I could do it, and to Hel with marsh magic and Witch Wars.

I opened my eyes again. We were outnumbered ten to one. It would be a death sentence, for all of us.

I reached down and touched the prisoner lightly with my fingers as I passed, tips grazing his shoulder. He didn't look up again.

Elan Wulf halted by the last fire. She lifted a slender arm and pointed toward a dark lump in a corner of the clearing, near what looked to be a large vegetable garden.

"Throw your cloaks onto the pile, girls. You are done with that life. Embrace the goddess Fen, and leave the death trade behind."

I walked to the pile. The air smelled of fresh-turned dirt from the garden, and I breathed deeply. It was a nice change from the heavy air of the dank marsh. I unclasped my familiar, hateful black Mercy-cloak and tossed it on top of the others.

Runa went next, then Ovie, and Juniper last of all. She dropped the cloak from her shoulders . . .

And her pale-green curls spilled down her back.

A Willow girl hissed. Then another. And another.

The girls began to chant. *Sea Witch, Sea Witch, catch her, snatch her, cut her, drown her, burn her . . .*

I stepped in front of Juniper, followed by Ovie, then Runa. We drew our knives and moved into the first fighting stance of the Seventh Degree.

"*Try to take her,*" I screamed. "*I dare you.*"

"*Quiet.*" The Cut-Queen's voice cut through the din. Her girls hushed. She stepped lightly around me and pushed her fingers into the Sea Witch's hair, squeezing the curls into a fist. "You have very green hair for a simple Mercy-girl. Explain yourself."

I snapped my hand around Elan's wrist and squeezed until I felt her delicate bones move underneath my palm. *"Let her go."*

A flash of silver.

And a knife was pointed at my heart.

"Get your hand off our queen." The girl had dark brown hair and blue eyes. She was tall, almost six feet, and carried herself with the upstart arrogance of a new devotee. She pressed the tip of her blade into my tunic, scraping it lightly across my chest.

Hel.

The plan had been to lay low, take stock, and display our loyalty and commitment to Fen. I needed to end this. Now.

I dropped Elan's wrist and raised both hands, palms out. "Juniper was raised in the Merrows, it's true, but she left that life behind. She's with me now, heart, mind, soul. She longs to learn the magic of the marsh and to follow Fen, just as I do. As we all do."

I forced myself to stand still and hold the Cut-Queen's gaze. She gave me another shrewd smile, and then released Juniper's hair. "There will be no Sea Witch burning tonight. Lower your knife, Tarth."

The tall Willow withdrew her knife but stayed where she was, hovering beside me. I nodded at Ovie and Runa, and they put their blades away as well.

"I welcome all the homeless, the orphaned, the outcast, into my village." The Cut-Queen lifted her chin, shadows dancing across her face. She glanced out across the clearing, across the reed-girls. "I take you in, whereas the Sea Witch mother would let you die in the thorns."

Juniper said nothing. I said nothing. It was true, after all. The Sea Witches had let girls die in the thorns.

Elan lowered her voice, her eyes back on my green-haired Mercy. "Did you know Mother Hush takes those dead girls and gives them back to the sea as a sacrifice to the goddess Jute? She calls these girls to her. She sends the sea-wind to whisper in their ears. They heed her plea . . . and end their lives with Thiss Brambles wrapped around their hearts. This is the price Hush pays to keep her sea magic."

Juniper had remained quiet and calm when the Willow girls started chanting. She'd held still when Elan grabbed her hair. She understood the part we were playing here and had done well. But I felt her shudder beside me now. Her hand darted into her pocket and clenched her shells.

She hadn't known about the Jute sacrifices, then.

Juniper turned to the Cut-Queen, a twist of her thin shoulders. "You're telling the truth. I can feel it."

"Yes." Elan closed her eyes and the tight line of her mouth relaxed. She looked young suddenly. Very young. "I was one of those girls. I died in the thorns. But when the witches threw me into the sea, I didn't sink down into the deep, food for the fishes and an offering to Jute like all those before me." She paused. "I was resurrected. I washed ashore with the tide, not dead, not drowned, but alive. I ran back into the brambles and found my way here."

Elan opened her eyes and swept her hand out before her. "This was nothing but an abandoned marsh hamlet when I arrived. *I* created this."

"You've given us Mercy-girls a chance, Elan." I kept my eyes blank and open. "A choice. We want nothing more than to follow you and pledge ourselves to Fen."

Elan Wulf tilted her head to the side and studied me again. This was it. If she was going to call us Mercies out as frauds, she would do it now.

I noticed she had a handful of freckles across the top of her nose. They seemed out of place, too sweet, too whimsical. The Cut-Queen was a full foot shorter than Runa, and yet she carried herself with the gravity of a king.

A part of me was in awe of this tiny twelve-year-old girl. I could see why they followed her. I could see why all of Vorseland was afraid.

She was a *force*.

Elan blinked, then reached forward and touched the ax at my waist. "So how did a group of Mercies get Elsh hatchets? I'm curious."

"We dug them up from an Elsh graveyard," Runa snapped, the old bite back in her voice. "Want to try to take them from us?"

I shot her a warning look, but Elan just laughed, a sweet sound that made her seem, for a moment, like the girl she was.

"Weapons stolen from a graveyard. I haven't heard that one before. Come, Frey can tell me about it over supper."

So that was it. We'd made it in. It hadn't been that difficult, in the end. One quick kill and we'd be done and on to Blue Vee.

"But first," Elan said, "you need to prove yourself a true Willow. I found a Quick wandering my marsh yesterday. Drown him. Sacrifice him in the name of Fen."

Hel.

I'd given up the death trade, but the death trade hadn't given up me.

"Death tracks us, unwilling to let us go."

Ovie had been right. I couldn't seem to leave death behind no matter which choice I made or what path I took.

Tarth pulled the Quick to his feet and shoved him toward me. I could see now that his back was bleeding, his tunic in tatters. He'd been whipped hard and was weak from it.

I put my arm around his waist and let him lean on me.

Most of the Willow girls had retreated into the thatched houses, unwilling to watch what was coming next. Proving that despite the Cut-Queen, despite abandoning the Mercy-trade or whatever life they'd had before this, some compassion still endured within them.

But Tarth lingered nearby, as did a dozen or so other girls, each with that raw, hollow look to them. One young, wiry Willow in particular made me uneasy. She had curly brown hair and cold ice-blue eyes—I'd seen half-starved wolves that looked friendlier.

The girl stared at the Quick, and her hands twitched. She was eager for this. For his death.

"Back off." I gave Tarth a hard stare, and then looked at the rest of the Willows, ending with the wiry girl. "Get away, all of you. The queen can watch. No one else."

They didn't move. I didn't move.

Elan made a dismissive gesture with her hand, and the girls slunk back into the shadows, all except Tarth, who refused to leave the queen's side.

Runa held her dagger in one fist. Juniper fiddled with her shells. Ovie stood, one leg forward, hand on the hilt of her ax, in the third starting position of the Seventh Degree.

The Quick shifted against my shoulder and sighed. I felt his breath across the side of my neck.

"What is your name?" I asked.

"Warrick."

I pulled out my water flask and held it to his lips. "Drink, Warrick."

He tilted his head back and let the cool spring water drip down his throat.

A twist of fate and it could have been Trigve drinking from my flask, about to die. Instead of this stranger.

"I'll make it quick, lamb."

He nodded. His dark eyes were sad, and wistful. I grabbed my dagger from the sheath on my calf and cut the rope around his hands.

He didn't try to escape. Where could he go? He was too weak to run. There was only one way this was going to end.

"The world is cursed," he whispered. "And yet, I do not want to die."

I faced him. I didn't shy away from his gaze but met it head-on.

"You will go to Holhalla as a warrior," I said. "Kiss me, as a hero from the sagas kisses his lover before he leaves for battle."

His freed arms slipped around me, and I pressed my chest into his. He put his hands to my cheeks, and I felt the calluses on his palms—the trademark of an archer.

My lips parted, and he kissed me deeply, and slowly, as if no one were watching, as if we had all the time in the world, as if this were the beginning of something, rather than the end.

If Elan Wulf was surprised, she didn't show it.

The Quick and I waded into the marsh together, the water lapping at my waist, his long arms brushing past the white reeds. He hissed when the brine hit his wounded back.

I looked over my shoulder at the Cut-Queen. She stood on the wooden dock at the edge of the village clearing, her small body tense and regal.

Forget the plan, Frey. Grab your ax, give Warrick your dagger, don't think, just do it, strike, attack, kill her now, kill her NOW.

I glanced at Runa—she knew what I was thinking. We were Mercies. We were sisters. I looked to Ovie, then Juniper. They were ready. They would take Tarth, leaving the Cut-Queen to me.

I went for my blade . . .

"Don't," Warrick said. "It won't work—"

"I know everyone who moves through my marsh, Frey."

I looked up.

Elan Wulf eyed me calmly as I stood in the water, ax held high. "I know you have a companion out there. I let him pass through. He's almost reached the Blue Vee border, but I could have him dragged back here with one nod of my head, with one jerk of my finger."

She paused.

"Kill the Quick, or your friend will die in his place."

Hel.

I slid the handle of my ax back into the sheath at my waist.

I turned and pulled Warrick into my arms, my heart against his. I could feel the warmth of him through his clothes, despite the cold, stagnant water. I felt him sigh again, his ribs moving against mine.

He smelled of forest, of pine and juniper and dirt, of cold nights and warm days, of wool and leather and wood smoke, of youth, of life.

He tilted his head down, as if to kiss me again. His lips touched my ear, and he lowered his voice. "She's holding two other Quicks. They're locked in the building near the garden. Help them."

I stepped back and clasped his forearm, hand near his elbow. "I will. I swear it."

"Think of me sometimes," he said.

"I will. I swear it."

"Kill me quick," he said. "Kill me merciful."

I shook my head. "No. I want you to fight me. Fight me like a warrior so our Vorse ancestors will shout your name when you reach the Great Hall of the Slain."

"I will," he said. "I swear it."

It took a long time for him to die. He gave me all he had left, and it was enough. It was a hero's death. We wrestled in the water until his strength gave out, and then I pushed my knee into the small of his back to keep him down until the end.

A group of Willow girls waded out to us when it was done. They pulled him from the water, onto dry land. They doused his wet clothes in a strange-smelling nut oil and lit him on fire. The oil sped the burning, and the flames danced.

The Quick would be nothing but ash by morning.

FOURTEEN

"*Come into my den,*" *she said.*

That's what the Willow girls called their huts . . . *dens*. As if they were foxes.

"Come, Frey. Warm yourself by my fire. You are now a true Willow. You have sacrificed to Fen and are protected by her power. You are entitled."

The Cut-Queen had sent Runa, Ovie, and Juniper to eat with the other Willows in the long communal building on the other side of the clearing. I hated being separated, but I was soaked with dank marsh water and melancholy beyond caring. I followed the marsh witch into her home meek as a child.

The Cut-Queen's den was plain and simple. One large round room, a few square windows, a plank table with a homespun linen cloth. A shrine to the goddess Fen stood off to the side, complete with small wooden carvings and figurines made from woven reeds and marsh grass.

I flinched when I saw the straw bed beside the plain red rug. This was it. The place from my sea vision.

I dropped my pack and my ax and sat down by the hearth. I took off my leather boots and warmed my toes, letting the fire steam my tunic and leggings dry.

Eventually a graceful black-haired Willow brought us food, and it was simple, like the hut—a bowl of cabbage stew boiled with garlic and onions. I had no appetite and wanted to refuse it, but I hadn't eaten something warm in days.

Besides, I was used to eating after bringing death.

I sipped the salty broth, and then felt guilty at the pleasure it brought when it slipped down my throat and warmed me from within.

I should have given the Quick my dagger and let him make a run for it. He would have preferred to die fighting the Willows in the marsh.

But even as these thoughts crossed my mind, I knew it wouldn't have worked. Elan had me kill Warrick not because she couldn't do it herself, but as a way to show my loyalty.

I glanced at the Cut-Queen over my soup bowl. Elan sat beside me near the fire, eating her dinner cross-legged, head bowed, honey hair slipping over her shoulders.

I never could have gotten this close to the queen if I hadn't killed Warrick.

I could still feel the Quick's calloused palms on my cheeks. How could someone be so alive one moment, so warm and vital and *real*, and then so cold and still the next?

If anyone would know, it should be me.

I watched Elan from the corners of my eyes as I sipped the

rest of my soup. I imagined reaching over, shoving her narrow, childish chin to the side, and slitting her throat right there before the fire.

And then I thought of Runa, Juniper, and Ovie eating in the longhouse, surrounded by the Cut-Queen's followers. Some of the Willows were former Mercies—they would know how to use knives and bring death.

I would wait for them to fall asleep. We would win this battle by stealth, not numbers.

Meanwhile, I had a part to play, and I would play it well. I owed Warrick this, at the very least.

I finished my soup and set the bowl down in front of me. Elan glanced at my bare feet, and then began to take off her boots as well, her short, slender fingers pulling at the leather laces. She wriggled plump, bare toes in front of the fire and sighed softly.

It was such a natural gesture, easy and relaxed.

She began to massage her feet between small, pale hands. "How did your parents die, Frey?"

"Snow sickness, when I was twelve."

Elan nodded. "I lost mine at nine. I was ten when I was snatched while I slept in a corner of the village inn and sold into a Bliss House. I killed the woman who ran it." She paused. "Eventually I went west, planning to join the Sea Witches, like many other lost girls. I hoped to find a family again. To find a home." She paused again. "All I found was thorns."

Her green eyes met mine. They didn't look so cold, in the firelight. They were kinder. Softer.

"Your story is similar to my own," I said. "I've often wondered what would have happened to me if my Mercy mentor, Siggy, hadn't come along. I suspect I would have ended up like the girl we found hanging at the crossroads outside Levin."

"It is a story shared by many of us." Elan nodded toward the shrine in the corner. "It was Fen who brought me back to life after the Sea Witches dropped me into the deep and left me for dead. Fen drew me here, to this place. I was called to build this haven for all the lost, abandoned girls of Vorseland."

I undid my thick braid and spread my hair over my shoulders so it could dry. "Some people don't believe in divine crusades."

Elan tucked her knees under her chin and wrapped her arms around her thin legs. "Are you one of those people?"

"No. I have faith."

She nodded.

"And yet, you didn't want to kill the Quick."

"No."

"Because you don't truly yearn to follow Fen, to learn the magic of the marsh?"

"I didn't want to kill him because I'm tired of death. That's why I quit the Mercy-trade. That's why I came here."

"Death is part of life. There's no point in running from it." Elan rubbed the end of her pink-tipped nose with the palm of her hand. "Killing these men in my marsh ensures that rumors of my ruthlessness will spread across Vorseland."

She paused. "Did you see any fences around this village? Any guards?"

I shook my head.

"No magic is as strong, or as powerful, as fear."

I watched the Cut-Queen as she stared into the fire. I was once again filled with an unsettling sense of awe.

I was beginning to see why the Willows followed her.

"You killed for Fen." Elan turned her head and gazed up at me. "And you will need her help, I think, for you are answering a call of your own."

I narrowed my eyes. "What do you mean?"

"You're after the Blue Vee Beast. The reeds whisper to me of all the doings in my marsh, and they told me this." She paused. "You did right to come here. You will want Fen behind you if you're going to try to kill this creature. You will succeed with her on your side."

A marsh breeze blew in and made the candle on the table flicker. The wind didn't smell as foul as it had when I first entered the Red Willow Marsh. The earthy, salty smell had become familiar. Almost . . . pleasant.

"You wouldn't have died in the thorns, Frey. You would have fought the sea when the witches threw you in, just as I did. I can see the anger in you. And the fire." The Cut-Queen stretched out her arm and put her hand on my heart, pressing in with her palm. "It radiates from your core, a warm, bright glow, the color of sunset and blood."

I squirmed under her touch, and she dropped her hand.

"Do you want the rest of my soup?" She held out her wooden bowl. "They always give me too much."

I took it and drank the rest of the broth in one long swallow. "Thank you for the food," I said quietly.

She nodded, and then tilted her head and rested her cheek in her palm. I saw pale blue veins running down her forearms.

Elan Wulf seemed fragile suddenly, soft skin, soft veins, one simple knife slice separating her from death.

"You're meant for greater things than dying in this marsh, Frey. Or in the Sea Witches' thorns."

I shrugged. "Perhaps."

"Many heroes of the Vorse sagas started off as mercenary wanderers, seeking food, shelter, coin, and a quest. But they were all men. There are no sagas about Boneless Mercies. Nor songs, either."

It began to rain outside, a gentle tap on the thatched roof.

I turned my eyes back to the fire. I wouldn't be tempted into a confession of my glory hunger. Elan Wulf could guess all she liked, but I wouldn't confirm it.

"It is not possible to avoid death, Frey, but you can rise to meet it. I learned this the day I rose from the Merrows."

She yawned then, and stretched, smiling as she reached her thin arms toward the ceiling, just like any other girl.

But when she rose to her feet, arms at her sides, she was the Cut-Queen again, back straight, eyes cold. "I've seen her."

"Who?"

"*Fen*. I've seen her roaming the marsh, floating on the water, glowing with magic, righteous and powerful. I saw her the first night I came to this village. I knew then what I was supposed to do." Elan cast another glance toward the shrine in the corner. "When the Willow girls are ready, we will raid the Sea Witches and take the Merrows for ourselves. We will move into their Scorch Trees and trade with ships. The Sea Witches who convert will be allowed to live. The rest will drown. We will take what they have, but we will not keep it selfishly to ourselves, as they do. We will share."

I kept my face calm, my eyes serene. Serene as Mother Hush.

So that's her plan. She's going to attack the Merrows.

"I thought you wanted to live peacefully here in the marsh." I kept my voice light, almost indifferent.

"Who told you that?" Elan clenched her fist and raised her arm. "I want *vengeance*. I plan to bring about a Great War. The Sea Witches have held the Merrows for long enough. It's time for a change. I'm not content to live among these reeds forever, just as you were not content to stay a Mercy. Let's make something happen, Frey. Let's see what we're made of. *Let's force the world to its knees*."

My blood began to pulse harder, my heart beat faster. I was on my feet, fist to my chest.

"Yes," I said. *"Yes."*

The Cut-Queen turned and walked to the shrine. She picked up a three-foot reed leaning against the wall and began to tap it gently against her legs. "Pain is a part of life. Pain is a *sign* of life. The dead feel nothing. Without pain, people become lazy and selfish and mean. It is a blessing to feel the sting. Fen sends it to me as a gift. It clears the mind and opens the senses. Watch and see."

Elan approached her bed. She slipped her tunic over her head and knelt on the red rug, just as I had seen in my vision. I flinched when she turned her back to me and I saw the crisscrossing wounds again, slashes of pink and red against her pale skin.

She lifted her arm . . .

And began to strike.

At first, her face was hard, lips pulled tight against her teeth, the grim whistle of the reed ripping through the silence of the night, cutting through the gentle sound of the rain.

The reed hit its mark again and again. And again. And again.

The blood smelled bitter against the sweet, fresh rain.

The strikes of the reed, the sound, the rhythm . . . It was like the beat of the drums, as dependable as waves hitting the shore.

I began to feel dreamy. My mind began to settle and *slow*.

It was just a tickle in my ear at first. A whisper, a murmur.

The reeds spoke of the stars, of the trees, of the murky water, of the fish, of the wind, of battles and deaths and births, and all things past and present. They spoke of me and the Mercies and of a dark-haired man in fur.

My mouth filled with the taste of the bog, of peat, of mud, of roots and bark, grass and endless gray sky. I put my palm to my heart and dug my fingers into my flesh.

Mother Hush said I had no magic in me, but I heard the Cut-Queen's reeds all the same. I didn't have sea magic, but marsh magic pulsed in my veins, and it was as real as a slap across the face.

Elan screamed, and I trembled at the sound.

It was the glory scream from my vision, the scream of victory, of triumph.

My eyes drifted to the window, out to the marsh, then back to her, to this marshland girl-queen . . .

She was *glowing* now, soft yellow light beaming through her skin like sunshine.

I stretched toward it, arm out, hand out, chest out, heart open wide.

I felt it. I felt the magic. I felt *Fen*.

I cleaned her afterward, wiping away the blood with a soft, wet cloth. I rubbed her skin with a wound-healing salve from my pack, one Juniper had made from lavender, rosemary, sage, and beeswax. I could feel the heat of the cuts through my palm.

Elan sighed heavily under my hands. "Thank you, Frey. It doesn't sting so much now."

I looked down at her, stretched out on the simple, straw-filled mattress, her cheek turned toward me. I saw her back, naked and raw, and the delicate blue veins of her eyelids, and the wisps of honey hair on her neck—she was no longer a queen or a leader or a marsh magic witch. She was just a child.

One summer night, under a shining full moon, Trigve told me about a book written by an Elsh queen, one who had lived so long ago she'd almost dissolved into myth. Her name was Lilt, and she had written of many things: her lovers, the gods, aging, the changing of the seasons, memorable feasts, and long, dark nights spent alone. She'd also talked of ruling and the wisdom she had gleaned through the years.

Lilt had said the most successful rulers knew that displaying vulnerability, carefully, in the right way, could be as powerful as ruthlessness.

I'd wanted to kill the Cut-Queen earlier, when she'd ordered me to drown the Quick in the marsh. I'd ached for the feel of her hot blood spilling across my hands.

But now?

She lay on the bed, bone-weary after the reed-whipping, unprotected, exposed. It was long after midnight, and she yawned and rubbed her eyes like any child who has stayed up too late.

I couldn't do it.

I couldn't fight a child.

I'd killed children before, yes, the sick ones, the ones in pain, the ones at death's door. But to *fight* one, one as small as this girl? To slay her as I would a beast?

Was there glory in this?

"Sleep here with me." Elan reached out and put her hand on mine. "Be my sister, my marsh-sister, just for the night. Ever since . . . Ever since I died in the thorns, I don't like to sleep alone."

She sat up when I didn't answer. She carefully pulled her tunic back over her head, wincing when the wool touched her skin. "Stay here tonight, Frey, if you are brave enough."

"What about my companions?"

She laughed, and it was quiet, sweet, and tired. "They will sleep in one of the dens with the other Willows. They are safe."

I had gone with the Cut-Queen to her den. I had swallowed my rage. I'd shared her food and seen her magic and tended her wounds. I had played along, and done well enough.

But Runa, Ovie, and Juniper were waiting for me out there in the night. There had been no chance to speak after the death of the Quick, but we knew one another's thoughts, and hearts. They would be waiting for me to come find them, so we could finish this.

"Do you know the myth of the Red Willow Marsh?" Elan yawned again and lay back down on her side. "There was a legend about this bog from long ago, from the time of the sagas. This marsh was said to be a place of deep magic. People believed that if you rested here for a night, you would wake as either a poet, a mystic, or a god." She paused. "Which would you choose?"

"None of them. I would wake as a conqueror."

She smiled. "Just as I thought, Frey. I would choose the same."

I gently pushed up her tunic and rubbed another round of salve into her skin, from her neck down to the last welt near her waist. She was asleep by the time I finished, soft, even breaths, rib cage rising and falling.

I climbed into the bed next to her, sliding underneath the sheepskin covers, and she curled into me, instinctively, like Ovie.

FIFTEEN

T*he rain had stopped, and the crescent moon was high in the night* sky.

I'd left Elan sleeping deeply, still curled toward me.

Runa, Juniper, and Ovie were standing in the shadows near Elan's den, underneath a great Red Willow Tree.

"Is she dead?" Runa whispered, arms crossed, eyes sharp.

I shook my head.

"Why not?"

"She . . . She fell asleep right beside me, unguarded and careless as a child." I paused. "It all just seems too easy. I tried to play the part of the devoted Fen follower, and I think I succeeded, but something feels off."

Juniper glanced over her shoulder toward the Cut-Queen's den, then back to me. "I befriended one of the Willows—she used to be a Mercy and still has a heart left, unlike some of the other girls here. She told me over dinner that whenever a new group of Mercies arrives, Elan takes one of the girls into her den and bewitches her."

My eyes met Juniper's. "I went into Elan's den wanting to bleed her slowly until she begged for mercy. But some of the things she said started to make sense. Then she reed-whipped herself in the name of Fen and . . . and I saw her *glow.* Glow like sunshine. I heard the reeds whispering to me and felt the marsh magic running through my veins . . ."

I paused. There was a fervent note in my voice that had never been there before. It sounded pious, borderline devout.

I shook my head, trying to clear my thoughts. "We need to get out of here, Mercies."

"Yes." Ovie looked troubled and uneasy. Her fingers strayed toward the dagger at her ribs. "This place is corrupt. I can feel it."

I glanced at Runa. "How did you get away from the Willows? That Tarth watched us like a hawk."

Runa nodded at Juniper. "Our witch did a spell."

Juniper waved her hand toward the nearby reeds. "There is seawater in this marsh. I said a salt prayer over the den, a simple one for sleep. They will wake, though, if given reason."

I turned to Ovie again. "Did you check to see if any Willows were on night watch?"

She nodded. "Yes, but there are none, which worries me. Whatever you're going to do, do it soon, Frey."

Runa turned and stared across the dark marsh. "It's too quiet. Too still. We kill the queen, and then we get out of here. I feel . . . watched."

"Yes. It's as if the reeds have ears and the trees have eyes. And they are all whispering to one another." Juniper pulled the seashells from her pocket—orange, white, and pink spirals, fragile and pretty as blown glass. She began to pass them from one palm to the other.

I knelt and dug my fingers into the dirt at the base of the willow tree. This was a trick Trigve had taught me—a way to get grounded if my mind ever felt as if it were drifting and lost.

But the soil smelled of marsh, of wet and bog and mud. I breathed in deep, and then stood and brushed the dirt from my hand.

"The Cut-Queen wants to start a Witch War with Mother Hush," I whispered.

Juniper and Runa jerked their heads toward me, eyes wide.

Ovie simply nodded. "I guessed as much. We must kill her, Frey."

I didn't answer.

The reeds had started whispering again, a soft rustle against the wind. I strained forward, toward the marsh—I could almost make out words . . .

"You are wavering." Juniper made a harsh gesture with her hand, one to ward off evil. "*Nante, nante.* Ovie is right. She has to die."

I still said nothing. The voice of the marsh was breathing in my ear now, the whispers going through my skin, wrapping around my heart, whispers of *Fen*, of *magic*, of *battles and glory*, of *blood and death* . . .

Runa grabbed my shoulders and shook me. "She's bewitched you. Get that girl-queen out of your head, and do what you came here to do. Frey, are you listening?"

Runa shook me again, harder, and the sounds of the reeds began to fade.

My eyes drifted over to the smoldering remains of Warrick in the clearing.

"Yes," I said. "I will kill her. I swear it."

I looked out across the hamlet and found the building near the garden. "The Quick I drowned had two companions. I swore I'd help them. We'll need to free them first."

I motioned for the Mercies to follow me. The prison was a square building with a turf roof and thick log walls—it had probably been used for food storage when this place was a regular Vorseland village.

The iron lock on the door was the size of my hand. Runa grabbed it and gave it a hard yank. It would not break easily. Or quietly.

"Here." Juniper reached into her leather pack, pulled out a large iron key, and tossed it to Runa. "I took this off Tarth while she slept."

I knelt and slid the dagger from the sheath on my calf. "Runa, Juniper—get the Quicks free while I deal with Elan. Ovie, stand guard. Be ready to run when you see me."

I kept my mind on Warrick as I crept back to the Cut-Queen's den. I thought of the final moments, when he fought me in the water, of how hard he had clung to a life that I helped the Cut-Queen take from him.

I wondered if his summers had been happy, filled with cloud-berry wine and wild hunts and sunlit forest naps. I wondered if his winter nights had been long, the dark hours spent telling sagas by the fire in one of the Endless Forests.

The Cut-Queen was waiting for me.

She stood beside her bed, hair tangled, cheeks pink with sleep. She didn't look regal or ruthless. She just looked like a twelve-year-old girl.

"Come back to kill me, then, Frey?"

I went *savalikk*, still as death, one foot forward, blade in hand.

"Yes," I said, simply.

She knelt at my feet and lifted her chin until I could see the veins in her slim neck.

"You're a glory-seeker." Elan looked up at me, green eyes wide. "You want to matter. You want *more*. You shouldn't be ashamed of this feeling. These thoughts drift through all women's hearts."

"Do they?"

"Yes." Elan lifted a finger and ran it across her neck. "Cut my throat, then. I won't stop you. Reality isn't fixed, like hills and mountains, but shifts like the wind. Life is just a cloud passing by the sun. It is nothing. It is everything. Take it away from me, if you wish."

I looked away from her, from the soft skin of her throat, from the vulnerable tilt of her head, and toward the window, to the reeds, to the marsh.

I shut out the whispers this time. I heard nothing at all, only silence.

I turned, drew my ax, and held it out to the Cut-Queen. "Come. Let's fight like warriors, girl to girl, knife to knife. Don't make me kill you while you kneel at my feet."

"No." Elan pressed her hands flat against her thighs and leaned her head back another inch. "Run your knife across my neck. Watch and see and learn."

"Fight me," I said again. *"Please."*

Her thin ribs rose and fell. "Don't worry, Frey. We will meet again."

I watched the blood pulse in her neck, *beat*, *beat*, *beat*.

Elan Wulf was going to slip into Holhalla as quietly as any of my other Mercy-kills, and there was nothing I could do about it.

I offered her a drink of water from my flask, and she took it, one long last swallow. Then I reached down and gripped her honey-colored hair in my left fist. I pulled her head back until she was looking at the ceiling.

I closed my eyes and slit her throat.

I cradled Elan as the life flowed out of her, blood warm, like summer sunshine.

I watched as she grew paler and paler, fading into death.

When it was done, I gently laid her on the floor and smoothed the hair away from her forehead. She looked peaceful. Somehow, under all the blood, she seemed at peace.

She had told me she was going to bring about a Great War. Instead, she had knelt at my feet and let me run my knife across her neck.

I understood nothing.

I wished I knew one of Juniper's farewell prayers.

It's over. Time to leave.

I stood and took one last look at the infamous Cut-Queen of the Red Willow Marsh . . .

A *glow.*

She was *glowing.*

It started near her heart, a faint yellow pulse under her skin. It grew brighter and brighter. It ran down her torso, down her legs, up her arms, and out the top of her head.

Her skin was *shining* suddenly, bright, blinding sunlight, yellow rays beaming outward.

The Cut-Queen blazed. She was nothing but glow, nothing but light.

I felt Fen.

I felt her tingling down my spine and shooting through my fingertips. I felt her beating in my heart and rippling through my blood.

I looked down . . .

Elan exploded into a thousand brilliant drops of sizzling sun.

I was blinded. Stunned. I pressed my palms to my eyes until the light-burn faded.

I blinked, and moved my hands. I was alone in the room, blood on my knife, blood on the floor, and no queen.

She was gone.

I hadn't believed Elan when she'd spoken of her resurrection after dying in the Thiss Brambles. I thought she'd been weak when the Sea Witches found her, but still alive. They tossed her into the Quell Sea, and the salt water healed her wounds—she'd woken up from a spell, of sorts. After all, she was young and strong and a fighter.

But now . . .

The Witch Wars raged for decades during the Lost Years. A witch-queen would die, and everyone would believe the battle was over and peace had returned. But then she would turn up again a few years later in a different place, leading another group of women, preparing to start another war.

It had all happened before, and now it was happening again.

I found the Mercies where I'd left them, near the prison. The two Quicks beside them—one dark, one blond—looked young and strong. Good.

"Is it done?" Runa whispered.

"Yes. It's done." I glanced at the Willow dens. Could I hear girls moving inside? Or was that just the whisper of the reeds?

"How?" Runa hissed. "How did she die?"

"Later, later. Fetch your Mercy-cloaks from the pile. I think I hear the Willows waking up. We need to *move*."

I grabbed my cloak, swinging it around my shoulders with a practiced sweep of my arm, then turned to the Quicks. "Ready?"

They both nodded, expressions weary, but steady. They would not slow us down.

"Let's get the Hel out of this marsh, then." I pointed toward the path leading east, on the other side of the garden. "It will be hard to see the trail in the dark, but we can follow the Elver star—"

"Traitors."

Tarth. She stood in the doorway of Elan's house, blade in hand, her gaze shifting from me in my blood-covered tunic to the freed Quicks and back again.

"I will cut you for this. I will cut you all to pieces for this. I will drown your parts in the marsh. You will never reach Holhalla. You will spend eternity wandering the reeds, I—"

Juniper, our tiny, gentle Sea Witch, ran forward, green curls flying, and planted her knife between Tarth's ribs before the Willow could take her next breath.

"Run." She yanked her dagger from the tall girl's chest. *"Run, Mercies."*

Tarth fell to her knees, clutching her side.

"*Juniper*," Runa shouted, pointing to the left. *"They're coming."*

Willows began to pour out of the dens, knives flashing in the dying firelight.

The reed-girls screamed—*screamed*—and the sound stopped my heart and made my hair stand on end.

It was fierce. *Raw.*

Juniper jumped the garden fence in one leap and took off toward the open marsh.

Ovie and Runa turned and followed her, the dark-haired Quick right on their heels.

"Run," I screamed to the blond Quick, who still stood frozen in place, eyes on the advancing Willows. *"Run."*

"*The world is ending*," he yelled.

I grabbed his arm and yanked him forward. "I won't let you die. Run with me. *Now.*"

His eyes cleared, and he nodded.

We ran.

THE BEAST

SIXTEEN

We left a trail of dead Willows all the way to the border of Blue Vee.

The Quicks were named Vital and Leif. Vital was shorter and blond and solid, and Leif was taller and dark and lithe. They fought with us side by side through the Red Willow Marsh. They hid with us in cold, snake-infested salt water, and pulled Willows in by their feet as they passed. They jumped with us from Red Willow Trees onto the backs of screaming girls.

The Quicks killed, and we killed, and the night stretched on in one long battle of blood.

A Willow jumped from a tree and slid a knife into Ovie's shoulder, but our Mercy still slew three girls with her ax before we'd gone a half mile. Runa drowned three more. Juniper stabbed two in the throat, and I knifed two in the back.

I lost count after this.

We fought quietly, and we fought well.

Vital and Leif had lost their bows in the marsh when they were taken, but one of the Willows was also an archer. I drowned her in the marsh, arm locked around her neck, her feet kicking up sprays of salt water. Afterward, I gave her bow and quiver to Vital when Runa refused it. His aim saved our lives more than once over the next few hours.

The last Willow attacked near dawn. She was brown haired and slender, and I held her arms behind her back as Juniper slit her pretty throat. We tossed her into the marsh and didn't look back. I could see the pine trees of the Blue Vee Forest up ahead, and I cared about little else.

When I finally dragged my numb legs from the cold marsh water and put my feet on the solid earth of Blue Vee, I was so grateful I said a prayer of thanks to Valkree.

We'd survived.

The six of us wearily picked leeches off one another as we walked toward the small village of Mista, flinching as our fingers closed on slick, plump bodies.

A trail of dead Willows. A trail of black leeches.

It felt as if we'd been wandering the marsh for years, not days.

After a few dozen yards, I noticed Vital was limping and trying hard to hide it. Droplets of sweat had gathered at his temples, and his skin had gone moonlit pale.

"Viper," he said when I caught his eye.

"Let me see." I dropped to my knees and felt his right ankle—it was swollen and hot to the touch. "You can't walk much farther on this."

"I know," he said. "Leave me here. Come back when you can."

I shook my head. I had no intention of leaving the Quick behind.

I motioned for Runa to look at Vital's ankle. She knelt beside me and held her palm to his skin. We exchanged a glance.

Runa rose to her feet and put her arm around Vital's waist. He slid his arm around her shoulder and leaned against her. The pain faded from his face as he took the weight off his right leg.

"I can walk now," he said. "Let's keep going."

Runa half carried the Quick the rest of the way to the village, though she was just as tired as the rest of us.

When I finally caught sight of the little houses of Mista, just as dawn began to streak across the sky, I put my fist to my heart.

Smoke rose from two dozen stone chimneys, and painted shields glinted in the early-morning light. The scene felt Vorse. It felt like home.

We dragged ourselves through the town square, and then simply stood still, dazed with exhaustion, until Ovie spotted a squat, snug building with a sign hanging in front of the door.

"The Cowardly Raven Inn," she said.

Trigve was inside, waiting for us, as promised. He stood near the stone fire pit in the center of the room.

I went to him.

"I worried about you," he said softly, lips near my ear.

I didn't answer. I was too weary, too spent, to tell him everything that was in my heart. I nodded, then reached up and slid my fingers into his hair. I pulled his head down toward mine until his forehead touched my own.

"*Trigve*," I said. And it was enough.

The innkeeper had a well-kept herb garden, and Trigve found Blood Onions for Vital's wound. He made a poultice to draw out the snake poison, and then used a Cloud Yarrow compress to stave off infection in Ovie's shoulder. It would have to work until we found the village Mender.

The inn was full, and all the rooms taken, so after Trigve tended to Ovie and Vital, we threw ourselves in front of the fire and slept like the dead, not waking all through the day. Nothing stirred us, not the coming and going of travelers, or the noise of the noon meal, or the thunderstorm Trigve said hit midday and shook the roof with its fury.

The sun was sitting low when I finally opened my eyes, its slanting autumnal rays shooting across the freshly scrubbed oak floorboards of the inn. Juniper and Ovie slept close on either side of me, and two gray, long-legged deerhounds were lying at my feet. I didn't move for a few moments, but just lay still, watching the innkeeper's children. They were playing Sword and Dragon in the long, rectangular room, jumping over benches and running across tables and giving stirring speeches about their brave deeds.

I smiled at their game, then untangled myself from the girls and the dogs, careful of Ovie's wound. I stretched, and every part of me was sore, from my scalp to my heart to my toes. I was bruised from our battle in the marsh, and I'd taken a handful of shallow knife cuts as well.

Vital, Runa, and Leif were in a pile near two more dogs on the other side of the fire. They rose when I did, and we all stumbled over to one of the thick wooden tables. Trigve wandered in from outside a few moments later and called for the innkeeper.

A thin man in his forties appeared from behind a set of double doors leading to a kitchen. He brought us a loaf of rye bread, a wedge of cheese, and steaming bowls of pork sausage stew. We all ate silently, deep in the pleasure of hot, well-made food.

The innkeeper stood nearby and cheerfully chatted with us as we cleaned our plates, kindly ignoring our dirty, marsh-smelling clothing and our reticence. He told us he had seven young daughters and four dogs, which "ran wild all over the damned village." His wife was a traveling mystic and had trained with the Orate Healers in Iber. She visited them only rarely.

The innkeeper's eyes flashed when he spoke of his nomadic wife. He was proud of her.

I sat with my thigh next to Trigve's, our shoulders touching. It was good to be near him again.

I was reluctant to leave the inn when we'd finished eating. After the marsh, it seemed such a warm, happy place. I liked the chaos of the dogs and young daughters and the comfort of the blazing fire, but we hadn't enough coin left to stay the night.

Besides, I knew the Quicks longed to get back to the forest. Those roaming archers never liked to be indoors for long.

I gave the innkeeper the last of our coin, minus two copper klines, and we went in search of the healer. We passed a group of milkmaids near the well—four pretty girls on their way to the cows in the nearby meadows, wooden pails swinging at their sides. I asked them how to find the village Mender. They smiled and pointed out a small, turf-roofed home tucked into a secluded corner near the blacksmith.

The healer opened the door on our first knock, as if she were expecting us.

She was young and slender, my age, with straight blond hair and an easy, laughing look to her gray eyes. She glanced at our Mercy-cloaks, shrugged, then told us her name was Fife and let us in.

Her one-room home was neat and smelled fresh and faintly floral, like a field of wildflowers in full summer. Herbs hung from every inch of the rafters, along with purple stems of lavender, mesh sacks of dried marigold blossoms, and long strings of garlic and onions.

The seven of us took up most of the empty space in the room, and it was very crowded, but somehow this made the place feel more comfortable and welcoming.

Fife motioned Vital over to the fire and had him take a seat on a small bench. She knelt, pushed up his dark Quick leggings, and peered at his ankle. Juniper, Trigve, and I hovered near her shoulder, watching her, and she didn't seem to mind.

The poultice had taken down Vital's swelling, but Fife drained the remaining poison away with a strong-smelling sunshine-colored powder that she retrieved from a glass vial kept in a locked cabinet near her large bed in the corner.

"What is it?" Trigve asked, eyes fixed on the yellow dust as she poured it into the palm of her hand.

"A spice from Iber called True Ermic. It's rare and costly, but I've had some luck growing my own. This was made from roots grown in my own garden." Fife knelt again, pursed her lips, and blew the powder across Vital's ankle.

Green drops immediately began to ooze from the snakebite and drip onto the floor.

Vital sighed as the poison left him, and the color began to come back to his cheeks. "Thank you," he said, his blue eyes on the healer's. "Truly."

Vital's gratitude to Fife was written plainly across his face. His injury, if it had been allowed to fester, could have taken his foot or even his leg. He wouldn't have been able to join his Quick brothers during their snowy hunts in the upcoming season, or, indeed, ever again.

The healer stitched up Ovie's wound next. She motioned for the Mercy to take off her tunic, which Ovie did with no ceremony or shame, dropping first her cloak, then her ax.

Fife didn't seem surprised at Ovie's having such a weapon, which made me like her all the more. She unbound Trigve's compress and clicked her tongue at the open wound—a three-inch gash of crusted blood. "You did good to use yarrow on this," she said, looking at Trigve.

He smiled, one of his quick, amiable grins.

Ovie shook her head when Fife offered her a drop of poppy oil before she began to sew the cut, which made the healer laugh. She heated a needle over a candle flame and began. Ovie made no sound during the stitching, though it must have hurt like Hel.

Whenever I tried to picture the Mercy goddess, Valkree, I imagined Ovie standing on a snow-covered mountaintop, holding a shield.

When it was done, Fife applied a thick ointment that smelled of garlic and black walnut, and bound the wound with clean linen. Ovie stood, rolled her shoulder, and then gave the healer a rare smile. "This will serve. Thank you, Mender."

Trigve pulled our last copper coins from his pocket and tossed them to Fife. She caught them in one hand and tucked them away into a hidden pocket of her flowing yellow-gray tunic.

"Will you all share a mug of cider with me?" Fife began to pour out honey-colored liquid from a nearby jug without waiting for our answer. "I make it myself from apples I pick in the hills."

The cider was delicious, both tart and sweet, with a fiery bite that landed at the back of the tongue. It lessened the ache of my bruises and warmed my marsh-frozen blood.

It didn't seem possible that I'd been in the Red Willow Marsh the day before, drowning a sweet Quick named Warrick, and then watching a girl-queen whipping magic into herself with a bone-white reed.

The marsh was death, and this was life. Apple liquor on the tongue, drying herbs scenting the air, twilight turning the sky outside the windows a vivid midnight blue.

"So are you going to tell me where you got those wounds?" Fife eyed Vital, then Ovie. "That shoulder laceration was given by someone who knew their way around a knife, and that was no ordinary snakebite—it came from a marsh viper."

We drank our cider in silence and didn't answer.

Fife just nodded. "You crossed through the Red Willow Marsh then. I'm surprised you're still alive. We get very few travelers from that direction of late."

"You are right," I said, finally. "We've come from the marsh."

"You are either very brave or very stupid." Fife's gaze traveled slowly around the room, taking in the seven of us. "Brave, I think."

"Perhaps we're both," I said, softly. "And the marsh is safe again because of it." I ran my fingers over one of the feathers in my Mercy-cloak, eyes on the fire. "As safe as it ever was, at least. The Cut-Queen is gone, and we killed a fair number of the Willow girls as well. The rest should scatter shortly. Spread the word, if you will."

Fife cocked her head, and candlelight flickered off her heart-shaped face. "Sometimes I would hear drums in the night, coming from the reeds. It made my blood run cold. That's one less monster lurking in the dark, crawling through my nightmares. Thank you for whatever it is you did. For however long it lasts."

We finished our drinks and set the mugs on the wooden table in the center of the room. The fire blazed up, and I noticed for the first time that Runa had dried blood on her tunic—the garment was stiff with it. Juniper had blood under her fingernails, as did Leif. Locks of Vital's hair were stained red, and Ovie had dried droplets on her right temple and on the top of her ear.

I wondered where the blood lurked on me.

I thought again of the comment Ovie had made in the brambles, about how death was tracking us, unwilling to let us go.

"I would not refuse another round of cider, if you're offering." Leif held out his mug to Fife and winked at her in a pleasant way.

I looked at the Quick, fully noticing him for the first time since the Cut-Queen's hamlet. There was a shine to his dark eyes that I quite liked. He seemed easygoing, like Trigve, whereas his fellow Quick, Vital, was perhaps deeper and more thoughtful.

Fife smiled but shook her head. "You've had enough. It's stronger than you think."

Leif laughed and ran a hand through his thick, dark hair before turning to his fellow Quick. "Ankle better?"

"Yes."

"Ready to go back to the forest?"

Vital put a strong archer's hand on his friend's shoulder. "Yes. A thousand times yes."

Fife walked across the room, tunic flowing, and grabbed a gray cloak from a hook near the door. "There is a sulfur spring nearby. You should visit it before you leave—it will help with the healing. And you all need a bath. You smell like a bunch of marsh rats. Come, I will show you the way."

I'd heard that hot springs were common enough in Blue Vee, though rare elsewhere in Vorseland. I'd never been to one. Warm baths were a luxury, and Boneless Mercies had little to do with such things, even when they were offered to us during the rare nights we spent at inns. Siggy had said they would make us soft and unfit for the death trade, and perhaps she was right.

But we were no longer Mercies. We would take our pleasures where we could.

The hot springs were about half a mile from the village, under a canopy of tall pine trees. Trigve asked Fife many questions as we walked, about her herbs and her training, and she answered them all willingly enough. More than willingly.

The springs consisted of three small stone pools, each of which had been lined with smooth rocks. Mist rose off the milky water in great clouds, the steam hitting the cold night air and turning pale. It smelled faintly of sulfur, but a gentle night breeze swept most of the scent away. Besides, I'd take sulfur over the dank, evil smell of the Red Willow Marsh any day.

Runa retrieved the flint box from her pack and lit the torches that stood on wooden poles near each of the pools. Light blossomed across the water. We gathered at the edge of the largest basin, and the warm mist caressed our skin.

Fife pulled Trigve off to the side before she left and invited him to spend the night in her bed.

I said nothing. Trigve could do as he liked. I might even have stayed with the healer in his place.

But in the end, he shook his head.

To her credit, Fife merely smiled. "The offer stands. And if you ever desire to learn the healing ways, I will consider it a fair trade—share my bed and I will share my knowledge." She reached forward and touched Trigve's cheek with her fingertips. "I've always had a weakness for men who lead with their hearts. I liked you from the first moment you stepped through my door."

She kissed him, a gentle kiss. A healer's kiss.

She broke away, and then swept her hand in our direction. "I believe part of your company is on its way to Jarl Roth to fight the beast."

"We are," Trigve replied quietly. "Will you wish us well?"

"Yes." She paused. "I will be here, if you change your mind."

And with that, she left.

Trigve joined me beside the pool a moment later. "I take it you heard Fife's offer?"

"I did, indeed. You could have accepted."

"I know." He paused. "Jarl Roth must be a tolerant man if a young healer in Blue Vee is allowed to live alone, to take men as she pleases and teach them her skills. He must be a fair ruler, not a follower of the old ways, like Jarl Keld."

I shrugged. "Maybe Roth knows nothing about it."

Trigve tilted his head, eyes on the rising steam. "It's more than this, I think. Mista has an air of . . . ease. Friendliness. Even with the Red Willow Marsh on one side and the beast prowling the villages on the other side of this forest, the people of Mista weren't suspicious or wary. Their eyes weren't hollow from fear and grief. It could be a sign of a good ruler."

I shrugged again. "I guess we will find out."

"Are we going to stand here all night talking, or are we getting in the water?" Leif's low laugh echoed across the pools.

"Come on, then," I shouted. "Let's do this. The first one in gets to sing 'Four Old Crones Go A-Bathing' from *Ergill's Saga*."

I unclasped my cloak and dropped it on the ground. I set my ax beside it, and then plopped down on a nearby rock and began to pull off my boots. Vital sat down beside me, tossed his blond hair, and began to unlace his boots as well. I looked over my shoulder at him and smiled. "I plan to enjoy this."

"So do I," he said.

"No more than me." Runa dumped her cloak at my feet. She'd already shucked her boots and wool leggings. She pulled her tunic over her head and strode over to the pool naked as the day she was born.

The rest of us stripped down to the skin and slipped into the scalding water, hissing as the steam hit our wounds, then heaving sighs of contentment as the pain faded away. We were too tired, and had been through too much together, to feel any awkwardness. And the mist and milky white water provided some level of privacy, as much as it mattered.

The heat melted my muscles and my mind. I released my hair from its braid, tilted my head back, and let the water lap at my neck. We didn't talk or sing. We just took pleasure in the silence.

SEVENTEEN

L*eif and I could hear his screams from the prison.*"

Vital's voice was deep and sad. We had set up camp a few miles into the Blue Vee Forest, and now all stood by the fire, waiting on Juniper. The Sea Witch was off alone, readying herself for the long prayers that were needed when a friend died too young, or for an unjust cause.

We would hold Warrick's last rites as the moon rose high in the sky, in the way of the Quicks.

Vital glanced at me, and I nodded for him to keep going.

"The Cut-Queen hit him with her reed, over and over, in the name of Fen. She meant for us to hear his pain."

"She planned to kill one of us next, then let the other go to spread word of the horror." Leif stood by Vital's side, shoulder to shoulder.

Trigve pulled out a flask and handed it to me. "I bought some *Vite* in Mista before you arrived," he said. "I figured we'd need it."

I took a long, fiery drink, and then gave the flask to the Quicks.

"He died bravely," I said. "He fought me with all he had. The Cut-Queen hadn't crushed his spirit—he was fierce right up to the end."

Vital sighed and nodded. "Then we will see him in Holhalla."

Juniper returned and began her prayers. They were part dance, part gestures, part song, part chant. Midway through, she had me kneel and hold my hands over the flames so the heat could burn away any dark spirits that might have clung to me as the bringer of Warrick's death.

We all felt better afterward. Warrick was gone, his soul sent on to Holhalla by a loving Sea Witch. Now the Quicks could heal.

I passed around the *Vite*, and we talked long into the night. I told Trigve what had happened in the Cut-Queen's village, and I told the Quicks about our time with the Sea Witches and Mother Hush.

Last of all, I spoke of Elan Wulf, of her refusal to fight me at the end, of how I slit her throat and spilled her blood, of how she died in my arms, of how she dissolved into a blinding beam of light.

"A witch resurrection," Vital whispered a few moments after I'd gone quiet.

"Yes," I said.

It was well after midnight, but I could still feel the warmth of the hot springs in my bones. Warrick's funeral had spent me emotionally, but I was calm. Content.

"So Mother Hush sent us into the middle of a witch battle." Runa took a long drink of the fire liquor and swallowed. "As if it were nothing more than another Mercy-kill, as if we were nothing more than mercenary warriors, paid for slaughter. As if we didn't deserve to know what we were getting into."

Juniper put her hands up, palms out. "It is not that simple, Runa. She thought we could help. And so we did. Her plan wasn't as heartless or cunning as you make it out to be. She was seeking the greater good."

Runa gave Juniper a shrewd look. "Did she tell *you* the truth, Juniper?"

Juniper paused for a moment, and then shook her head.

Runa shifted on the ground and kicked another branch into the fire. "Everything I've heard of witches confirms what I saw in the Merrows. They take no interest in the wider world and are mainly concerned with themselves."

Ovie leaned back, crossed her ankles, and shot Runa one of her rare half smiles. "Aren't we all?"

I held up my hands like Juniper, palms out. "It didn't work anyway. The Cut-Queen might be gone for now, but she will rise again. She knew I had planned to kill her. She'll come back all the stronger after this resurrection."

Runa shrugged, her strong shoulders pressing into waves of dark hair. "Let her start a Witch War then, if she lives. What does it have to do with us?"

"It will be the first Witch War in centuries." Juniper pulled up the hood of her Mercy-cloak, and her face fell into shadow. "This is no small thing."

I nodded. She was right.

Leif and Vital had been quiet during our talk of the Cut-Queen, sipping *Vite*, eyes on the fire, thoughts on their dead companion, no doubt.

I turned to them and took the flask when Vital handed it to me. He was younger than I'd thought at first. His fear and exhaustion in the marsh had made him appear older. But no beard grew on his smooth face—he was seventeen at most.

"What will you both do next?" I asked. "Where were you headed when you were forced to cross the marsh?"

Vital looked up, blue eyes meeting mine. "Warrick had a twin brother named Calder. They hadn't seen each other in two years, ever since his brother took up with a band of Quicks who left to hunt the Green Wild Forest, north of Blue Vee—they crossed the marsh before the Cut-Queen ruled the reeds. Warrick had gotten word that his mother had died, and he wanted to see Calder and tell him. We knew the risks and went anyway. We were Warrick's Blood Brothers."

"Blood Brothers?" I raised my eyebrows.

"Quicks tend to have two or three close companions—they take an oath of blood to never leave the others' side." Leif ran his finger across his palm. "We slit one another's hands and let our blood mingle. It's an old tradition, passed down from the warrior blood pacts in the sagas."

I pressed my thumb into my palm and remembered the blood oath the Mercies and I had taken the night we'd decided to go to Blue Vee.

Trigve nodded. "In *Ergill's Saga*, Ergill makes a blood oath with his closest friend, Jerrick, before they set off to hunt the dragon. And they both keep the oath to the end."

"Yes." Leif paused. "We won't break our blood pact. We will carry Warrick's message to Calder and spend the winter with the Green Wild Quicks, hunting the red deer and caribou that run through those woods—it's the northernmost of the Seven Endless Forests, a sea of pine and juniper trees that stretches on until the edge of the world."

Leif's eyes lit up when he spoke of the woods.

"You are all welcome to join us," Vital added, "if you like to run and hunt and are good with a bow."

"Liar." Runa eyed the arrow-filled quiver on the ground beside Vital, and then nudged it with her toe. "We aren't welcome. The Quicks don't take in Boneless Mercies. We are too grim. We aren't boisterous or merry."

Vital grinned. "We will make the rare exception." He picked up his bow and held it out to Runa. "Here, let's see what you can do."

Runa reached for the bow . . . and then brought her hand back to her side. "No. We can't join you. Not yet. We are headed down a different path."

Vital dug in his pockets and pulled out a bit of beeswax,

which he began to rub into the bowstring. "Aye. You are going to try your hand at the Blue Vee Beast, I think."

"Yes," I said.

Both Quicks looked at me then, but it was Leif who spoke first.

"Give up that path, I beg you. Come hunt with us this winter. The other Quicks will accept you after I tell them what you did in the marsh, how you freed us and killed the Cut-Queen. We will spend the season running through the snow, eating what we kill, visiting Night Markets, getting drunk by the fire, telling old tales. It's a marvelous life."

Vital nodded at his Blood Brother's words, then leaned forward and put a hand on my shoulder. "Don't be seduced by that beast and by the gold. Don't let the creature take you as it has everyone else, Frey. Come with us. It is a wonderful life, as Leif said."

"It does sound marvelous, Vital. Truly." I took another swig of Trigve's *Vite* and stood. I motioned to Runa, and she rose and followed me into the dark beyond the fire.

"What do you think?" I took Runa's arm and pulled her closer to me so we could whisper. "We might not get an offer like this again. Should we give up Blue Vee and go with the Quicks?"

Runa opened her mouth, closed it, and then shrugged. I slid my arm around her waist, and we stood in the dark, side by side, pondering.

I attempted to send my mind down two paths again, as Trigve

had taught me. I slowed my breath and imagined one path, north, to the Green Wild Forest, and one path west, to Blue Vee. I closed my eyes and waited for the light to come, to shine on the right road, the correct choice . . . But after several breaths, both paths remained shadowed.

"We can ask Ovie," I said, finally. "Or Juniper. See if they've changed their minds."

Runa's eyes met mine. "What about the beast?"

"Someone else will kill it."

"Will they?"

I didn't answer. I was thinking about what Runa had said earlier, that the Sea Witches were only concerned about themselves.

If we followed the Quicks north and ignored Jarl Roth's plea for help, would we be any better?

Later that night, I lay awake beside the dying fire, staring up at the stars as if my future were written there. My limbs were intertwined with Ovie's, our breaths in rhythm. I heard wolves howling in the distance—we were in the far west now, and they were much more common here. Their song sounded wistful, full of hidden meanings and long-lost secrets.

Juniper slept beside Vital. She seemed to like the thoughtful blond Quick. She lay wrapped in her cloak, Vital's arms around her, his chin buried in her thick green hair.

The sight of it made me smile.

Trigve was nestled into my back, in Juniper's usual place.

"I killed a Willow," he whispered, when the wolves had quieted and everyone had fallen asleep. "On my way through the marsh. A scout, I think."

"You did? How?"

"She had a knife to my throat before I heard her coming. She held me captive for several hours and seemed to be listening to the reeds, waiting for further commands. She was tall and strong and swift, but that didn't protect her from the marsh snakes. One bit her leg, and I saw my chance. I drowned her, Frey."

"Good," I said.

But he turned away from me, toward the fire. "Is it? I want to heal, not kill. Violence is not in my nature."

"I know." I shifted forward and pulled Ovie closer into me, careful of her wounded shoulder. She breathed in deep, and I felt her ribs move against my chest. Her hair was free from her braids for once, and I rested my cheek on her head. She smelled like snow.

"All of us will now arrive in Jarl Roth's Great Hall with blood on our hands," I said. "We are true warriors."

"Does it matter?" Trigve paused. "I thought you and Runa might have changed your minds about going west, after the offer from the Quicks."

"We talked, yes, but made no decision. Part of me wants to follow my heart and go with Vital and Leif. The thought of it . . . It makes me glow inside, like the Northern Ice Lights dancing over fresh snow. But part of me also hungers to go on to Blue Vee and do the right thing. The *greater* thing."

"You will have to decide soon," he whispered.

The wolves started howling again, and the sound made me think deep things, dark things—our saddest Mercy-kills, Siggy's death, dying children, the sagas, the witches, all the things the Vorse have forgotten, and all they never knew.

EIGHTEEN

L*eif had heard that Calder's band of Quicks was hunting near the* village of Nils, in the northwest. Nils was a tree town—meaning it was one of the few villages deep inside a Vorse forest, rather than hovering at the edge. We all had at least five days of walking the Blue Vee Forest together before the Mercies and I had to turn straight west, to Blue Vee.

If we were still going to Blue Vee, that is.

We covered about twenty miles a day, moving fast, even running when we hit clear, open stretches of the trail. Only a few main roads ran through the Blue Vee woods, but we didn't see many other travelers, which suited us fine. Our company numbered seven now, and the passing woodcutters and farmers tended to duck out of our way as we crossed paths, rather than the other way around. Which, I thought, was a nice change.

The pine trees in the woods were tall and straight, with an elegant, noble air, like thin, graceful kings and queens, nodding stoically as we passed. Our feet stirred up their brown needles as we walked, and I found the rustling noise rather comforting. The air was cold, but it had not snowed since those first early flurries the night we decided to seek out the Blue Vee Beast.

I knew, though, that the weather would not hold for long. I could feel the snow in the air, feel its frigid bite at the back of my throat when I breathed in.

On our second day with the Quicks, Juniper pulled me off the trail at high noon. She told me she'd appeared to Mother Hush in a dream the night before, and warned her of the Cut-Queen and her resurrection.

"Are you angry?" she asked. "I should have asked you first. I wasn't sure the dream-walking would work. We are moving farther and farther away from the Merrows."

"No, you did right, Juniper. Hush should know."

Juniper nodded, her gray eyes worried. "What do you think it would mean if the Witch Wars return to Vorseland?"

A raven cawed in the top branch of a nearby pine tree, and we both looked up. I watched it for a moment, then turned back to Juniper. "It would mean the world is shifting. Trigve says that time moves backward as well as forward and that the age of the sagas will continue to rise and fall throughout the centuries, like the rise and fall of the sun."

Juniper took my hand in hers, our fingers intertwining. "Runa was right. The Sea Witches have been too isolated, too caught up in themselves. A Witch War would end this, for better or worse."

. . . . .

It didn't take long for Leif and Vital to discover Runa's affinity for archery. She stared at Vital's bow with so much yearning as we walked—they couldn't help seeing it. They demanded she go hunting with them our second night in the forest, and she came back an hour later, laughing and joking, holding a pair of snow-white boreal rabbits in each hand.

I hadn't seen Runa this happy since the shooting contest with Aarne, and it warmed my heart.

Ovie, Juniper, and I continued to practice the Seventh Degree beside the fire, but Runa now spent her time constructing arrows out of pine branches. She and the Quicks had been taking turns using Vital's bow, but they hoped to run across a Night Market soon. I heard Runa tell Leif she'd take up the death trade again to get the money for her own bow, if that's what it took.

Runa had hated being a Mercy more than any of us, so it meant something when she offered this.

We feasted every night on stories, as well as *Vite* and wild game. We laughed and ate and drank, and we talked of everything and nothing. Trigve recounted obscure myths he'd read in books, and the Quicks talked of the Great Hunts of old. Juniper told tales of the Sea Witches and the goddess Jute. I tried to recall all the epic legends Siggy had shared with me on cold winter nights when it was just the two of us, from the tale of the Lone Girl in the *Blood Frost Saga* to the story of Midnight, of her bravery during the Raven War, as told in the *Sea and Ash Saga*.

I didn't tell stories from the *Witch War Chronicles*. None of us did.

Only Ovie and Runa declined to tell any tales. Ovie because she rarely spoke, and Runa because she was Runa.

There was an ease among us all, even after so few days. Killing the Willows had brought us close.

Juniper slept next to Vital now, and I often caught them talking softly beside the fire or standing shoulder to shoulder, praying to the stars.

On the fifth night, the mood around the fire shifted from contented and carefree, to thoughtful and melancholy. Everyone seemed to move slower, shoulders hunching as we gathered firewood.

No one spoke of it, but we all knew a crossroads was coming. We'd passed the tree town of Welkin earlier, and the path would fork soon—one direction going to the Destin Lush Valley of Blue Vee and Roth's Great Hall, and the other north, toward Nils, and the Skal Mountains, and the Green Wild Forest.

Runa, Ovie, and I sought out our Sea Witch during her evening prayers on that last night. We found her underneath a twisted, ancient juniper tree, a cluster of dusky berries dangling above her head.

I grabbed a handful of the berries and rolled them between

my palms, releasing the sharp, earthy scent. "Which is it to be—north with the Quicks, or west to Blue Vee?"

No one spoke for a moment. This was a decision that would not be made lightly by any of us.

I closed my eyes and listened to the soft voices of the Quicks in the distance, preparing food by the fire. I listened to the wind blowing through the tops of the pine trees far above. I listened to the sound of my heart beating out its strong, Lion Star rhythm.

I turned to Runa. "Your desire to follow the Quicks is as clear as the midsummer sun."

She nodded. "Never have we had so much as now. Let's follow Vital and Leif and spend the winter in the Endless Forest. We will hunt and live and be free . . . And nothing evil in this world will be able to touch us."

I turned to Juniper. "You must choose a path as well. Which is it?"

Juniper pursed her lips and blew over her right shoulder. "Mother Hush wouldn't have given us the secret to slaying this giant if she didn't think we stood a fair chance. The people of Blue Vee need us. We stick to the original plan and go west."

I nodded. "What say you then, Ovie?"

Ovie's eye met mine. "If we don't like the look of the place when we get there, or feel we truly can't defeat this monster, then we will leave. But if we can aid Jarl Roth in this battle, then we are obligated to do so. It is right. It is heroic. It is in keeping with the old ways. The hearts of Boneless Mercies beat just as strongly as any Vorse warrior's."

Ovie's speech stirred me, as she had meant it to. I wanted to raise my ax in the air, tilt back my head, and shout *heltar* into the night sky.

Juniper made a Sea Witch sign for valor, and then stepped forward. "One vote for the Quicks, and two for Blue Vee. What will you decide, Frey?"

I held the Sea Witch's gaze. "Ovie is right. We should try to kill this beast if we think we can. It is the heroic choice. I say we go west to Blue Vee."

Afterward, I stood in the shadows next to Trigve. We both watched Runa as she split wild goose feathers with her knife and attached them to arrows with nimble fingers, eyes intent upon her work, lips pulled tight.

She'd accepted the decision with silence and grace, but she was the one who would suffer the most from it.

Siggy and I had met Runa three years ago. She'd sought us out in the southern village of Gyda and hired us for a Mercy-kill. It wasn't until we arrived at an isolated crossroads near the Black Knife River that we discovered the Mercy-kill was for herself.

Mercy-suicide was rare in Vorseland, but it wasn't against any laws, old or new. Siggy had done a few throughout the years, a dozen perhaps. Though I learned later that she'd never had a request from someone so young.

I remembered Runa as looking very beautiful and very tall. Her expression was solemn in the light of the fading sun, and determined.

She'd looked straight at me, then Siggy. "Can you shoot a bow? I'd like to be pierced with an arrow through the heart."

I was still an apprentice at the time and didn't have my Mercy-cloak, so Siggy had taken Runa's bow from her. She aimed, drew back the arrow . . . and then lowered the bow again. Siggy handed the bow back, eyed the dark-haired girl head to toe, and then smiled. "There will be no Mercy-kill tonight. You are coming with us to learn the death trade. We don't have much, but we have each other."

Runa nodded, just once, and that was that.

She burned the bow later. She threw it into the fire, and we never spoke of it again.

"Tell us a tale, Runa," Leif said. "You have yet to do any story-telling. Tell us a tale of heroes and tragedy and archery."

The Quicks were no fools, and they knew by our moods that we had chosen to continue to Blue Vee. We'd all finished our meal of wild mushrooms and grouse in silence, no one wanting to broach the subject.

Runa looked up at Leif, and to my great surprise, nodded. "I know such a tale."

She paused, just long enough to glance at me before turning back to the fire. "There were once two sisters who roamed the dark and mysterious southern Ebba Woods. Their father had married a woman forty years younger, but she made a good bargain of it, for he kept her well. He was the best archer in the jarldom—he had gone on some of the last Elsh raids with Jarl Oluf's son and brought back what wealth was left on those foreign shores.

"The father taught his daughters the skill, and the two young girls were better shots than any grown man in the nearby village. They always had enough to eat during the long winters and spent many happy nights beside the hearth, crafting arrows using the feathers of the rare Red Wren, the scarlet tips marking them as unique and special to their family alone.

"Time passed, and the sisters grew up. Their father began to feel his age. He could no longer run through the forest graceful as a deer. He forgot little things, then bigger things, and soon he could remember nothing at all. And so their mother had him Mercy-killed—an arrow through the neck at sunrise on a hill covered in wildflowers. The sisters came home from the Ebba Woods to find their father burning to ash. The mother left, declaring a desire to roam and see the wilderness of the eastern plains, but the sisters stayed in their father's home and spent their days hunting and running and keeping him alive in their hearts.

"One winter a pack of Fremish men crossed the border into Vorseland. They were a group of wolf-priests—the unsanctioned clerics who drink yew berry poison until they lose themselves to it. Many had been driven from their own land for performing dark, secret rituals on kidnapped villagers, and this group was worse than most.

"They entered the town of Ebba on a moonless winter night, and the sisters awoke to screams. They grabbed their cloaks and their bows and ran to the center of the village. The Fremish men broke down doors and invaded homes—cries of pain and terror filled the air. The younger sister went from house to house, shooting the wolf-priests through open windows. She was cunning as a fox, and ten times as brave. Meanwhile, the older sister climbed a roof, aimed, and fired off every arrow in her quiver. She killed with perfect, mindless precision, and bodies began to cover the ground.

"The last pack of men moved toward the village well, howling at the night sky, their shaggy gray cloaks rippling in the wind. The older sister slaughtered them between one breath and the next. By dawn, all two dozen of the wolf-priests lay dead. The elder sister rejoiced. She went searching for her younger sister, to celebrate their victory and the heroic rescue of their village . . . And she found her, facedown near the town well, a red-feathered arrow through her heart."

The flames of the fire rose up, and a log crumpled into the embers with a thud. Runa jerked, her head twisting to the left.

I saw her expression, and it was grief and pain and remorse.

Runa held out her hand for the flask of *Vite*, and drank long. "The village of Ebba praised the sister for what she'd done," she said. "*The night had been dark*, they said. *It was an accident. Think of how many lives you saved.* But she didn't listen. She burned her younger sister on the hill where her father had died, and left the town for good."

Runa took another sip of *Vite*, stood, and then walked away from the fire and into the shadows.

She had killed her own sister. She'd been carrying the weight of it all this time.

I found her a while later by the same ancient juniper tree.

"This is why I set aside the bow for so long," she whispered when she saw me.

"Yes. But you have mourned long enough." I took a deep breath and again smelled the sharp, herbal scent of the juniper berries. "Let yourself be happy, Runa. Go with the Quicks. I will come find you afterward, if I survive, and will stay with them for as long as they will have me. I swear it."

She hesitated, and for a moment I thought she would agree. But then she reached forward and grasped my forearm, her fingers closing around my elbow. "No. You and Ovie are right. Blue Vee is the noble choice. I will join you, and together we will attempt to kill this giant. It's courageous and heroic. It's what my sister would have done."

I returned her grasp, wrapping my hand around her muscled forearm. "*Heltar*," I whispered. *"Heltar."*

. . . . .

We parted ways with the Quicks the following day, when we reached the forked path in the road. We said our good-byes, and they turned and walked north.

The Mercies and I watched them until they disappeared between the trees.

NINETEEN

All the villages we passed were quiet, unnaturally so.

The people eyed us warily as they moved about, with none of the warmth and easy welcome we'd found in Mista. Even the animals seemed quiet—dogs didn't bark and birds didn't sing. It was as if the entire world were holding its breath, trying not to draw attention to itself.

Vee was the old Vorse word for valley, and *Blue* referred to the blue mist that often rose up from the sweeping grasslands come evening. There was one main road to Blue Vee's Great Hall, passing through the fertile valley of Destin Lush and crossing through steadings and villages and open woodlands of birch and aspen.

I imagined it was a very beautiful place in the summer—sheep grazing in meadows and fields of barley waving in the breeze.

Or it had been, at least, before the beast.

Some people had nailed wooden bars across their doors, and others had put up fences of sharpened stakes. This wouldn't stop an attack, but perhaps it gave the residents some peace of mind.

"No men," Runa said as we crossed through the third hamlet. "There are no young men. Only elders, women, and children."

A hollow-eyed woman with a dark-haired infant on her hip heard Runa's comment and looked over at us. "They've all fled. The ones who still live, that is." The baby began to cry, and she rocked back and forth to soothe it. "They are hiding in the Blue Vee Forest."

"They should have taken their families with them." Ovie's expression was cool, but there was fire in her voice. "It was cowardly to run off and leave you all."

The mother gave a tired shrug. "Then who would tend to the injured? Who would see to the chickens and the cows and the pigs? And how would our children survive the winter without a home and hearth? We have no choice but to stay." She paused. "The beast attacks the men first—if they returned, they would die like all the rest."

I turned and watched a girl our age leading a cow across the muddy town square. She was strong, with muscled arms and a graceful gait—there was something of Runa about her, which I liked.

She caught me staring and drew closer. "You seek Mercy-work? There is none. Not here. We all die soon enough without your help."

I shook my head. "We wear the cloaks, but we no longer deal in the death trade."

"You come to offer yourself to Roth, then? To hunt the beast?"

"Yes."

If she was surprised to see four women offering themselves as warriors, she didn't show it. "The beast comes in the night," she said, green eyes hard. "Always in the night. I haven't slept in weeks. I'm turning into shadow."

Juniper reached forward and put her hand to the girl's cheek. "I will pray for you."

"It won't help. You should leave here. Return to where you came from, and don't look back."

I took a step toward her and rested my hand on the cow's side, letting its heat warm my fingertips. "You should flee yourself. Take this cow and hide in the forest. You will have milk, and meat, if it comes to that."

"I can't." She moved brown hair off her forehead with two calloused fingertips. "Mother broke her leg and needs my help. She said the gods will protect us . . . but I'm not counting on it."

She smiled again. This girl had a sharp wit that had not yet been dimmed by her fear and exhaustion.

I might have asked her to join us if she hadn't mentioned a mother. And if we were still Boneless Mercies.

"We've come here to kill this night stalker," I said, "and don't mean to fail."

She tilted her head and scrutinized me for a long moment, then turned and disappeared into one of the thatched homes without another word. No doubt she believed me about as much as she believed her mother about the protection of the gods.

. . . . .

On the second day, we came across the first fully abandoned village.

Most of the houses had been burned, and the town was nothing but piles of gray ash. We explored the huts that were still standing, looking for bodies. Juniper found a young boy behind a bed. His tiny skull had been crushed.

"Dead for a few days, maybe longer," Ovie said.

"And yet no one has come for him." Juniper touched the boy on the temple. "He's so young."

Runa pulled her flint box from her pack and looked at me. I nodded. Juniper said a prayer over the boy, and then Runa set the house on fire, with him inside. His soul would reach Holhalla.

We first caught sight of the Great Hall on the morning of the third day. We cleared a group of trees and there it was, capping the top of a high hill, overlooking the valley of Destin Lush, the Skal Mountains in the far distance. It was as beautiful as a Gothi tapestry.

Surrounding the base of the hill rose a stone wall with twenty-foot gates—it would take us several more hours of walking before we reached them.

We passed a handful of charred hamlets on the way but didn't stop to explore. These villages had been burned weeks ago, perhaps months. Besides, our eyes were fixed ahead, toward the Great Hall and all that awaited us there.

Its walls began to shine in the late afternoon light as we got closer, the sun reflecting off the metal of the many shields that hung from its sides. The Mercies and I had been in a handful of Great Halls during our travels in the death trade, but none so grand as this.

"Two hundred men could fit inside," Ovie said with a nod of her chin. "Easily."

"I doubt there are two hundred men left in all of Blue Vee." Trigve shifted his pelt of wolf to keep the cold wind off his neck, and then looked up at the sky. "It's a good thing we're close to the end of our journey."

Runa followed his gaze and nodded. "A storm is brewing."

Clouds soon drifted across the sun, and snow began to fall. We were covered in soft white flakes by the time we reached the thick wooden gates of the wall, pale flecks dotting our black Mercy-cloaks like stars in the night sky.

Two men stood guard, one young and one older, both with blond, braided beards and thick eyebrows—father and son, I thought. They wore leather armor over wool tunics, and fox pelts across their shoulders. The younger man eyed our cloaks with interest, but the older one merely glanced at them.

"You seek an audience with Jarl Roth?" The father's voice held a whisper of the Blue Vee accent, the same as the villagers we'd met earlier. The people here often spoke in lower tones, the vowels held on the tongue and drawn out. It was a pleasant sound.

I nodded. "Yes. We have answered his plea for aid. We've come to kill the beast."

The son raised his eyebrows. "Women, and Boneless Mercies at that. Very unusual. Roth will be pleased, regardless. No one has come in weeks. People are beginning to despair."

The accent also sang through his voice, an echo of his father's.

Trigve once said the western Vorse accent was the closest dialect modern Vorseland had to the cadence of the ancient sagas.

"Many warriors have come," the older man said. "They feasted in the jarl's Hall and boasted of their cunning and strength. All have died."

Trigve stepped forward, chin raised. "These four women are the Boneless Mercies who slayed the Cut-Queen of the Red Willow Marsh and drove the Willows out of the reeds. If you haven't heard of the deed yet, you will. The marsh is safe again because of them."

I took a step forward as well. "Mother Hush of the Sea Witches sent a raven to the jarl. He's expecting us."

The father eyed each of us slowly, then knocked his fist three times on the right-hand gate. I heard a man grunt as he lifted a heavy bar from the other side.

The twenty-foot doors creaked on their large iron hinges as they opened. The snowfall had lessened somewhat, and I noticed now that the thick wood was marred by two great dents, one on each side, where it had cracked under force.

The son saw me looking and swept his hand toward the doors. "Logafell. She tried to break in twice, early on, but the gates held. Then she began to attack the villages of the valley."

Runa jerked her head to the right and caught the guard's eye. "The beast is female?"

"Yes." He ran a gloved hand down the braid in his beard and shifted uneasily from one foot to the other. "A female giant with long white hair."

"Nante, nante." Juniper pressed her palm to her heart, and then swept her fingers out in front of her, making the Sea Witch gesture to cast off the dark.

Trigve and I exchanged a glance as we filed through the gates.

We made our way up the hill on well-worn steps, passing free-roaming livestock—ducks, geese, chickens, and a few cows. I spotted various huts, the blacksmith's, and then the barracks, now abandoned. The stables were also empty. Sheep roamed across a neglected training yard—no men had practiced there in some time. A bathhouse was off to the left, with steam rising from a hole in the roof.

Three older women tended a fire pit, which was lined with stone and covered with turf. I sniffed the air—roasted pig. My mouth watered.

No guards stood at the grand, iron-studded doors to the Great Hall, which surprised me little. If the rumors were true, Roth couldn't afford to waste men on unnecessary guard duty—he'd sent what remained of his best warriors out into the Sleet

Heath at the end of summer to track the beast to its lair. And the men had still not returned.

I put my shoulder against the carved wood of the heavy front door and pushed.

Snow swirled around us as we entered the Great Hall of Blue Vee, gusts of cold wind making the flakes dance.

We were alone.

I looked up at the soaring roof, rafters the size of pine trees, then glanced about me. I saw long trestle tables lined with simple benches, and a double-headed battle-ax hanging from a hook on the wall—it appeared well oiled and well used. An open stone hearth sat in the middle, wood crackling. Two rows of intricately carved pillars stretched the length of the building, depicting scenes of hunting and battle.

Richly colored tapestries covered the walls and gave the Hall a warm, cozy feeling, despite the vast, open space. I knew that some of them hid doors that led to passageways—passageways that opened to narrow sleeping quarters or led to back doors and underground cellars. It was the same in all Great Halls. As Boneless Mercies, we'd entered through these passageways. The main doors were for the jarls and their families. And for the warriors.

To the left, a giant yew tree rose in a blaze of red berries and narrow, bright green needles. Its trunk twisted up and up until its top branches broke through a hole in the timbered ceiling and stretched out into the sky.

I turned and closed the door behind us with another shove of my shoulder. The sound echoed down the Hall.

"It's too quiet." I blinked, waiting for my eyes to adjust to the darkness. There should have been warriors practicing swordplay and children running about and dogs sleeping under tables. "I hadn't expected Roth's jarldom to be as troubled as this."

Runa crossed her arms. "What, did you have grand dreams of pushing open the doors to this Hall and declaring us the Saviors of the Red Willow Marsh to a hundred men-at-arms?"

I shrugged. "As much as I allowed myself to think about it . . . yes, I did."

We strode forward, keeping our footsteps soft, until we reached the base of the yew. We stood underneath its branches, and waited for a servant to drift in and tell us how to find Jarl Roth.

"It's said only a few of the giant yews are still alive in Vorseland." Trigve put his hand on the bark and looked up toward the sky. "They were brought to our land by Tor the Wise, a warrior and naturalist who traveled far into Iber in the time of the sagas. I never imagined I would get to see one of his trees."

Juniper reached up and ran her fingertips down the soft needles. "Yew trees are filled with magic. According to a Sea Witch myth, there's a type of yew that grows only in Elsh graveyards. Its roots sprout through the mouths of the recently buried, inching down their throats until they encircle the heart. It's said that the graveyard yews whisper the secrets of the dead into the Elsh wind."

Snow drifted down from the opening in the ceiling, falling in gentle white clumps onto the tree's twisted branches. Runa brushed away a handful of delicate flakes and plucked one of the plump red berries. It was halfway between her teeth when Trigve grabbed her wrist.

"Yew berries are poisonous, Runa."

Juniper nodded. "It's true. The whole yew is deadly, needles and all."

Runa spat out the berry, and then crushed it under her foot with a scowl, as if it were an insect.

Trigve brushed snowflakes from his hair and smiled. "I read a tale of a Fremish wood-carver once—he carved spoons from yew wood and sold them in the nearby village. A dozen people died before they discovered the cause. The spoons brought poison to the tongue with each mouthful."

Runa stood on tiptoe and yanked on a slender young branch, bending it into an arch. "They may be poisonous, but I've heard yew wood makes a grand bow."

"Hmm." Juniper moved closer to the trunk, so close her freckled cheek almost touched the bark.

"What is it?" I didn't like the look in her eyes—curious, but worried.

Juniper backed away from the yew again and began to rub her upper arms with her hands. "There is a great deal of magic in this tree. My skin is tingling, and I taste dirt on the back of my tongue."

"Is it dangerous?" I looked up at the tree with new respect and wariness.

"No. It's the same with all ancient trees. They soak up magic from the earth, year after year. If anything, it's protecting this Hall. I think it's why the giant wasn't able to break in."

Ovie, who had yet to speak since we entered, stepped closer to the tree now and leaned against the trunk, hand on her dagger. "We are no longer alone. Someone approaches. Be on guard, Mercies."

As one, the Mercies and I grabbed our blades and shifted into the first fighting stance of the Seventh Degree, quiet as the moon.

"They sought the kiss of battle, and blood."

The voice came from the gloom near the back of the Hall. I could see nothing, not even a shadow. I heard only his footsteps, slow and irregular.

"Their hands were made for war, not for weaving. Their hearts were made to conquer, not submit."

It was a line from the *Witch War Chronicles*, about two witches and the Battle of Beggars and Thieves. I knew it well.

The stranger spoke with the same accent as the guards, though his words had a more refined lilt, a gentler touch. I could see his form now as he edged out of the dark, closer to the fire. He moved gracefully but slowly—his right leg was stiff, and he did not put his full weight on it.

He reached the yew tree and stepped into the light. He was tall, tall as Trigve, but broader, with bright blond hair flowing past his shoulders. An old scar under his right eye stretched three inches to his jaw. It added to his beauty, rather than took from it. He wore a thick wool cloak dyed a rare azure blue, the same color as his eyes, and there was a subtle gauntness to him—his jawline a shade too sharp, dark circles under wide-set eyes, waist too thin for wide shoulders.

Jarl Roth looked us over. His eyes went to our cloaks, then our weapons. "I have a dying jarldom that won't last the winter, and the gods send me a pack of ax-wielding Boneless Mercies." He smiled then, to take the edge off his words. "Life is . . . strange. So what have you Mercies to recommend yourselves over all the great warriors this beast has already slain?"

"Warriors are loud, and Mercies are quiet," I answered. *"There is strength in silence."*

This was something Siggy used to say if I ever griped about feeling invisible as we moved from town to town, never staying in one place, never lingering long enough to make friends or acquire neighbors or matter to anyone but one another.

Silence I could understand and accept, but not solitude. Siggy would have said they were one and the same.

Roth reached out and pressed his hand to the trunk of the great tree. "They built this Hall around the yew—it's said this tree is so old the god Obin played under its branches as a child. Some believe it hears us and understands what we say."

He paused, and his eyes met mine. "Mother Hush told me of your coming. She said you'd sworn to kill the Cut-Queen of the Red Willow Marsh on your journey here. Did you accomplish this feat with your Mercy-silence?"

I relaxed my posture and slid my ax back into its sheath. "Yes, we did. Elan Wulf is dead . . . for now."

He raised his eyebrows. "I'll need to hear more of that story later."

Curiosity flickered across his expression, and I liked him the better for it.

"I am Frey." I reached out, and Roth and I gripped each other's forearms in greeting. He was thickly muscled—he'd spent many days training with heavy weapons under hard teachers.

I turned and nodded at the others. "This is Runa, Ovie, Trigve, and Juniper. We cleared the Red Willow Marsh on our way here and made it safe again. We have come to kill the creature Logafell. Do you accept our offer?"

Jarl Roth released my arm and put his fist on his heart. "Yes, I accept your offer. You are most welcome."

TWENTY

W*e feasted that night in the Great Hall of Blue Vee.*

The air smelled of beeswax candles and roast pork. I sat by Roth's side at the high table, facing the front doors on the far end. Roth's younger sister sat to my left—a sweet girl named Vale, who shared her brother's blond hair and gentle, commanding air.

Of the hundreds of warriors who used to live here, there were now just sixteen. Sixteen still alive out of Roth's former army. These last men sat by themselves at a table near the giant yew and showed little interest in me or the other Mercies. No doubt they assumed we would die like all the rest who'd come to their aid, and even quicker, being women.

Trigve and the others sat together at a table nearby, amid a handful of hollow-eyed servants and unnaturally quiet children. The Mercies initially kept their eyes on me, shifting uncomfortably on the wooden benches, but they began to relax after the food was served—the delicious pork, along with honeyed apples, loaves of sourdough bread, and a salty cabbage stew.

Roth displayed none of the wariness of his warriors. Some people talk at length upon a first meeting and try to sway the listener's opinion of them, but this jarl said little, and when he did speak, his voice was low and easy. He asked me only basic questions as we ate—what path we'd taken to Blue Vee, and how long I'd been traveling the Borders as a death-trader.

The meal gave me an opportunity to study him in return, this isolated jarl whose name and troubles were now known across Vorseland.

Roth carried himself with the gravity of someone in his middle years, but I didn't think he was much older than me. The candles on the table were tall and bright, and I could see that his skin was smooth and unlined, except for the pink scar. He had a broad forehead and no beard, and his hair hung loose down his back, with one thick braid near each cheek.

His sister wore her hair in the same style, loose, with two braids. Vale looked to be about Juniper's age, and she had pale, arched eyebrows and a wide mouth. She picked up a nearby loaf of bread, tore off a piece, and drizzled it with honey from a bowl that sat between us.

"Blue Vee has the best honey in all of Vorseland," she said, handing me the bread.

I took a large bite. Syrupy sweetness spread across my tongue. "My mentor, Siggy, used to say that honey was too sweet for a Boneless Mercy and that death-traders should eat bitter foods."

Roth tilted his head to the side. "I disagree with your mentor.

I think we should seek what simple pleasures we can, while we live, regardless of circumstance."

Vale nodded, braids brushing her pink-tinged cheeks. "You are right, brother. Simple pleasures—like roaring fires during cold snowstorms. Soft, well-made clothing. Lazy, gentle dogs that sleep all day. Loyal family and old friends . . . What is better than this?"

"Nothing," Roth answered, "except honor. And glory."

He turned to me again and gave me a long look. Then he shoved his chair back from the table and began to pat his knee with one hand. "Vika, come here."

A gray skinny-legged dog near the fire shook herself and ambled over. She licked Roth's outstretched hand, black nose inching across his palm, and then sat very politely, as if expecting something. Roth gave her the uneaten food on his plate and a piece of honeyed bread besides. The dog took each morsel gently between her lips, and then swallowed it whole. Afterward, she settled down under the table near our feet and heaved a great moan of contentment.

"Dogs eat and sleep and chase rabbits," I said. "They have contentment and ease and the thrill of the glorious hunt. They live like the Quicks."

"What do you know of the Quicks?" Roth asked, the curious note back in his voice.

"We rescued two in the marsh. And we almost joined them, before deciding to come here."

Vale twisted toward me, eyes wide. "You rescued two Quicks? I've often dreamed of running off to the Endless Forests. Though I'm no good with a bow."

"I hear it's a marvelous life," I said, smiling. "You should hone your archery skills and join them. You seem merry enough to suit their liking."

"Frey, are you encouraging my sister to take up with a bunch of woodland rovers?"

I just laughed. "Yes."

Roth laughed then, too, though a dark look crossed his face soon after, as if he didn't think it was right to laugh when so many were dead.

All through dinner, I'd expected Roth to tell me of her. Of Logafell. He did not. Finally, I pushed back my plate. "Will the beast come tonight, Jarl Roth? I'll need to prepare with my companions."

"Please just call me Roth. And no, not tonight. The snow has stopped, and the moon is full and bright. Our beast likes to hunt in the dark." He paused. "What is your plan, Frey? How do you expect to kill this giant when it's taken the lives of so many others? You must have some plan if you came all this way to offer your services."

"How could I form a final plan until we arrived and learned what we were up against?"

He nodded. "Good point. The previous warriors waited for Logafell to attack, then raced out into the night, blades raised. Is that what you will do?"

"No. Being a Mercy has taught me how to be patient. How to be quiet. I do not plan to attack this giant on open ground, but to track her back to her den. That is how you hunt a wolf."

"You will not find her easy to follow. She leaves no footprints, despite her size. Not in mud or snow." He paused. "But I have called in mystics from the outer islands, and they will arrive soon."

I shrugged. "Yes, perhaps they can help us. Though I'm sick to the bone of mystics and magic after the Red Willow Marsh."

Roth leaned forward, elbows on the table. His cheeks looked gaunt in the candlelight. "You keep taunting me with that story, Frey. I would like to hear you tell it. Soon."

I nodded. "Supply me a few rounds of *Vite*, and I'll play storyteller."

I heard someone laugh and looked down the Hall to find Trigve deep in conversation with a petite girl who sat across from him at the table. She had dark hair and wore the yellow tunic of a Royal Healer.

Juniper had found someone to talk to as well, a young man in a heavy Arctic Bearskin cloak. He had sad eyes, but his smile was sweet and honest. He wasn't one of Roth's warriors—he must be the soothsayer.

Jarls have always employed seers and fortune-tellers to advise them when to plant or war or raid. These mystics often lived in solitary huts outside the Great Hall, spending their time communicating with the gods and seeking visions. I remembered seeing such a hut near the stone pit where the women were roasting the pig.

I searched the young man's face, trying to decide if his expressions seemed especially cryptic or prophetic. If he was a soothsayer, he wasn't very good. He certainly hadn't helped Roth defeat Logafell.

I scanned the crowd again. I found Ovie near Juniper, keeping her own counsel, as usual. I expected the same from Runa but was surprised to see her conversing with a girl her own age—one with a swirling blue tattoo on the left side of her face.

The tattoo marked her as a Glee Starr from the southern Skyye Islands, and she did look somewhat like my tall Mercy, with her dark hair. She was outgoing and cheerful, though, talking and jesting with all around her, whereas Runa was reserved and guarded.

I lost track of time after this. A servant brought out several kegs of mead, and I started to drink. And drink. And drink. As did all around me.

When Roth stood and sang the first bars of "Hook, Fire, and Snow," I joined him along with everyone else, my voice melding into the throng until it became one glorious tone, rising up to the roof.

We sang "Into the Dark" next, then "Follow the Wolves." Drink after drink, song after song. And as my lips mouthed the familiar words, something began to ripple through my heart—a feeling I'd experienced in the Merrows but hadn't recognized until now.

Belonging.

This Great Hall, for all its grand tree and soaring ceiling and intricately carved pillars . . . It was a home. A community.

The burden of being lone Mercies, of being wanderers and outsiders . . . I hadn't realized the toll it had taken, until now. We'd been greeted as warriors here, in the truest sense. Roth's household had put its fear and sadness on hold for the night and stripped its cellars bare to welcome us with food and song in the way of the sagas. Despite the lean year, despite the sorrow.

A bold, glorious welcome . . .

Before we fought the beast and died like all the others.

It was the least they could do.

It was everything.

By midnight I was very drunk and feeling rather sleepy. I was about to climb under the table and curl up next to Roth's dog . . . when Runa began to shout.

The beast. It's come, after all. Hel.

My cloak and ax lay in a pile behind my chair where I'd thrown them halfway through the feast. I fumbled for my dagger, knocking plates and goblets to the floor . . .

And felt a hand on my arm.

"It's just a skin-fight." Roth nodded down the Hall at the Glee

Starr girl. She was facing Runa near the yew. Both had drawn their weapons.

"Indigo is feisty and shameless," he said, "but all here love her. She came in last year with a traveling theater troupe and never left. I think she was tired of the road."

"I know the feeling," I said.

Roth's eyes met mine. "Indigo trained as an archer before she became an entertainer. She swore her fealty to me with her bow in hand. She has begged me to allow her to leave, to hunt the beast, but I've denied her request. She keeps my warriors in good spirits. I'd hate to lose her." He paused, and his mouth curved into a faint smile. "I wondered how long it would take her to pick a fight with one of you. She likes to show off to strangers, and there haven't been many of late."

Indigo. All the Glee Starr people were given blue names, like "Cobalt" and "Sky." It was a charming trait. One I'd forgotten.

Runa swore again, loudly, then threw off her cloak and boots. She stripped down to her thin under-shift, and the Glee Starr girl did the same. It was a gesture of good faith—no daggers could be pulled from hidden pockets. They would fight skin to skin, bone to bone.

Roth's warriors rose as one and pushed back their table to clear a space on the floor in front of the giant yew. Runa moved to one end of the clearing, opposite the blue-tattooed girl. They began to circle each other.

I caught a glimpse of green hair moving across the Hall, and then Juniper was at my shoulder.

The girls continued to circle each other, both sizing up the other before making the first move. This was clearly not the first fight for either, though I'd never actually seen Runa skin-fight in all the time I'd been with her.

Roth and I rose to our feet and drew closer to the crowd that was forming around the two girls, Vale and Juniper following close behind. I could see that Runa was furious, lips tight. And her eyes looked glassy as well—a surefire sign she was drunk.

Indigo, by contrast, seemed invigorated by the prospect of a battle and was alternatively laughing and yelling harmless taunts.

Runa made the first move. She threw herself at Indigo, shoving her into a nearby table, and then jumping lightly out of the way when the girl snapped forward, right fist swinging.

Both girls were thickly muscled and strong as wolves. Roth's warriors began to cheer, for it was already proving to be a good fight. Runa took an elbow to the ribs, then slammed her fist into the other girl's lower back. Indigo coughed, turned, and kicked Runa in the face.

On and on it went. One would fall, then the other, neither staying in one place long enough to be pinned to the ground.

I caught Trigve's eye through the mob, and he winked at me. He was enjoying the fight as much as the rest.

Runa slammed her forehead into Indigo's nose, then in turn was sent sprawling when Indigo kicked her in the stomach. Bright red blood dripped down Indigo's face. Both girls were shouting insults now, though I couldn't catch their words over the cheers of the crowd.

Next to me, Juniper looked anxious and worried. I wanted to comfort her, but my heart was also stirred by the fight, and I couldn't keep from grinning.

Runa won in the end, but barely, finally pinning Indigo when the Glee Starr girl tripped over a nearby deerhound that was somehow managing to sleep through the noise. She dug her knee into Indigo's chest, swearing as the girl writhed underneath her.

Indigo howled in frustration . . . and then began to laugh.

"*Good fight*," she shouted. *"Good fight."* She pulled her hand across her face, wiping away blood. "Shall we go again?"

A moment passed, and then both girls were laughing.

Runa held out her hand and helped the girl to her feet. They got dressed, still laughing, and then approached Jarl Roth at the front of the crowd to ask his forgiveness, as was tradition.

Roth looked slightly bemused. "It was a welcome bit of entertainment," he announced, "and you each fought well."

Afterward, I went to Runa's side and touched the purple bruise that was blossoming near her left eye. "What in Hel did she say to make you skin-fight her?"

Runa just shrugged, but Indigo looked at me and grinned.

"I asked this Boneless Mercy if she'd ever killed anyone who wasn't sick or dying, and then I asked her what on earth made her think she could slay our giant." She laughed again, an infectious rolling sound that filled the Hall. "She didn't like that much."

"Is that all?" I glanced at Runa. "I'd have wondered this, too, in her place."

"I have a temper." Runa put her hand to her ribs and flinched.

"And I never get angry." Indigo moved closer to Runa and slid her arm around her shoulders. "So let's be friends."

I laughed. "Now go to the healer and get fixed up, both of you." I nodded at the dark-haired girl in yellow—she was standing near the hearth, still talking to Trigve.

The two girls moved off together, their long dark braids swinging.

Leave it to Runa to get into a skin-fight our first night in Blue Vee.

The Hall was beginning to empty now, for the mead was gone and the fun over. Servants disappeared behind tapestries. Warriors fetched furs and threw them beside the open hearth.

I returned to the high table and gathered up my cloak and ax. We would sleep by the fire if the men would make room for us.

I heard someone say my name, and I turned, expecting to see Trigve. I found Roth instead.

"Will you come to my room and take some *Vite* with me?"

I hesitated for a moment, and then nodded. "Just let me speak with my companions first."

I scanned the Hall. Trigve was with the healer, examining Runa while Indigo looked on. Juniper stood beside the young man in the bearskin cloak—they were both petting one of the dogs. I finally spotted Ovie near the yew tree. She must have been quite drunk, for she was sitting cross-legged behind Vale, weaving several small braids into the girl's hair.

I'd asked Ovie to braid my hair many times, but she'd never agreed. Yet here she was now with this stranger, quick fingers diving in and out of soft strands.

"Vale has that effect on people." Roth nodded toward the pair. "She's got a way about her. I've seen her tame feral dogs with just a look. Seems she's worked her magic on your stoic friend. Your companions are making themselves at home, Frey."

My eyes met his. "People tend to think Boneless Mercies are grim and solitary, but the reverse is generally true. We crave society and form friendships easily. It is the nature of a wanderer—settled folk can take their time and create bonds with leisure, but we meet people only in passing and have to make the most of it."

Roth smiled. "I agree. Let's make the most of it."

I followed the jarl of Blue Vee behind a large tapestry of two longboats at sea. It was woven in shades of yellow and black and blue, and mythical creatures danced along the border. We moved down a dark hall, steadily but slowly. Roth's leg injury was not recent—he'd learned how to walk fairly smoothly, without putting too much weight on his right side.

He made a quick left and opened a heavy door.

The jarl's bedroom was modest compared with the Hall, but it was warm and comfortable. Fire blazed in twin braziers, and shields hung from each wall—some were new, and some had dents and splinters and faded paint. Fur pelts covered the bed, and its heavy, carved frame was wide enough to fit four, perhaps five, full-grown Vorse men.

Roth crossed the room and took a tall bottle from a wooden stand in the corner. He began pouring *Vite* into two small black drinking horns. I threw my cloak and ax onto the floor and sat down in a broad, simple chair near the braziers. A sheepskin pelt lay near my feet—I picked it up and placed it across my knees.

"So how did you get that silver hair?" Roth asked over his shoulder.

"My mother was born into a Finnish band of Relic Hunters. She fell in love with my father when her family was passing through Vorseland."

"Have you ever been to Finnmark?"

"No, but I'd like to travel there someday and track down my kin."

"In what region do they reside? I have distant family near the Twilight Sea."

I shrugged. "My mother's family name was Sand, which is a very common Finn name, and they were roamers as well. I wouldn't know where to start looking." I paused. "You ask a lot of questions."

He handed me one of the drinking horns, and then sat down in the chair next to mine. "Yes. And now it's your turn. Ask me anything you like."

"How did you hurt your leg?" I've always found that some things are best approached directly.

"I climbed to the top of the giant yew as a child . . . and then promptly fell. We had no Mender at the time—the bone broke and didn't heal properly." He paused. "People used to whisper behind my back, '*a cripple will never become jarl*.' They said the gods wouldn't allow it. And the same people say it's my fault the beast attacks Blue Vee, for *a broken man leads a broken land*."

Roth was quoting the *Bloodbringer Saga*—one of the characters in the saga was a one-armed jarl named Scolt, who calls down a dragon from the high hills, and it brings destruction, fire, blood, and death.

I took a sip from the horn, and the *Vite* burned its way down my throat. I scrutinized Roth as I drank. He was lean with worry, almost haggard. He'd barely touched his dinner.

He would not live long like this. His jarldom was dying, and he was dying with it.

It was good that we Mercies had come.

I nodded at his right leg. "Does your injury prevent you from tracking the beast yourself?"

Roth downed his *Vite* in one swallow. He rose and refilled the horn. "Yes. I can't go to the beast, and she can't come to me. And so here we are."

"I'm sorry," I said, and meant it. "What about—"

"An Iber horse?" He shook his head. "The first time Logafell attacked, I rode out with thirty other men on horseback. She killed all but seven of the horses and the men riding them as well. I sold the rest, which is where I got the gold for the reward."

I was surprised. I'd assumed all jarls were wealthy beyond counting. Nothing was ever simple, it seemed.

I stood and went over to him. I poured myself more of the fire-spirit, and then eyed Roth's cheek. "And how did you get the scar?"

"Fighting Dennish pirates. They came up the Quell Sea, hoping to find treasure in Elshland. When they realized nothing was left on those shores, they came here. We met them on the sand one cold winter day. I was just a scrawny fourteen-year-old then, with a damaged leg. I demanded to come with, though I had to be carried on the back of a small Ice Horse. When I saw my father fall, I jumped down and stood over his body. I fought shoulder to shoulder with his men until every last pirate lay dead. I earned the jarldom that day, in their eyes at least."

He paused. "Is that the last of your questions?"

I laughed softly. "Not quite. Tell me, do you invite all the Logafell glory-seekers to your room for a drink after the feast?"

"No. Not all." He rubbed his jaw with the palm of his hand and smiled. His blue eyes flickered, and I got a glimpse of the man he'd been before the beast. Proud and brave, but also lighthearted and quick to laugh.

I'd seen many people in my travels, but Roth struck me as rare—the kind you meet only a handful of times in life.

The kind who can change you for the better.

I sat back down next to Roth by the fire, and proceeded to tell him all my tales then, from Siggy to the dead girl at the crossroads. From Gunhild's last stand to the Sea Witches. From the Cut-Queen to the Quicks.

He was an excellent listener. Intense, but quiet. He interrupted only once, to ask detailed questions about the Cut-Queen's resurrection. I told him everything I could remember, from the feel of her blood across the back of my hands to the glow that began in her heart and grew until it pierced the room with blinding light.

Roth stretched out his right leg when I finished and began to massage his thigh in an absentminded way. "If you are right, and this signifies the beginning of a Witch War . . ." He paused. "The winds are shifting in Vorseland. Can you feel it?"

"Yes. Sometimes." I stood and fetched the *Vite* again. I refilled our drinking horns, and then refilled the flask in my pack as well.

I returned to my chair, and looked at Roth. "Blue Vee isn't what I expected."

"What did you expect?"

"A Hall of wild-eyed men shouting insults, full of scorn. I was prepared to defend myself and the Mercies. I was prepared to fight."

Roth smiled, but it was sad this time, without the spark from before. "They might have done this, at first. But they've seen too many friends die to be scornful or arrogant. They no longer have the luxury of rejecting help when it comes simply because it has a different shape than they're used to."

I nodded, and tucked the sheepskin around my legs. "Regardless, I didn't expect to be drinking liquor with the jarl in his room, telling stories by the fire."

He laughed softly. "Seek the simple pleasures, Frey. Don't ask questions."

We both were quiet then for a while, staring into the dying red flames in the brazier.

"What is it you want from life?" Roth asked a while later.

I lifted one leg and rested my arm on my knee. "I want glory. I want to be remembered."

"And do your companions desire this as well?"

"These thoughts drift through all women's hearts." It took me a moment to realize this was an echo of what the Cut-Queen had said back in her hut. I flinched.

Roth, who was watching me closely, saw it. "Perhaps you should have gone with the Quicks. You could be in the Green Wild Forest now, hunting every day, free as the water and the wind. Instead, you will die here, like all the rest. And I'm sorry for it."

"I might not fail," I said. "We could succeed. We stand a chance."

"Yes, you do." He paused. "But only fools seek greatness, Frey."

"My mentor, Siggy, used to say the same thing. I never believed her."

Roth just laughed.

He told me about Logafell, then. He said she was over twelve feet tall, based on the accounts of the few eyewitnesses who'd seen one of her attacks. The people said she was a Jotun—one of the giants of ancient Vorseland, spoken of in the sagas.

"I had a hundred and sixty-eight men before she came that first terrible night last spring." Roth began to grip the arms of his chair, and his knuckles turned pale. "The first two nights, she tried to break through the gates, but they held. On the third night, she started burning. Every last man, woman, and child were dead in the village by the time we saw the flames. She picked my warriors off one by one as we charged across the Destin Lush Valley in the dark. I lost thirty that night, and the rest over the course of the summer."

"And now you are down to sixteen."

"Yes. And now I have just sixteen." Roth sighed. "We are not rich here. Many of my warriors are also farmers and shepherds. Most lived in three of the larger hamlets nearby—and these were the first the beast burned to the ground. As if she knew."

"She *did* know." I swallowed another long sip of *Vite* and gasped as it burned the back of my throat. "The people of Blue Vee are right—this beast is a Jotun. Mother Hush said the same, that

Logafell is a remnant of the giants who used to live north of the Skal Mountains, in the Wild Ice Plains."

He nodded. "I thought as much."

I began to undo my long braid. I shook my silver hair free around my shoulders and rubbed my scalp with my fingertips. "Tell me, how many outsiders have come here, seeking to kill the beast and collect the reward?"

"Thirty-seven. All young. All men, until you. They come. They feast. They wait for Logafell to attack. They rush after her, though I warn them it's a trap . . . And they never come back." He paused. "The village burnings are simply a distraction—a way to draw my men out of the Hall until she's killed every last one of us."

Roth looked down at his leg and frowned. "Four weeks ago, Flinn had a vision of the giant—he saw her skulking through the Sleet Heath, blond hair to her waist, skin slick as stone, her fists clutching bones, fingers curving into blood-caked claws. Eight red wolves ran at her heels. I sent a band of twenty-five warriors east to that barren stretch of land to find her den. They never returned. If I still had my Iber horses, I would have led them into the heart of the heath myself. Instead, I'm stuck here, drinking and feasting and watching my people die. Which, some would argue, is worse than death."

Roth rose to refill his horn. I noticed that he swayed a bit as he walked.

How much has he had to drink? How much have I?

"What else happened when you visited the Sea Witches?" he asked when he returned to the fire. "You didn't say much about this."

I leaned back in the chair and laughed softly. "Mother Hush drowned me in the Quell Sea to give me a vision. Then she brought me back to life and gave me the secret to slaying the giant, in return for my promise to kill the Cut-Queen."

Roth gave me a shrewd look and leaned forward. "The *secret?*"

I nodded. "Hush said she has a weak spot on the back of her neck."

Roth pondered this for a moment. "Even if that is true, you'd have to get close enough to reach it. No easy feat."

"No, it's not."

"She's no fool, that queen of the Sea Witches."

"No. And she'll need that cunning for the coming Witch War."

"Won't we all." He paused. "Indeed, I have a feeling that Logafell is the start of something, rather than the end. Can you really kill this beast, Frey?"

I thought of *Ergill's Saga* again, of the brave farm boy who took on a dragon and won. Would I have the courage to face Logafell when the time came?

A breeze blew through a nearby window, and the fur-lined covering flapped against the frame.

Rogue winds are a sign the gods are watching.

I shivered suddenly, thorns up my spine. The flames in the brazier roared up as if in answer, and the firelight made the shadows dance.

"Frey?" Roth spoke my name sometime later, after we'd both drifted into silence again. I was nearly asleep, curled up with my sheepskin like a cat. The fire, the warmth, the feast, the mead, the *Vite* . . . I was done in.

"Yes?"

"Are you bound to the man who came with you?"

I hesitated. "Yes . . . and no. We are bound to each other as friends, but not lovers."

"Ah. That is a deeper thing, then."

"It is."

I looked over at Roth. He was getting tired, too—his eyelids were heavy, and he'd relaxed into an easy slouch, his shoulders nestled into the corner of the chair.

He looked young suddenly. Too young to be so troubled.

"Roth?"

"Yes?"

"Is your mother dead, as well as your father?"

"Yes."

"No uncles, or aunts, or grandparents?"

He shook his head.

"So you are like me and Trigve and the other Mercies. Alone."

"Except I have Vale."

That was true. He had his sister.

"Roth?"

"Yes?"

"What is your given name?"

"Esca."

I smiled. "Trigve has told me of the *Moon Serpent Saga*. A snake-eyed boy named Esca takes his magical sword, Wrath, on a quest to save the world."

"I used to love that tale as a child. Do you know the end?"

I shook my head.

"Obin attends Esca's wedding feast in the far north disguised as a beggar. He steals Esca's sword and plunges it into an ancient ash tree, a tree so old it has turned to stone. Obin then declares that whoever can pull the sword from the tree will inherit Esca's jarldom. They say the sword is still there to this day."

I sleepily raised my eyebrows. "Do you believe it?"

"I don't know. I was determined to find it when I was young. I had dreams of gathering my boyhood friends together and journeying through the Green Wild Forest until we found Esca's forgotten lands and the sword buried in the stone tree."

I sat up and put my hand on Roth's arm. "Is that an invitation? If so, then yes. I will accompany you on this Moon Serpent quest once I bring down Logafell. All I ask is that I get first chance at the sword."

Roth laughed. "Done."

I sighed deeply and then rose from my chair with reluctance. "Can I bring this sheepskin with me to the hearth in the Hall?" I'd grown rather attached to the black wool rug in the way only a wanderer could.

"Of course." Roth stood. He picked up my cloak from the floor and swung it over my shoulders, his knuckles grazing my neck as he fixed the clasp. "Feel free to take any other furs that you see here as well. And tell the men to make room for you in front of the fire. I don't want you freezing in the night."

I held his gaze for a moment—a long moment—then picked up my ax and adjusted my pack. "Wake me if the beast comes, Esca Roth."

"She won't come. Not tonight. Sleep deep, Frey."

And I did.

TWENTY-ONE

I *counted four of them, four slinking creatures moving through the shadows.*

How they'd gotten in, I didn't know. They hadn't entered through the main doors, and Roth barred the other entrances at night.

Stregas.

Also known as the Pig People.

I'd been dreaming, deep Sea Witch dreams, *driftwood and salt, smoke and spells, sun-warm trees and waves and sand and thorns* . . . when I felt Ovie shift beside me in my sleep. She whispered my name and gripped my wrist. I opened my eyes and followed her gaze.

Blue dawn light was filtering down from the yew tree opening in the ceiling, casting shadows upon cloaked shoulders. Juniper lay against my back, sleeping soundly. Everyone in the Hall was still asleep, even the dogs. I touched Trigve, and he opened his eyes. I pointed at the Pigs with my chin, and he nodded. We stayed *savalikk*, not even reaching for our knives, not wanting them to know we were awake. Not yet.

We watched the Pig People as they moved silently about, scrutinizing the tapestries and the carvings on the pillars. They wore drab brown hooded cloaks, but their faces shone an eerie, unsettling rose-petal pink.

The Stregas crushed the dried coral found on their shores and dusted their skin with the powder. Some said they did it to resemble the pigs they hunted and used in their rituals, and some said they merely wished to scare their enemies and appear otherworldly, but no one really knew.

The Pig People lived on the Boar Islands off the far north coast of Iber. I'd heard the islands were wild and godless. But I'd also heard they did, indeed, have a god, and he was old—older than our Vorse gods, older than the world itself.

I saw a shadow pass near my feet, then another . . .

"Abomination."

A hand shot out and seized a chunk of Juniper's pale sea-green curls.

"Filthy Sea Witch. Abomination."

One of the Stregas started to drag Juniper backward across the Hall by her hair.

"*Drop her*," I screamed, reaching for my ax and scrambling to my feet, Ovie and Trigve right behind me.

"Abomination. Abomination." All the Pigs were chanting it now, their hissing whispers crawling out of the shadows.

Runa and Indigo jumped up, weapons held high. Indigo took one look around her . . .

And then ran, full out, and slammed into the Strega. She pushed her into a pillar, squeezing her windpipe between her fingers.

"Drop the Sea Witch, Pig."

The Strega shook her head. Juniper sat crumpled at her feet, the Pig's hand still in her hair. I lunged forward and hit the Pig in the stomach with the hilt of my ax. *"Let her go."*

Pink fingers released green hair, and Juniper slid to the floor.

Behind us, Ovie and Runa stood guard, axes raised toward the three hissing shadows near the giant yew.

I held up my hand, palm out. "Indigo, you can let the Pig go."

Indigo glanced at me, grinned, and released the Strega's throat. The pig-girl began to cough and clutch at her neck.

The entire Hall was awake now. Roth's warriors formed a half circle around us, blades facing the shadows.

"Filthy Sea Witch."

The Strega spat at Juniper's feet, and then coughed again. I helped Juniper up, and then turned and backhanded the Pig across the face. Pink dust burst into the air, particles dancing in the early-morning light like snowflakes.

"Say that one more time, Strega, and I'll run my blade across your throat." I wiped my hand on my tunic, and it left a long pink trail.

The Strega kept her mouth shut.

Her hood had fallen back when I struck her cheek, and I could see she was young, fourteen at most. Her head was shaved and dusted as pink as the rest of her face, but there was a delicacy in her features and in the small chest heaving underneath the brown shapeless cloak.

"I take it the Pig People have arrived." Roth stepped out from behind the longboat tapestry. "Warriors, lower your blades. Stregas, come forward."

The three Stregas approached silently, slowly, until they stood in a line next to the Strega girl whose pink dust still clung to my tunic.

Roth turned to the tallest of the Pig People, a young man about his own age.

"Attack one of my guests again, Een, and I will blood-eagle you in the way of my ancestors." He paused. "That is not an idle threat."

The leader nodded at this, and said nothing.

"The Sea Witches are *filth*. They take foul Iber sailors to their beds to beget more sea-haired girls like themselves. They trade their honor for spices and oils and wine. They are imposters, *blasphemers*—"

"Enough, Astrid." This time it was Een who struck the Strega girl across the face. She flew backward, fell to the floor, and then scuttled back into the shadows.

Roth turned to Juniper. "I called the Stregas here, offering them gold to perform their pig ritual and divination. I see now they have the manners of wild dogs. I am sorry."

Juniper gave Roth a small nod, then walked over to the

Strega girl, grabbed her wrist, and forced her fingers open. The Sea Witch picked up the green strand she found there and slid it into a side pocket on her tunic. "Stregas like to steal hair—they use it to put curses on their victims. Watch your locks, everyone."

I put my hand to my hair and gripped it in my fist.

So this was why the Stregas shaved their heads.

Most Vorse were familiar with the Stregas, even if they'd never encountered any. The Pig People were mentioned in the *Blood Frost Saga*, among others. In one story, a jarl named Vigga called the mystics to him, hoping they could tell him how to defeat the sea monster that had been sinking his longboats as they crossed the Quell. The three Stregas gutted a young pig and read the truth in its entrails—the sea monster, known as Jormund, was the half-serpent, half-human son of a Vorse woman and an Iber snake god. The Stregas told the jarl he should sacrifice his only daughter, Edda, to the sea, so Jormund could take her as his wife and live with her in the deep. Vigga had all three Stregas killed where they stood. But as the seasons passed, and the jarl lost all but three of his ships, and most of his men, he took Edda out in a boat himself and tossed her into the waves.

"Come," Roth said. "The sooner we get this over with, the better."

Roth walked to the front doors of the Hall, and we followed behind, the Pig People, Trigve, me, the other Mercies, and Roth's remaining warriors.

We stood outside, snow around our ankles. I watched the movements of the Hall servants for a moment—women washing clothes in icy water, feeding chickens, shooing children into huts—then turned and looked down into the Destin Lush Valley. It was stark white, sun glinting off frozen snow. I saw the three burned villages, then more hamlets, one after another, spreading from the forest to the barren Sleet Heath, far in the distance.

Roth motioned me to him with a flick of his chin. I drew near and stood at his shoulder, facing the Stregas.

"Watch," he said. "You will need to hear what they say."

He called for a servant, and a gangly boy of sixteen appeared, all arms and elbows and legs.

"Fetch one of the hogs, Olin."

The boy ran off. He returned a few moments later, tugging a pink young pig across the yard, rope tied around the animal's thick neck.

Een took the pig from the boy and held out a slim hand to Roth.

Roth reached into his cloak, and then dropped a fistful of gold coins into the Strega's palm. "Don't ask for more. I have none left."

"Except for the reward."

"The reward is for the warriors who defeat the beast. Unless you are offering to fight her yourself, Een."

Een blinked slowly and said nothing.

Roth nodded. "Right. Let it begin."

The pig wagged its piggy tail and side-eyed the Strega, its gaze lazy and pleasant . . .

The Stregas attacked.

Brown cloaks flying, knees in the snow, knives stabbing into the poor animal's flesh, screeching, squealing, blood, slaughter.

It reminded me of ravens on a corpse.

The pig gave a final squeal, then dropped to the ground and fell over onto its side.

It was Een who slit the pig from end to end and pulled out its entrails, a bulging mess of gray, red, and purple on the bright white snow.

It was Astrid who read them.

She dug her small hands into the steaming, stinking mess. I counted six heartbeats . . . seven . . . And then her hazel eyes began to turn pink, corner to corner, pink as the Coral River that ran through the southern Borders.

Astrid began to rock back and forth on the snow, red droplets of blood on her pink-dusted cheeks.

Een made a quick upward gesture with one finger. "It's starting."

Roth and I took a step closer. We dropped to our knees and leaned toward the petite, hairless girl.

"Winter missssst. Sssssmoke on sssssnow."

The girl's voice was throaty and deep, despite her age, with a strange hiss to it that made my blood run cold.

It reminded me of the reeds, whispering, whispering, in the Red Willow Marsh.

I shuddered.

"An arrow in an apple leaksss bloodred. Follow the crimsssson tearssss to her den. Mind the teeth."

The sun disappeared behind the clouds, and we all fell into shadow.

I sniffed the air. *Snow.*

Storms came on fast this far west.

Astrid began to shake, small shivers that shook her slim shoulders. She dug her fingers deeper into the innards, clouds of steam rising as the heat hit the cold morning air.

"The end comessss with a kisssss. Beware her bite. Death huntsssss you."

The Strega blinked, and the pink color began to fade from her eyes.

Snow began to fall.

The Stregas left not long after Astrid's reading, back down the hill, back to their ship, back to whatever dark hovel they lived in on their pig island.

Roth and I watched them go, brown cloaks fluttering behind them.

Een glanced over his shoulder at us, eerie pink cheeks catching the dim winter sun.

With the Sea Witches I'd felt peace, and with the Cut-Queen I'd felt strength and awe and fear. But the Pig People filled me with something just as primal—a deep, disquieting unease, like setting up camp on an ancient battlefield and sleeping in the dirt of the long dead.

Trigve and Juniper appeared at my elbow, their eyes on the mystics below. At the foot of the hill the two guards lifted the bolt, and the Stregas passed through the gates.

I let out a sigh of relief when the doors shut behind them.

"I have a feeling our paths will cross again," Trigve said, still staring into the distance. "I don't think we've seen the last of these Stregas."

Juniper nodded, then made a circular gesture with her hand. *"Nante, nante."*

I shivered as fresh snowflakes hit my cheeks. "I wish I'd cut Astrid's throat when I had the chance."

Roth pulled his blue cloak tighter about his shoulders and looked at me with tired eyes. "Then we wouldn't have gotten our prophecy."

TWENTY-TWO

T*wo nights passed, and we saw no mist and no beast.*

The snow fell and fell.

At night, I slept by the hearth with Trigve and the Mercies, Ovie on one side, Juniper on the other, Trigve nearby, just like always, except now the sweet dog Vika lay at my feet as well.

We were warm beside the fire, and we slept deeply, despite everything.

Trigve spent most of his time with Siv, the healer in yellow. She had her own hut near the Hall, and she and Trigve passed the afternoons mixing potions together, looking through ancient medicinal scrolls, and tending to the sick.

Runa and Indigo spent the daylight hours making arrows and shooting targets in the Great Hall as Roth's men looked on. Runa was also learning how to make a yew bow, under Indigo's instruction. She cut a branch from the ancient giant yew tree for the purpose, which required a ritual of forgiveness. Juniper and Flinn, the soothsayer, led the ritual at dawn, and it was filled with mysterious gestures and quiet chanting.

Juniper was often with the soothsayer, which surprised me little—he was gentle and handsome. They walked down to the valley each day and visited the Star River—Juniper said fast-moving water helped visions come easier. I often caught sight of them from the top of the hill, her green hair and black Mercy-cloak melding with his dark hair and white bearskin.

And Ovie. Ovie disappeared with Vale during the day, making rounds through the Hall, checking on the preparation of food in the kitchens, and the brewing of mead in the cellars, and the goats, pigs, and sheep in the outbuildings. She seemed to have designated herself the girl's comrade and protector and seemed content in the role.

I spent my evenings drinking *Vite* with Roth.

I soon learned that the jarl followed the ways of Obin. He did not sacrifice animals on the summer solstice, but instead set out offerings of bread and honey on the ancient stones near important rivers and streams. He believed in the power of nature—the magic of trees and earth and wind and sea. Obin was a poet's god, and the only one, it was said, who understood that life was an endless series of crossroads that led to both deep joy and great sorrow.

As a former Boneless Mercy, I still prayed to Valkree, when I prayed. But Obin started visiting me in my dreams—short flashes of a broad-shouldered man standing at a crossroads, leaning against a hangman's tree, his clear blue eyes narrowed against the setting sun.

And in my dreams, Obin looked like Roth.

Roth and I spoke a great deal and drank a great deal. He seemed to value my companionship, and I was happy enough to give it to him. He was a natural storyteller, with a deep, expressive voice. Late at night, after the *Vite* took hold, his mood would lighten, and he'd tell me exciting tales from his childhood.

"When I was ten, I went troll-hunting and treasure-seeking in the Skals," he told me on the second night. "I ran off without my father's permission, determined to find monsters and glory in the deep, dark Sleet Heath Caves that stretch for miles under the mountain."

"You went alone? That was brave."

Roth shook his head. "No, I went with five close boyhood companions, all sons of my father's best men-at-arms. And all dead now."

"Killed by Logafell?" I reached out, and Roth refilled my horn with *Vite*.

"Yes."

"Did you find one?" My voice was starting to slur. I'd lost count of how many times I'd filled my drinking horn. Four? Eight?

"Find a troll, you mean? No. And we found no treasure, either. Just endless dark caverns, some empty, some filled with bones, animal and human."

Roth's talk of the caves gave me a sudden craving for fresh air. I rose and lifted the flap across the window. I breathed in the snow-scented night, and then sat down and was quiet for a long while, thoughtful from the drink and from watching the orange flames dance in the brazier.

"What are you thinking of, Frey?" Roth asked a few moments later.

Most Vorse would have considered this a rude question—our thoughts were our own business. But I didn't mind.

I looked over at him. Roth's eyes shone purple-blue in the moonlight streaming in the open window. I wondered if his mother really had been a Sea Witch, as Mother Hush had claimed. Some of the Sea Witches had eyes that turned a lilac shade under the moon. I hadn't seen it when I was in the Merrows, but then, I hadn't been searching for it, either.

"I was thinking about my friend Sasha and her son, Aarne," I said. "I hope they are doing well with the Sea Witches and passing a warm winter among the Scorch Trees. I think of them often." I paused. "There is something in me that makes it hard to forget people, no matter how short their presence is in my life. I always wonder about them afterward, who they were before we met, and what paths they take after we part. Siggy used to say this was a lousy trait for a Mercy, that it only made the job all the harder. She was right."

Roth nodded. "If remembrance is a curse, then I suffer from it, too. I often see the faces of my dead companions in my dreams."

"That is not a curse. You are keeping your friends alive. As long as you remember them, they still live."

Roth tilted his head and then smiled. "I will try to see it this way from now on."

I reached out my arm, and Roth refilled my horn.

"I heard your mother was a Sea Witch," I said, slurring the last two words. "Is it true?"

"Aye, it is."

"How did she end up here in Blue Vee, married to your father?"

Roth paused. "That is a long story, one that's best told under the midnight sun, on a warm summer night."

"Fair enough," I said. "I can wait."

We sat in silence then, watching the fire.

I took the last sip of my *Vite* and drifted into sleep, chin on my chest.

I woke up sometime later, Roth asleep in his chair next to me, head tilted back, face serene.

On the third morning, I gathered the Mercies to me after our simple breakfast of oats with honey and milk. We walked down to the empty training yard and began to practice the Seventh Degree under a blue sky that stretched all the way across the valley to the mountains.

Indigo joined us after an hour or two, and Ovie began to show her the steps. The Glee Starr girl was a quick learner, and soon we were all flowing through each phase with ease, white snowflakes flying around us.

On the fourth morning, we gathered all the women in the Great Hall and asked them join us, including the healer, Siv. The training yard, once devoted to male warriors, was now the domain of four former Boneless Mercies, one former theater troupe performer, and two dozen women and girls ranging in age from ten to seventy. The servants from the kitchens held knives, but the rest grabbed sticks from the ground. It didn't matter—they still learned.

The beast still didn't come. Not that night. Not the next.

On the sixth morning, I looked up from my practice and saw Roth standing nearby. He stayed for over an hour, shifting positions occasionally to rest his right leg.

The *edge dance*. All of us women moving in unison, Ovie calling out the steps, the hiss of our blades as they moved through the air, the thump of our boots hitting the ground—it gave me joy, sharp and pure, straight to the heart. I could taste the power of it on the back of my throat, like a long drink of *Vite*.

I was no longer a simple wanderer, alone in the world except for my companions. I felt linked to these people, these women, to Roth, to this Hall. We'd been in Blue Vee only a week, but it was the longest I'd spent in one place since running away from the Bliss House at fourteen.

On the evening of the seventh night, a gray-blue mist rose and spread across the valley.

Roth and I stood together on the hill outside the Hall and watched it come—the rare sight of smoke on snow. The haze moved swiftly, covering Destin Lush in the span of a few hundred heartbeats.

"I wish I could take them in," Roth said, nodding down at the wall below. "I wish I could keep all my people safe behind these gates. But how many could I fit inside? A tenth at most, elbow to elbow? And who would decide which ones lived and which ones died?"

I understood. I had the same urge. "We traveled through several villages on the way here—it seems that the ones who could flee, did. The men hide in the forest. It's the sick and injured who are left in the villages, the elderly, and the young. They must wait it out and live or die, relying on fate and luck."

Roth turned to me, eyes on mine. "I'd die in their place, if I could."

"I know."

Thunder echoed across the valley, so loud and deep I felt it ring through my heart. A moment passed, and then I heard it again. And again.

I scanned the horizon, but all I saw was mist. I looked at Roth. "That's not thunder."

"No."

I reached for the dagger at my calf and held it down at my side, sharp side out, in the fourth position of the Seventh Degree.

Logafell's howl was the sound of *breaking*, of slaughter, of ruin, of *crush* and *beat* and *burn*.

"Look, Roth, there." I pointed.

A girl was running through the mist, toward the gates in the wall. She was young, maybe four or five.

Her white wool dress was red with blood.

Roth looked down at his right leg, then back at me. "Save her, Frey."

I ran.

No guards stood at the gate. Roth had called them in when the mist started to rise—the guards never survived the attacks, and he couldn't afford to lose any more men. I lifted the bolt myself, straining, *straining*, until it finally shifted off the latch.

I pushed the tall doors open and was met with a wall of mist. I took a deep breath, and ran blindly toward the girl's screams.

My shoulder smacked into the trunk of a tree, and I staggered backward.

My feet tripped on stones buried under snow, and I fell, knees smacking into the ground.

Finally, the wind shifted, and a patch of mist cleared.

I saw her near a group of three tall pines, running hard, her chubby arms and legs pumping. I raced toward her, close . . . closer . . .

I bent down and swept the girl up into my arms.

I unclasped my Mercy-cloak and tucked it around her cold

little body. She was still screaming, the sound muffled now by my shoulder.

I held her close and *ran*.

Her legs bounced against my hips, her breath warmed my neck.

I *felt* Logafell's howl when it came again, the sound boiling my blood, pounding my bones.

I spun around, eyes squinting through mist and snow . . .

A wolf, a Giantine Wolf, shaggy red fur, yellow eyes, five feet at the shoulder, eight from nose to tail.

It was magnificent.

It was monstrous.

It raised its front paw, in a point.

Run, Frey. RUN.

Roth met me at the doors. He slammed the gates shut behind me—

The wolf crashed into the other side. It rammed the wood, blow after blow.

The gates began to shake. To *moan*.

The girl screamed again, and I clutched her even closer to me, so close I could feel her pulse. I counted the beats, waiting for the blows to end. One hundred. Two hundred. Three hundred.

The blows stopped.

The wolf retreated, back into the mist.

It knew it would get another chance at us from the other side of the wall.

We saw the smoke from the village when we reached the top of the hill, a darker shade than the haze. Below the smoke, flickering orange flames danced with abandon, like Elvers after a Midsummer feast.

"Thorsten burns," Roth said, looking down at his valley, his voice low, and sad as twilight.

Siv took the girl from me when we reached the Hall. The poor thing panicked when I handed her to the healer, fingers clutching at my tunic, eyes wide and terrified.

"Shh," I whispered, rubbing my thumb across her cheek, "Siv will take care of you. You're safe."

Siv hushed the girl, rocking her back and forth. I hadn't spent much time with the Mender, but I could see she had a tender way about her, like Juniper.

Siv caught Trigve's eye, and then gestured to the girl's pearl-white toes. "Rub her feet. She's been running on snow."

Trigve took both of the girl's feet in his palms and began to massage them until the color came back, his touch gentle and expert. "What village did the giant burn?" he asked, softly.

"Thorsten."

He nodded and said nothing.

Roth was by the yew tree, talking to his men-at-arms. I noticed for the first time that none of the men was younger than thirty. I understood now that these last sixteen warriors were the best of Roth's fighters—the seasoned veterans who'd outlasted the rest.

Roth looked up and saw me watching. He motioned me over with a nod of his chin. I went to him, the Mercies at my side.

"So what is your plan, Frey?"

I put my hand on the hilt of my ax and let the warriors run their gaze over me. "We go out beyond the wall and meet her."

The men began to shout and swear. I'd expected as much.

Roth raised an arm, and they fell quiet. "Logafell has lured us out before. It is certain death."

I nodded. "Yes, it's a trap. But this time we will not try to kill her. We only need to stand our ground until we wound her. If we can believe the Stregas' vision, then I will be able to follow her trail of blood back to her den and slay her in her lair."

Roth held my gaze. It was the right choice, and he knew it. Even if it meant more of his men would die.

Their blood would be on my hands.

Juniper stepped forward. "We go after Logafell tonight, and we don't hold back. We make it count."

Runa glanced at me, then gripped her new bow in one fist and turned to the men. "I, for one, am not afraid."

Ovie drew her ax and faced Roth. "We do this in the old way, with steel and blood."

I saw the faces of the last sixteen Blue Vee warriors slowly shift from wariness to . . . pride.

Roth walked over to the wall and grabbed the double-headed battle-ax that hung there, lifting it easily, strong shoulder blades sliding down his back.

"We won't cower," he said, deep, accented voice ringing down the Hall. "We won't huddle behind locked gates while a giant sets our villages on fire." He raised the ax above his head and let his voice rise to a shout. *"We fight, for Blue Vee."*

"*We fight*," I said, louder, loud enough for all to hear, "*because we are Vorse*."

We moved slowly toward Thorsten, the mist curling around our bodies like claws, clinging to our skins like icy spiderwebs.

If this was a hunt, we were the prey.

Trigve, Indigo, the Mercies, and I made up the middle of the pack, along with Roth. His warriors surrounded us on all sides, weapons out.

Silence.

Nothing but the crunch of our feet on frozen snow. I breathed in and felt the fog moving down my throat, settling into my lungs.

Sweat trickled down my spine, despite the cold.

Roth had given Trigve a large ax with a hickory handle, and he gripped it in his fist, eyes on the mist. Despite his prior claims to know very little of fighting and weaponry, Trigve looked confident with the blade. Brave. I would have preferred he stayed safe at the Great Hall, with Siv, but I knew better than to ask it of him.

The smell of burning drifted in from the direction of

Thorsten, and this is how we stayed on course, for we could barely see the ground six feet in front of us. We flinched at every sound, every snap of a twig, every whistle of a Great Owl. On and on, through the clammy fog.

I prayed.

Not for victory, but for the mist to clear, so it could be a fair fight, and so I could see this creature, this last remnant of the northern giants, before I was killed.

I heard a sharp intake of breath to my right.

One of the warriors, a tall man with sorrowful eyes, had fallen to his knees, weapon on the ground, hand to his waist, blood seeping through his tunic.

The second man was taken as I watched, yanked backward by his hair, a flash of white fangs, his ax dropped at my feet.

I felt the swish of air as the third man was pulled from our circle. I heard the snap of his bones as they broke under giant teeth.

We squeezed into a tighter circle. I felt the fear coming off the men. I felt it pouring off myself.

Fear would overtake us, then panic, and then we'd simply run back to the Hall.

"*Enough*," I screamed. I turned to Roth, squinting in the haze. "Logafell's wolves are going to pick us off one by one. We need to lure her out of the mist."

Roth shifted the battle-ax to his right hand. "*Kill the wolves*," he shouted, his deep voice cutting through the fog. "*Force her out of hiding.*"

I raised my voice to match his. "*Go by scent, not by sight.* Run into the mist and attack them before they attack you."

Mercies and men-at-arms scattered into the dark mist. I moved blindly to the east, arms out before me, weapons ready. I breathed in, and smelled juniper berries and snow . . .

And also fur. The wet, earthy stink of fur, like a whip across my face.

I lunged into the haze, my ax in both hands—

I *screamed*—

And buried the blade in the creature's flank until it crunched through bone.

I wrenched my weapon free and hit it again, this time lower down.

It howled . . .

And howled . . .

And then it fell. The thud echoed up my legs.

I would make this quick and clean. A Mercy-kill. I screamed again, and hewed open its neck. Blood splattered my face.

The wind swelled, and a patch of the blue mist dissipated. I looked up. Ovie and Trigve stood off to the right, a dead wolf at their feet. One of the warriors, a lithe man with red hair, had taken another. I spun to my left and saw Roth, battle-ax raised, a dead wolf by his side.

Our eyes met.

"*Back to the circle, everyone,*" he shouted.

I called out to Juniper and Runa and heard the answering cries. They were alive and well, thank the gods.

Together we stumbled our way through the mist and moved into position, back-to-back. Silent. Waiting.

"That will have gotten her attention," Roth whispered. "Prepare yourself, everyone."

The wind swelled again.

Ovie lifted her blade and pointed. "There."

Logafell.

She crouched near a tall, snow-covered pine, elbows hugging bent knees, white-blond hair flowing around her muscled, half-naked body, like a Gothi nun's veil.

She stared sat us, eyes the size of apples.

Logafell curled back her lips and *snarled*, pearly teeth the size of oyster shells . . . then she tilted her head back and *howled*.

It was raw and ancient and *primal*.

She rose up from the ground as we watched, up and up, as tall as a tree, as tall as a god, arms as thick as pillars.

The ground shook as she circled around us, the thud of her footsteps rhythmic and deep, like the Cut-Queen's drums. Thick muscles rippled under her worn wool tunic.

Indigo and Runa exchanged a glance, and then moved to stand shoulder to shoulder. In unison, they pulled back their bowstrings.

We all watched the arrows as they soared into the air, felt the thrum—

Each bounced off the giant's skin, leaving only faint lines of blood.

"What now?" Runa screamed. *"What do we do, Frey?"*

The wind shifted again, and the mist swept back in, great patches of milky haze. Indigo and Runa spun in the fog, arrows ready . . .

Logafell dodged forward. She gripped one of the male warriors by the shoulder, fingers like tree branches. We watched his body rise into the air, and then disappear into the fog.

Blood dripped down on our faces like rain.

She tossed his limp body aside and lunged forward again. One swift move of her arm . . . Roth flew backward and landed on his right leg. Hard.

Somewhere, off to my right, I smelled wet fur.

Somewhere, off to my left, I heard Trigve scream.

"Trigve." Everything was happening too fast—I couldn't see, the damn mist—*"Trigve."*

No reply.

I smelled wet fur again. *Close, too close—*

Juniper spun around, eyes wide. She grabbed my arm. *"Kneel, Frey."*

I crouched down, and the Sea Witch jumped onto my back, and then into the air, swift and light as a deer. She cut the wolf's throat with one quick jerk of her hand, its teeth gnashing inches above my head.

The wolf dropped to the ground. It began to writhe on the snow, red blood, red fur.

Juniper and I backed away from the beast and into the mist. A breeze brushed by my cheek, and a patch of fog cleared . . .

Logafell. She knelt next to her dying wolf, her hands on its neck, trying to stanch the blood.

"*Now, Runa*," I shouted. "*Quick. Aim for her eye.*"

Runa ran to my side, Indigo at her heels. She raised her bow . . .

And missed.

"*Again*," I screamed.

Another arrow hissed through the air, this time from Indigo.

Then another.

And another.

Runa shifted position. She took a deep breath—

The fifth arrow flew straight and true. It sank deep into Logafell's eye, the tip disappearing into iris-black.

Logafell howled.

The sound cut through my mind like fire, burned my skin, my eyes, my scalp. It went on and on . . .

And then suddenly . . . *silence*.

I put my hands to the earth and felt the thud of four beasts fleeing back into the mist.

I found Trigve under a juniper tree. His arm was broken, but he was alive.

I knelt there in the snow and gave thanks to Valkree and to Obin.

Roth lived as well. His leg was badly hurt, and he suffered a deep gash to the back of his skull, which bled like a stuck pig.

We found the remains of his warriors in pools of blood . . . missing limbs, crushed skulls, sharp teeth marks on tender skin. Nine of the last sixteen, gone.

It was a slow journey back to the Hall, the injured and the dead dragged in on hastily constructed sleds made of pine boughs, spilled blood freezing hard in the cold night air.

Roth fell unconscious on the way back to the Hall. We brought him to his room so Siv could tend to him.

Indigo and the men-at-arms burned their comrades, the Mercies and I went back into the valley to search for survivors.

Thorsten had a scattering of homes, two dozen at most, and more than half were burned to ash by the time we arrived. We found no one alive.

Ovie discovered the bodies of three young girls near a smoldering outbuilding. Three bruised, broken corpses, the oldest eight years at most.

I dropped my ax in the snow. "Logafell will die for this. I swear it on my life and every life I've ever taken."

Juniper made a Sea Witch sign for justice, a cross with one long line, one short.

Runa pushed back her Mercy-cloak and knelt beside me. "We came here to kill this giant. We will keep our promise."

My eyes met hers. *"I swear vengeance. For Jarl Roth and all the people of Blue Vee. For these three dead girls, and for Vorse girls everywhere."*

We found the trail of blood on the way back to the Hall, each drop the size of a gold coin, glowing crimson in the snow.

TWENTY-THREE

"O*nce upon a time, in the final days before the Salt and Marsh* Witch War, four Boneless Mercies turned their backs on the death trade and went west, seeking immortality."

I said this with my fist on my heart, my back to the Great Hall of Blue Vee, my gaze scanning the Destin Lush Valley, the sun rising pink in the east.

Ovie nodded. "Even if we fail, we still succeed, Frey."

Juniper pushed back the hood of her cloak, and her pearl-green curls shone against the white snow. "We are doing something that hasn't been done before. That is what matters."

Runa simply lifted her chin and stared ahead, past the valley, to the Sleet Heath.

Indigo had joined us as well, claiming she didn't want Runa to get all the glory. She moved to Runa's side and grinned. "Let's kill this monster, Mercies."

The Glee Starr girl, for all her boasts and bravado, had blood of fire and a heart of gold.

We'd stayed at the Hall only long enough to report on Thorsten, clean the grime from our faces, and gather supplies. Logafell's blood trail would last only until the next snowfall, which could come any moment. It was now or never.

I went to Roth's room and sat by his side for several minutes, as long as I could spare. He still hadn't woken. His leg was bandaged, and his head wrapped in a clean linen cloth. He looked . . . young. I thought of the stories he'd told me about his childhood, of hunting trolls in the caves.

Lastly, I sought out Trigve, in Siv's hut. He was pale but awake, lying on a cot with his arm in a sling, dried herbs hanging overhead.

"So you're off to slay the beast," he whispered.

"Yes."

He wrapped his good arm around me and pulled me close.

"Don't die," Trigve whispered, his lips near my ear. "Don't die, Frey."

I gripped his tunic in my fists and held him tight. "I won't, Trigve Lothe."

We tracked Logafell across the open plain, black cloaks fluttering over white snow.

"They haven't left a single print," Runa said a few hours into our trek. "Neither she nor her wolves. As if they run on air."

"It's a spell." Juniper tilted her head, staring at the ground. "It's ancient northern magic, older than Sea Witch magic. We don't know the way of it."

We followed the drops north, on and on, until the trees gave way to berry-red lichen and purple heather.

It was drier in the Heath, the snowfall slighter. We picked up speed, heels kicking up flakes as we ran.

We stopped at noon, just long enough to start a fire. We rubbed the cold out of our tired limbs and melted snow for chicory tea. Ovie found winter lingonberries, and we ate these by the handful, grateful for the tart spice that heated our bellies, even if it didn't fill them.

Juniper, cheeks glowing red from the chill, swallowed a mouthful of berries and then lifted her arm and pointed north toward a small hill. "Look. A milk-white doe."

I saw it, a faint outline against the snow, tall ears, dark eyes, standing in a pocket of sunlight. It watched us as we watched it, before suddenly turning and bolting off, thin legs leaping easily over the drifts.

Juniper smiled and made a witch sign for luck. "It bodes well. The gods are with us."

I looked at my Sea Witch friend. The lack of sleep was getting to us all, but she was suffering the most. I could see it in the dark circles under her eyes and in the tightness of her mouth. The white deer seemed to cheer her, though, and give her comfort, and I was glad of it.

Runa took a sip of chicory tea and glanced at Ovie, who sat on a fallen tree, sharpening her ax with a small stone. "You and Logafell have something in common now."

Ovie tapped her finger on the patch over her eye. "True."

I heard a raven caw and looked up at the sky—it was a crisp, striking blue, though the winter sun provided little heat.

I wondered when we Mercies would sit like this again around a fire.

Perhaps soon.

Perhaps never.

The trail of blood eventually led us to a river and a narrow canyon.

The canyon was deeply shadowed—the tall, jutted sides blocked the sun. Yellow Cave Crows lived in the small, dark cavities at the top of the cliffs, and their songs were lonely and mournful.

There was an eerie feeling about the chasm, one that made my spine tingle and my jaw ache.

We stood at the entrance to the ravine, toes near a giant drop of blood, and squinted into the shadows.

Ovie pushed back the hood of her cloak and took a step forward. "We will be trapped inside this canyon once we enter. We can't climb these steep walls."

I nodded. "My instinct tells me Logafell does not yet know we are following her. She is in retreat, wounded, with five of her wolves dead. She's thinking only of her den."

And with that, I entered the ravine.

We did not run now, but walked, feet on soft snow. Quiet. Silent. We followed the edge of the canyon stream, keeping watch on all sides. The Cave Crows flew overhead—a burst of yellow across the black cliffs. One came so close that I reached out and touched her wing as she passed, fingers sliding down feathers. They are brave birds.

I heard the waterfall before I saw it—a misting white stream slipping down over black rocks, crashing into a small pool at the bottom. I came to the last bead of blood and stood, toes pointed forward.

It was the end of the trail.

I gripped my ax in one hand and reached for my dagger with the other. "Logafell might have been able to pull herself up those rocks," I whispered, "but her wolves sure couldn't. Get out your weapons, Mercies. She went behind the waterfall. It must conceal the entrance to a cave."

Juniper raised a hand, palm out. "In the *Blood Frost Saga*, the Lone Girl finds the entrance to the Ice Elver's cave behind a waterfall. It is right that the giant led us here. It feels . . . balanced."

Ovie stared ahead into the white surge of water, body tense, ready to spring.

Indigo grinned and lifted her bow. "We will kill this giant or die in the attempt. If we die, then we will drink and feast tonight in the golden Great Hall of the Slain, and all of Holhalla will kneel at our feet. I'm ready, and I'm eager."

I smiled, despite myself. "You are fierce, Indigo."

Runa nodded. "She is Vorse."

We waded into the pool, feet treading carefully on the icy stones.

I closed my eyes and stepped through the water.

The cave tunnel was dark, pitch dark, new moon dark. I shook off droplets of water, like a dog, then gripped my ax in my fist so hard my bones ached. I couldn't see the girls next to me, but I felt them, felt their tension and their warmth.

"Fire," I whispered.

I heard Runa fishing around in her pack—she always carried one or two unlit torches—oiled strips of wool tied to a stick of green wood. I saw sparks, and light cut through the dark, banishing it back into the corners.

She handed me the torch, and we moved forward. I heard water trickling, a soft patter like rain.

We walked on and on. The air smelled stagnant and clammy, with a faint earthy tinge. I had the unnerving sensation that we'd entered the belly of some ancient, gargantuan sea beast. The hero of the *Sung and Told Saga* was swallowed by a whale when out fishing, and he lived in its belly for several weeks before escaping. I would not wish for this fate.

Something brittle cracked loudly beneath my heel, and I flinched.

Bone.

I lifted the torch. We had entered a large cavern, the roof as high as the ceiling of Roth's Great Hall. Higher.

Bones. Stacks upon stacks of them, some taller than me, some almost as tall as Logafell. The skull of a wolf sat near my feet, cradled against a human femur. I saw the rib cage of a bear and a pile of delicate, tiny bones that looked as though they belonged to mice. I saw the skulls of birds and cats and cows. The far corner was filled with the tangled antlers of giant red deer.

"Troll cave," Juniper whispered. She drew a circle in the air. *"Nante, nante."*

I spun around slowly, eyes on the shadows. "Trigve said trolls don't exist."

Ovie shifted position, gaze circling the room. "All the same, the giant didn't do this all on her own. There's a hundred years' worth of kills here."

We picked our way through a century of skeletons to the other side of the cavern, careful not to touch any of the larger piles—a clatter of bones would not aid our stealth. We came to another tunnel, this one leading farther down. Runa lit the second torch and went first, fire held high.

I had felt safer in the dark.

Ovie's fingers touched my elbow and I slowed.

"Logafell will send out her wolves first," she whispered, "and they will find us with or without light."

Indigo halted in front of us, drew her bow, and fired an arrow into the dark. It flew down the tunnel and struck a stone in the far distance. "I thought I heard something," she hissed. "Feels like we're being watched."

We moved closer together, shoulder to shoulder. The tunnel opened again, this time into a slant-roofed cavern with a wide pool.

White cave icicles hung down from the roof like teeth.

"Careful, Mercies." I went up to the edge of the pool and stared down. "I don't like the feel of this place."

I lifted my torch until I could see my reflection. The water was unnaturally still. *Savalikk.* I reached my foot forward and gently touched the edge with the tip of my boot . . .

I heard a noise, and looked up—

Dripping red fur—

White teeth—

The Giantine Wolf burst from the pool and lunged at Indigo. They both hit the ground. Indigo jerked her body to the left and sank her blade into its neck, just as the wolf sank its teeth into her shoulder.

"Indigo." Runa dropped her torch and drew her bow. An arrow hit the wolf's flank. Then another. It growled but didn't release its grip.

Ovie charged forward, ax raised—

The last two wolves leapt from the pool, spraying water. One hurled itself toward Juniper . . .

And the other rammed into my left side.

I fell, arms covering my face. My head hit the floor of the cave, and I saw stars.

I felt heat near my ear, the wolf's breath, teeth snapping . . .

Use your dagger, Frey.

I sliced the wolf across its tender black nose. It recoiled, and I gained a few seconds of freedom. I jumped to my feet and skidded on wet stone. I dropped my dagger, and it skittered across the cave floor.

Hel.

The wolf shook its head, and its eyes cleared. It turned to me—

I grabbed my ax—

It jumped forward—

And I buried my blade into its side.

I grabbed the handle in both hands and began to drag the beast back to the pool. It gnashed its teeth, but I held. Its blood spattered my cheeks, and I held. I dragged the wolf in, step by step, until the water hit my waist.

I took a deep breath, *deep*, and pushed the wolf's head under water.

I *held*.

"Frey."

I turned and saw Juniper astride the second wolf's back.

"*Juniper,*" I shouted. I craned my neck toward her—

My foot slipped on the rocks at the bottom of the pool.

I let go of the ax and fell.

The wolf lunged upward. It broke the surface and *howled.*

I heaved myself out of the water and howled back. I scrambled forward, hands reaching for the hilt of my blade, still in the wolf's side—

It snapped its jaws, close, too close. I shielded my face—

It snapped again, and bit down.

I screamed.

Pain. Pain like fire. Pain like death.

I pounded on the wolf's nose with my free arm, again and again and again. Its jaws slackened. I yanked my hand from its mouth.

The first and second fingers on my left hand were gone.

Blood. Blood everywhere.

I wedged my wounded hand into my right armpit and *screamed.* I grabbed the ax in my right fist and shoved the wolf under the water again. I held, through the haze of pain and blood loss, straining, panting . . .

I smelled fur and blood and fire and steel. I *held.*

The wolf went still.

I yanked my ax free, caught my breath, and looked over my shoulder—

Ovie was slicing the first wolf across the throat, blood streaming until I couldn't tell where girl ended and wolf began.

Runa knelt over Indigo. She was tearing at her tunic, trying to get to her wound.

Juniper.

I waded out of the water and went to the Sea Witch. She lay on her side, eyes closed. She had a large red welt at her right temple. I put my ear to her chest and winced at the pain in my hand when I shifted forward.

Her breathing was shallow but regular. She would live.

I rose to my feet and went to Indigo. Her shoulder was ripped open to the bone, a raw mass of muscle and skin and blood.

"What a fight, Frey," she whispered, as Runa fussed over her shoulder. *"What a fight."*

Runa cauterized my wound. She held her knife over the flame of her torch until it turned red, then she pressed it to the stumps of my fingers. I screamed. And screamed. But I didn't faint.

I'd seen many things as a Boneless Mercy. I'd *done* many things as a Boneless Mercy. But I'd never smelled the scent of my own flesh burning. Yet I was ready for it when it came, and I did not shame myself.

Runa wrapped a clean woolen rag around my hand when it was done. I would still be able to use it, if necessary. I took a long swig of *Vite*. Then another.

Ovie bent down and picked up Juniper, one arm under her thin neck, and one under her knees. She carried her across the cavern and set her next to Indigo.

Her eyes met mine. "So it's down to the three of us."

I looked at my bandaged hand, then at Runa. "You still with us?"

She nodded. "Of course."

I nodded. "Then let's give this giant a good death."

TWENTY-FOUR

Logafell's cavern glowed like the moon. Patches of phosphorus mushrooms grew along the cave floor. The eerie, blue-white light made her bare skin shine like wet stone.

She sat at the far end, her muscled arms wrapped around knees the size of cauldrons, thick white-blond hair hanging down over broad shoulders. She looked up at us when we entered, but didn't rise.

She was beautiful.

And she was vulnerable, without her wolves, without the mist.

I looked around. A giant pile of furs was in the far corner—her bed—as was a simple wooden table, legs as tall as Juniper. It was set with golden plates and wooden mugs. Bones were scattered here and there—remnants of past feasts.

The walls of the cave were not slick and damp, but rugged, with jutting black ridges like misshapen steps. A worn tapestry hung in the corner—it showed a snow-covered mountain under an orange sun. There was a hearth in the middle of the cavern, cold now, but with iron cookware nearby.

This was not some deep, dark cave of carnage and horror.

It was a *home*.

I looked back to the beast, to the *woman*, at the far end of the cavern. Caked blood covered her left eye. She'd ripped the arrow out, leaving an empty black hole.

Even after all the destruction she'd caused, all the death, those three young girls in Thorsten . . . I didn't like seeing that wound.

"These tunnels lead under the Skal Mountains." Logafell's voice was softer than I'd expected. It echoed across the cavern like the hush of ocean waves. "There is treasure to be had there if you are brave enough to go after it. I found those gold plates down one of these tunnels. There is plenty more."

She spoke in perfect Vorse, though not with the Blue Vee accent. Her accent was . . . *colder*. Crisp and tinged with frost.

She glanced toward my bandaged hand. "Lose something?"

"Just a few fingers. Nothing I'll miss."

"Are all my dogs gone now?"

I nodded.

"Pity. I raised them from pups. Little Torvi was my favorite, but they were all loyal pets. I'd hoped to take them home someday, back to the north, and set them free to run with the last Giantine Wolf pack in the Ice Plains."

Logafell heaved a great sigh, and then rose to her feet.

She was *giant*. Hill, tree, *mountain*.

"So you've come to kill the famous Blue Vee Beast. The Lean

Ones, the Night Stalkers, the Jotun . . . My people have been called many things throughout time. Well, what do you think, now that you've seen me and my home?"

"I think you are beautiful."

She laughed, and it was a pleasant sound, low like thunder, soft like rain. "Nothing is simple, is it? Not quests, not heroes, not beasts, not glory."

I craned my neck and stared up, up, *up*. I met her gaze. "No. Nothing is simple."

She nodded, and her white hair fell like silk across her shoulders. "Well, if you're going to kill me, girl, then get on with it."

I lowered my chin and glanced at Runa, then Ovie. As one, we unclasped our Mercy-cloaks and let them fall to the ground.

We charged.

Runa yanked the thick rope out of her pack as she raced toward the giant. She took one end and threw the other to Ovie, who caught it midair. They pulled the rope taut and ran it straight into Logafell's tree-trunk thighs.

Logafell swatted at us, great arms swinging. I scurried to the far wall, deep in the shadows, and started to climb. I wedged my ax into a narrow cleft and pulled myself up with one arm onto a four-inch ledge.

I glanced over my shoulder. Runa and Ovie darted across the cavern floor, dodging the giant's fists. They wove the rope around Logafell's legs, once, twice . . .

Logafell took a step forward, stumbled, and nearly fell.

If she falls, we have her.

I pulled my ax free, and climbed higher.

Runa wrapped her end of the rope around her waist and cried out as it cut into her flesh. Ovie tied the other end around her shoulders, and they both began to move backward, away from each other, step by step, pulling the rope tight, rigid as the string in Runa's bow.

Logafell tossed her head and then jerked her shoulders backward, wrenching the ropes around Runa and Ovie until they screamed.

They couldn't hold her.

"*Now, Frey,*" Ovie shouted.

I dropped my ax and ran across the ledge. I bent my knees, jumped—

I landed on Logafell's back, fingers clutching her hair.

She *howled.*

The giant began to writhe, her whole body twisting. She dragged Runa and Ovie across the cavern floor, their boots scraping across stone. I dug my feet into her back and held on.

Logafell howled again. She arched, then wrenched forward—

I went flying. I hit the ground. Hard.

I couldn't move. Couldn't *breathe.*

I willed my eyes open—

I saw a shadow, rising above me . . .

A foot. Logafell's giant foot.

"Frey." Runa let go of the rope and drew her bow. An arrow ripped through the tender part of the giant's ankle.

Logafell screamed. With one flick of her wrist, she threw Runa into the wall, near the tapestry.

I forced my arm into the air and pounded my fist on my chest, once, twice. My breath came back, a big wave of pain that lifted my ribs.

"*Runa*," I choked.

She didn't move.

"Runa."

The cave seemed to grow hazy, as if the blue mist had risen again. My hands began to tingle, and my body felt limp. Numb.

I was losing consciousness.

"*Finish it*," Ovie shouted. *"Finish it, Frey."*

I blinked and turned my head. Ovie had grabbed the other end of the rope when Runa dropped it and was sweating and swearing, struggling to hold both. Logafell swung at her again, fists like boulders. I felt the air shift as she moved, strong as a wind coming off the sea.

I heaved myself up to my feet, bent over, and was sick on the floor. I wiped the back of my mouth and glanced to the left. Runa's body was twisted at an odd angle, head turned one way, legs another.

Behind me, Ovie screamed my name. I spun around. Logafell was moving back into the far corner again and dragging Ovie with her.

Finish it, Frey.

I ran to the wall and scrambled back up, bruising muscles and scraping skin. I scuttled across the jutting ledges. Close . . . a little closer . . .

I leapt.

My arms flailed as I hit open air. I unclenched my fist—

And grabbed a handful of Logafell's tunic. I squeezed my right-hand fingers, tight, until my knuckles turned white. I felt the giant's skin underneath me, hard as stone. I pulled myself up, foot by foot, heels sinking into her giant spine until I could feel every curve of her vertebrae.

She writhed and twisted, trying to shake me off. But I clung on and held.

I inched upward.

Inch by inch by inch—

I tilted my head back and saw it. *The soft spot at the base of Logafell's neck*, just as Mother Hush had said. A fist-size piece of translucent flesh, a blue cluster of veins, blood pulsing behind delicate skin.

The chink in the monster's armor.

Below me, Ovie was straining, face red, sweat dripping. *"Hurry, Frey."*

I lifted my wounded hand and reached for my knife. I clutched it in my fist, *the pain, oh Hel, the pain* . . .

Logafell reached forward and grabbed one end of the rope. She yanked it backward—

Ovie flew.

She hit the wall near the pile of furs and lay still.

I clung to Logafell's back and howled, just as she had howled, and her wolves had howled.

My voice soared across the cavern.

I lifted myself with my right arm, slowly, slowly, muscles quivering. I dragged my body up, up, one more inch, almost there . . .

"Don't you want to know why I did it, Mercy?"

Logafell's words echoed softly off the cavern's walls.

I froze.

"Before you stick me with that Mercy needle, you should know that this was not simple cruelty, the wild rampage of a mindless beast."

She had stopped writhing and twisting. She stood still. *Savalikk.*

Why?

I felt the deep intake of her breath, her giant ribs expanding against me. She knew. She knew I had the dagger to her neck and she was about to die.

I was shaking, with exhaustion, with anger. *Just slide the blade in and be done with it, Frey.*

But I hesitated. Just as I'd hesitated with the Cut-Queen. Logafell was a beast. A monster. But she was also a woman.

I would hear her last words.

"What was it then, if not cruelty?" I asked.

"Men, many of them," she said. "White-haired pirates that came from the sea. They saw my three daughters on the shore, hunting for clams—the oldest was only ten, though they were tall as trees. The men filled my daughters with arrows—their skin had not yet grown hard, was still as soft as yours. I found their bodies on the shore, bloodied and broken. Why did they kill them? For what reason? Because they were different?"

I took a deep breath and steadied my grip, toes digging into her spine.

"I'm sorry," I said. And I was.

Sweat trickled down my face, and I wiped it away with the sleeve of my left arm. The blade caught my reflection, my bloodshot eyes, as I hung in midair from the giant's back.

I looked . . .

Fearless.

"Throw down your dagger, girl. Let us be allies. Let us wander this world together, crushing all before us."

"I would," I said. "In another place, in another time, I would go with you, and we would bring the world to its knees."

I paused. I thought of Roth's broken warriors and the three young girls in Thorsten. I thought of the hanged girl at the crossroads. I thought of the girl in the Thiss Brambles. I thought of all the Mercy-kills through the years, on and on and on.

I thought of Runa, and Ovie.

"No. I'm done with death."

Her neck twisted to the side. She looked at me over her

shoulder with her one remaining eye. "I gave you a purpose, a quest, a chance to be noticed by the gods. *I* gave you this. Never forget."

I squeezed my fingers around the hilt of my knife and groaned with pain. "I'm in your debt, and I won't forget. I'll see you in Holhalla, giant."

I sank the dagger in deep.

Logafell screamed.

It was my very last Mercy-kill.

I felt the Blue Vee Beast shudder under me—

And then the blood came.

It ran and ran, like the waterfall that hid her den, great waves of it, a giant's torrent. It coated my hair, my face, my body. My hands grew slick with it.

Logafell began to sway from side to side.

I let go.

Down, *down, down, down.*

Her body landed on top of a pile of bones—they were crushed to dust, a white plume misting into the air.

The ground shuddered, tremors echoing through the cave like thunder.

I fell onto the furs near Ovie. I lay still for a moment, then dragged myself over to her. She was unconscious, but breathing.

Thank you, Valkree.

I crawled my way to Logafell, slipping twice in blood.

She seemed smaller now that she was on the earth instead of

towering above. Smaller and more . . . fragile. I put one palm to her giant cheek, and then slipped my flask of *Vite* between her lips.

"Here, drink this, lamb." I emptied the bottle between her teeth.

She swallowed, and then sighed.

I sat, knees touching her shoulder, and waited for her heart-beat to slow, a slight pulse of heat against my skin, growing fainter and fainter.

"I wanted to die," she whispered.

"I know," I said.

"I've already wandered the earth too long. The last of our race fled the far north, where we'd been hunted down one by one. We used to walk the ice, proud and regal as gods. But when we came to Vorseland, we hid in caves, crawling like demons in the dark, withering for want of sun, for want of purpose. My people died by the dozens, until it was just the four of us, me and my daughters."

She took a breath, and it was shallow, soft as a breeze. Blood seeped from the back of her neck, soaking my clothes.

"They would not bring me a good death, all those men of Blue Vee. You . . . you five girls finally gave me the end I needed. The end I deserved."

Logafell, the Blue Vee Beast, took her last breath and died in my arms.

. . . . .

I got up slowly and crossed the cavern floor, my bones heavy.

I slid down next to Runa's limp body. I wrapped my right-hand fingers around her pulse. Nothing. I pushed my palm into her chest. Held.

Nothing.

I heard a faint shuffle of feet and smelled salt and wood smoke and pine resin.

Juniper.

She knelt beside me, her tunic in tatters, her forehead a mass of welts and bruises. I released Runa, slowly, carefully, and took Juniper in my arms. I pressed my face to her neck and gripped her tight.

"How is Ovie?" I asked when I finally let her go.

Juniper nodded over her shoulder. "She has a few broken ribs, but she lives."

Ovie stood near a patch of the glowing mushrooms, one hand clutching her side. I rose to my feet and limped over to her. I held her as I'd held Juniper. We didn't speak. There was no need. I felt her heart against mine, and it sang the same sad song.

TWENTY-FIVE

It took seven strikes to sever Logafell's head.

My left arm was useless. I couldn't move it without my knees going weak from pain. So I decapitated the Blue Vee Beast with one hand, my right fist clamped around the hilt of my grave-dug ax. I swung and swung, the hiss of steel, the crunch of bone.

We burned the rest of her in the cave, gray smoke melting down dark passageways. I wanted to burn her body under the open sky, to release her spirit into the fresh Vorse air, but her head would have to be enough.

Juniper, our tiny Sea Witch, carried Runa's body through the long, dark tunnels. Between Indigo's shoulder wound and Ovie's broken ribs and my injured hand . . . Juniper was the only one of us still strong enough to see it done.

I would have carried Runa all the way back to Blue Vee in my arms if I could have, the way she carried the hanged girl at the crossroads.

I'd heard Juniper say that waterfalls caught evil spirits and trapped them like flies in a web. And I did feel protected by the rapids, the cool mist dusting my cheeks like snow as we passed through.

"We will drink to Runa's memory," Ovie said as she cleaned her ax in the snow outside the cave. "Each night beside the fire. Wherever we are, whoever we become, we will not forget."

"No," I said. "Never."

We slowly cobbled together two sleds of pine branches. One for Runa. One for Logafell's head.

I knew the people of Blue Vee would need to see what remained of the giant. They'd need it to feel safe again, to truly believe the horror was past.

It took us two days to return to the Hall, slowed down by our wounds and our heavy hearts as much as the heavy sleds behind us. We spoke little on the journey and ate little and slept less. I rubbed a black walnut balm from my pack onto Indigo's shoulder, as often as she'd let me. I used an Arctica balm on Ovie's ribs and the vicious-looking rope burns that crisscrossed her palms, arms, and back, red as the Cut-Queen's welts.

I used the same balm on the stumps of my missing fingers, when I could bear it, always remembering to hold my breath so I couldn't smell the burned flesh when I undid the bandage.

When I'd imagined killing the beast, all those weeks ago in the Hail Inn, I'd mostly thought about the glory, the *triumph*, of four former Boneless Mercies marching into a Great Hall as heroes, as conquerors.

Or I'd thought about death. Not a quiet Mercy-death, but an honorable death, one of steel and blood and screams, and the smoke of my pyre rising up to the sky.

But as we crossed through the gates and trudged up the hill to the Great Hall, my thoughts were not bright and vivid, lingering on our victory.

I glanced over my shoulder at Runa on the sled, the cold winter wind whipping the edges of her Mercy-cloak, a strand of her dark hair spilling out, the tip touching the snow.

No, my thoughts were on my friend, and the remains of the giant on the sled beside her.

A girl gone.

A giant gone.

They cheered as we entered the hall.

Heltar, heltar, heltar.

They yelled out our names, and the sound of it echoed off the rafters.

We halted under the giant yew tree, half-dead with exhaustion. Word had spread quickly as we'd moved up the hill, and the crowd in the Hall was growing thicker by the moment.

I heard a shout, then another.

The mob parted.

Roth entered.

I'd asked the guards at the gates about his welfare, and they'd said he'd woken not long after we'd left. I'd smiled for the first time in days.

The jarl of Blue Vee came to me, blond hair loose, blue cloak rippling. If he was still wounded from the fight with Logafell, he didn't show it. He clasped my forearm, warm palm cupping my elbow, and my heart beat stronger at his touch.

He looked down at the sleds beside me, first at Runa, then at Logafell's head, which we'd covered with a sheepskin rug from her cave.

"Frey," he said softly. "It is done."

"Yes," I said.

I turned to the crowd. I gripped my ax with my good hand and raised it in the air. "*This is the head of Logafell, the Blue Vee Beast.* Treat her with respect. Dennish pirates killed her three young daughters, and they were the last of their kind." I paused, my eyes scanning the crowd. "*We have slain the last Vorse giant, and I want her burned alongside the warrior Runa the Archer, on a great pyre that can be seen by the entire valley.*"

Siv took one look at us and began to bark orders.

We were in the bathhouse. It held several long wooden tubs, each with a fire lit underneath to heat the water. Steam drifted out the small hole in the ceiling. The air smelled verdant, floral—Siv had added dried herbs to the water to stave off infection and help us fight fatigue.

We couldn't sleep, not yet. We had a friend to burn.

Siv handed me an ice fever tonic, and I drank the green glowing liquid with a quick toss of my head. The potion gave me a numb feeling, first my tongue, then my mouth, then arms, torso, legs.

The pain in my hand lessened for the first time in days.

The pain in my heart stayed bright and sharp as ever.

We climbed out of our clothing, Siv helping when needed, and then sank into the tubs. I stretched out my limbs, keeping my wounded hand out of the water. I sighed deeply.

Indigo hissed as Siv poured a red-colored oil onto the wolf bite. "Do that again, healer, and I'll skin-fight you."

Siv looked at the Glee Starr girl and gave her a mild smile. "Not with that shoulder, you won't."

She did me next, gently patting an ointment onto my stumps. It smelled of honey and frankincense. The last scent of burned flesh disappeared.

"You lost a lot of blood," she whispered. "I'm not sure how you all made it back here, hauling two sleds."

"We are Vorse," I said.

She met my gaze and held. "Trigve is in my hut, waiting to see you. Go to him when you're done here."

I found Trigve in Siv's small, warm hut, attempting to mix potions with one arm in a sling. He dropped the glass vessel he was holding when he saw me. It crashed to the floor, leaking oily purple fluid everywhere.

"I didn't die," I said. "I kept my promise."

We held each other and didn't let go for a long, long time.

We burned them together that night on a pyre made of mountain birch.

The girl and the giant.

The flames rose higher and higher, orange against a black night sky, up and up, twenty feet, thirty feet, until they licked the stars.

Indigo watched the flames with approval. "Birch burns fast and hot. Runa would not want her body to burn slow."

"She will soon be in Holhalla." I threw Runa's bow on the pyre. She would take it with her to the Great Hall of the Slain.

"The time of monsters and men has passed," Ovie said. "This end is a beginning."

Juniper made a witch gesture of truth. "Logafell was the last of the Vorse giants. The Sea Witches dreamed it, and the wind confirms it."

"We will never see her like again." And I meant both Logafell and Runa. "We turned away from the death trade, and our path led to joy and glory. And loss and sorrow."

"Such is life." Ovie put her fist to her heart. "Such is life, Frey."

I watched the flames and thought of Runa.

Beside me, Juniper began to weep.

Ovie, my stoic Ovie, went to her and wrapped an arm

around the Sea Witch's waist. "Don't cry for Runa. It was a good death."

Juniper blinked and put her palms to her cheeks. "I don't cry for Runa. I cry for Frey. She is Vorse and will not weep. I must do it for her."

I couldn't sleep those first nights after we returned. I told everyone that my hand pained me and kept me awake, but it was my heart more than anything.

I'd pace the Hall, thinking of Runa, and eventually Trigve would rise and come find me.

"She should have gone with the Quicks," I'd say.

"It was a good death," he'd reply. "Don't take that from her."

I'd agree and keep pacing.

On the fourth night, it was Indigo, instead of Trigve, who found me in the small hours wandering a dark hallway. I turned to find her standing at the end of the corridor, watching me. She wore her arm in a sling, but her shoulder was healing. Siv said she would fully recover, though she'd always have a scar.

I went to her. "What is it, Indigo?"

"I've made a decision." She slipped her hand into her tunic and pulled out Runa's dagger. "I will join the Quicks, as Runa longed to do."

She lifted the blade to the nape of her neck.

"Will you help me?" she asked.

I nodded. I took the knife and began to saw through her braid as she held it still. Dark strands fell in soft waves at my feet.

"I told the Sea Witch of my plan," she said when it was done. "Juniper agreed this would restore the imbalance created when Runa died. There's no need to mourn now, Frey."

I reached up and ran my right hand through her shorn mane. "Roam the Endless Forests, Indigo. Hunt and rove and be free."

Indigo grabbed my hand in hers. "Let us be Blood Sisters. Let us spend the seasons running through trees, sleeping under the stars, Runa's name on our lips."

I closed my eyes and pictured myself *moving quietly through a winter woodland, my feet turning up freshly fallen snow, Indigo at my side, bow in hand, lone deer up ahead, a song on my tongue . . .*

"Together we can go back to Logafell's cave, and follow the tunnels under the Skal Mountains, looking for treasure . . ."

I saw us, torches in hand, *moving down dark halls, chasing an underground stream, into the mountain, deeper and deeper, until the cave opened up, a cavern strewn with gold . . .*

I opened my eyes, and shook my head.

"I can't join you, Indigo. I've decided to go south with Trigve, so he can study with the Orate Healers." I paused. "I will come back one day, though. And I will find you, if I have to search every Endless Forest in Vorseland. And when I do, I will stay with the Quicks for as long as you wish. Forever, if you ask it."

Afterward, I went back to the hearth and slid into the pile of warm bodies. I wrapped my arms around Ovie and closed my eyes.

Indigo would join the Quicks in Runa's place.

It was right. It was good.

My mind found peace, and I slept.

Esca Roth lost almost all his men to the giant Logafell. Only seven remained, out of all his dozens of warriors.

So the women of Blue Vee began to train in earnest. To become masters of the *edge dance*. The widows and the fatherless daughters came up from the villages of the Destin Lush Valley to fight, to live in the Great Hall, as only the men had done before.

I joined them at sunrise on that final day. I squinted in the cold winter light, watching them move through the steps of the Seventh Degree.

Jarl Roth would have the first female army in Vorseland, something that hadn't existed in living memory, not since the time of the *Witch War Chronicles*.

I refused his reward in the end.

Juniper, our thieving little Sea Witch, had snuck off and stolen the giant gold plates from Logafell's cave before we left, hiding them in her pack until we returned to Blue Vee. Those plates would be enough to see us through to where we needed to go, with some to spare.

I would even be able to pay for Trigve's education with the Orate Healers in Iber.

Roth could use his gold to rebuild his jarldom. And buy his Iber horses back.

On the last evening before we left, Trigve went down to Siv's hut to say his farewell, and I met Roth by the giant yew. We sat at its base, on one of its great, twisted roots, and drank from a black horn filled with *Vite*, as we had on the first night.

"So you're off to Iber now?" Moonlight filtered down from the hole in the ceiling, and Roth's eyes shone violet.

"Yes."

"Won't you miss the cold and the snow?"

I leaned back against the large trunk of the tree and sipped the *Vite*. "Not one bit."

He leaned back as well, his shoulder touching mine. "I'm writing a saga about you and your companions and the fall of Logafell."

"You're a poet?" This surprised me, though it shouldn't have. Roth had the depth of feeling needed to create fine verse, and the heart as well.

He nodded. "As was my father. Storri Sturlson is one of our ancestors—he's the author of the *Blood Frost Saga*."

I turned and wove my eight remaining fingers into Roth's long blond hair, something I'd been wanting to do since I'd first set eyes on him. I squeezed his locks in my fist until the stumps of my fingers ached.

I kissed him.

When Roth went to his room after the meal that night, I followed. I shed my clothing by the light of the brazier's fire. He helped me when I needed it—my hand would not be fully healed, not for a long while yet. It would take months to learn how to use the remaining fingers with grace, instead of fumbling. It was a small price to pay, all in all.

When I was naked, Roth reached up and undid my silver hair from its braid. He sighed when it flowed loose and free down my back.

The night was cold, and the wind had teeth, but we were warm as fire.

Roth slid out of the furs and went to the side table to refill his horn. I watched him as he moved around the room, and smiled.

"Esca?"

"Yes?"

"Do us justice in your saga. It will be the first Vorse tale to mention Mercies."

He took a long drink of *Vite*, head tilted back, and then swallowed. "I will. And when I'm done, I'll lure the famous bard Odenna to Blue Vee and have it put to song."

"It is right that the Boneless Mercies are finally given a story after so long—that they are given victory and glory after serving Vorseland quietly for years upon years."

"True." He nodded, but then narrowed his eyes. "Just remember, Frey. Triumph is a beast of its own. It hungers and craves and yearns, and it is never satisfied. I've seen success ruin more people than failure. Be careful. Don't let glory-seeking get in the way of your happiness."

I threw back the furs and went to him. He gave me the horn, and I drank deeply.

Roth bent his head and kissed my shoulder.

I slid my right hand up his torso, resting my fingertips on his ribs. "I'll seek no more fame. Adventure, yes, but not glory. I've felt its pulse. It is enough."

We went back to bed. I crawled under the pile of furs, and he pulled me to him. I pressed my chest into his. We kissed long and slow.

"What is it about the nighttime that makes us dream impossible things?" he asked a while later.

"Why, of what do you dream?"

"Oh, many things. My jarldom is safe, and I have much to be thankful for. Yet . . ."

Roth's gaze met mine.

"I hope to return to Blue Vee one day," I said.

He nodded, eyes soft in the firelight. "Don't make me wait too long, Frey."

We fell asleep in each other's arms, his face nestled into the hollow of my neck. I slept deep and dreamless until dawn.

. . . . .

Ovie chose to come with Trigve and me, south to Iber. I could do nothing but stare at her and grin when she told me, I was so pleased. She finally turned and simply stalked off, in a hurry to pack her things and say farewell to Vale.

Indigo would go north to the Quicks and to our friends Leif and Vital.

Juniper would finally head home to the Sea Witches.

We held one another on that last morning before she boarded Roth's longboat—it would sail down the coast and land on the banks of the Merrows, a much easier journey than our trek through the Red Willow Marsh.

"I will come to you in your dreams," she said. "This is a parting of body only. Not mind."

I held her tighter, her curls pressed against my neck, soft rose petals on my skin.

Juniper struggled, and then pulled back so she could look up into my eyes. "There once lived an ancient Sea Witch mystic who used to wander Frem, preaching of the balance, of living in harmony with the earth. At the end of every sermon, she would hold her hands out, palms down, and say: *All will be well, all will be well, all manner of things will be well.* All will be well, Frey. I will come to you in your dreams."

I let her go.

She pressed her palms together and blew over her right shoulder, lips pursed, setting a wish out on the air. "We will meet again soon, Frey."

I'd often thought it would have been easier for me to lose my life, rather than my Mercies.

But in the end, I let her go, as I'd let Runa go.

I endured.

All will be well.

All will be well.

All manner of things will be well.

EPILOGUE

W*e booked passage on an Iber trading ship in the Blue* Vee port and made our way down the coast. Traveling is simple when you have coin.

I thought of many things as we sailed, standing on the wooden deck, sea-wind in my silver hair. I thought of the Cut-Queen and Mother Hush. I thought of all the people who had come into my life since leaving the death trade, however brief . . . Gunhild and Warrick, Vital and Leif. I thought of my missing fingers. I thought of Roth and the ache he'd left in my heart.

I thought of Runa.

For the final leg of our journey, we hopped a beautiful, red-and-white-striped spice ship from the city of Delphi to Santor.

Santor. The Iber island that held the school for Orate Healers . . . also known as the Iber Institute of Physick, or, more commonly, the Hall of Potions.

We spent our first night at one of the inns near the port. Iber inns weren't cowering, dark places with low ceilings and dirt floors. They were great stone buildings with pools of cool water, decorated in beautiful tiles, with circular holes in the roof to let in the light.

The people of Santor didn't sleep in beds, but in hammocks hung on sturdy ropes from the ceiling. I was rocked to sleep in a blue-tiled room like a child in a mother's arms.

Juniper came to me in my dreams that first night on the island. As if she knew we'd finally reached our destination. She was dressed all in green again, like the Sea Witch she was, and sitting in the black crook of a Scorch Tree.

I smelled salt and wood smoke and pine resin.

She told me many things. She said that Sasha and Aarne were happy and well and that she'd persuaded Mother Hush to teach Aarne some of their sea prayers, despite his being a boy and an outsider.

She told me that she'd appeared to Vital in his dreams as well and that the Quicks were deep in the Green Wild Forest, living in the trees and feasting every night on giant snow hares.

She told me of the rumors spreading across Vorseland about the Cut-Queen. It was said she had reappeared and was raising an army among the Pig People on the Boar Islands.

She told me that Mother Hush, in response, was training the Merrow Sea Witches in the art of battle and war.

I woke in my hammock with a jerk, some hours before dawn.

• • • • •

It was the heart of February, a Vorse month of endless dark, endless cold, endless snow. But Trigve, Ovie, and I walked together down narrow stone alleys and felt no chill.

The buildings on Santor were squat and heavy—but they had been painted white and cerulean blue, which gave them the light, airy appearance of clouds.

The white and blue houses climbed up the main hill, up and up, alongside rows of olive trees, eventually leading to an open plain that stretched to the other side of the island.

Olive trees grew everywhere, in courtyards and on street corners. I remembered the olive oil I'd tasted during the meal with the Sea Witches, and smiled. I plucked one of the green fruits from a branch as we walked by and took a bite. It was bitter as poison. I spat it out and swore. A nearby Santor grandmother shook her kerchiefed head at me and laughed.

"No, not that way," she said in stammering Vorse. Santor was a port city, and many languages were spoken, but most of the residents spoke a variation of Iberik. I'd tried to pick up the language on the voyage over and had learned a few basic words, but I had a long way to go before I'd be able to converse freely.

"Not for eating. Oil only." The woman fetched a pitcher from inside her blue-roofed home and poured the green-gold liquid into a tiny cup before giving it to me to sip.

"See?" she said after I'd tasted the oil.

I wiped my lips with the back of my hand and smiled at her, nodding my thanks.

The people of Santor were friendly and welcoming—how could they not be, living under that warm, ever-present sun? I tilted my face to the sky as we walked, basking in the glow.

Eventually we found our way into the bustling market, and I bought figs, a salty white cheese, and a delicious flatbread dripping with herbs and olive oil. The farmers gazed at my three-fingered hand when I reached for my coins, but they asked me no questions.

Trigve and Ovie and I stood shoulder to shoulder by the sea and ate the food standing up, glancing peacefully at the water while we chewed. The ocean in Santor was not like our sea back home, gray and moody and passionate. It was calm and blue. Blue as the sky.

We found a tailor and changed out of our wool tunics and into the flowing silk garments everyone wore on the island. The fabric was soft and cool.

Trigve also had a handful of red linen robes made—the traditional attire of students on Santor. He would attend school for a year, or perhaps two if he excelled and wanted to specialize. Perhaps we could rent one of the cool, tiled houses on the hill. Ovie and I could earn money picking olives and doing a bit of fishing. There would be no freezing winter months to worry about and no shortage of food, either. Bright, plump fruits grew easily here, all year long. It would be a pleasant life, as long as it lasted.

I thought of the woman in black silk and her dark features

and delicate dress. How homesick she must have been, alone in that shadowed house in the forest.

I took her lock of hair from my pack and clutched it in my palm as I strolled.

"We will have to go back to Vorseland, someday," I said after a while. "And take part in the upcoming Witch War."

"Yes." Ovie wove her arm through mine. "But not yet."

Trigve just glanced at me and smiled. "It's an offense to the gods to think such melancholy thoughts in such a beautiful place on such a beautiful day. Let yourself be happy, Frey."

My eyes met his. "I will. I promise."

We passed through the main market and watched young girls selling fruit, and dark-haired fishermen haggling prices with busy mothers. I saw a stall with archery bows for sale, beautiful ones made from the wood of olive trees. I thought of Runa.

We walked on and soon came upon a crowd gathered near a fountain in the main square. Two bards sat together on the white stone. A sister and brother, based on their similar appearance—dark hair, freckles, lively eyes.

They were singing softly in the lazy afternoon heat, a bowl out for coins, a stringed instrument on the sister's knee. Children sat at their feet.

The pair finished their song and began another. The melody was beautiful, bittersweet, with long, soaring notes. They had strong, pure voices.

It dawned on me after a moment that I could understand the words of the ballad, for they were in Vorse.

The song told the story of four Boneless Mercies who faced a terrible beast in a deep, dark cave. They defeated the monster and took its head back to the people, who sang their praise and feasted in their honor. Their brave act soon sparked a change in the world, that led the land into a golden age.

I put my fist to my heart, and smiled.

I am Frey, former Boneless Mercy, ally of the Sea Witches, failed slayer of the Cut-Queen, mourner of Runa the Archer, companion to Trigve, friend to Jarl Roth. I defeated the giant Logafell. I am woman, wanderer, warrior.

This is not the end of my story.

GOFISH

QUESTIONS FOR THE AUTHOR

APRIL GENEVIEVE TUCHOLKE

What inspired you to write *The Boneless Mercies?*

I decided to write a fantasy inspired by ancient Scandinavia after a trip to Iceland. It's a majestic country, raw and wild and cold. I reread *Beowulf* while staying in Reykjavík, and I thought: This tale has nearly everything an epic story needs—a hero, a monster, brutal battles, tragedy, victory . . . but where are the women warriors? What are they up to? What are their stories?

Strong women play such large roles in your novel. Are there strong women that you were inspired by when creating these characters?

I wrote about brave, loyal, adventuresome women as a result of my experiences with *conformist* women—women who refused to take risks, refused to stay curious about the world, to go against the crowd, to embrace each other's unique personalities.

I've read (and loved) fantasies about female wanderers (such as Garth Nix's *Sabriel*), but these books often feature a lone hero. I was curious to explore the friendship and love between a group of female characters, to have them work together to accomplish something daring and noble.

What kind of message do you want readers to take away from this story, if any?
I want the reader to walk away with a joyful feeling of triumph and possibility, wrapped in a comforting glow of profound female friendship.

What challenges did you face while writing this book, and how did you overcome them?
One of the challenges I faced was deciding how much of the original *Beowulf* story I wanted to keep in my book. An author has to strike a fine balance when doing a retelling—paying tribute to the original story, while also creating something new. In the end I kept the monster, the mead hall, the blood, and the glory. I *almost* kept the dragon. And I added a lot of witches.

What is your favorite scene or moment from *The Boneless Mercies*?
Spoiler alert!

My favorite scene might be when the characters race through the prickly Thiss Brambles on their way to the Sea Witches.

Hmm . . . actually it's the final scene, in the epilogue, where the glory-seeking Frey is strolling through the Santor marketplace and hears two bards singing of her and her companions.

What's the best advice you ever received about writing?
The best advice I received about writing didn't actually come from my creative writing degree—it evolved from being a hardcore reader-kid, and then working four years in a bookstore right out of college:

If you want to be a good writer, start by simply reading, everything, every genre—high literature, classic literature, obscure literature, religious literature, commercial literature, nonfiction, romance, westerns, choose-your-own adventure, picture books, graphic novels, new age, occult, comedy, travel writing . . . read it all. It's how I learned what I wanted to write, and how I learned the cadence of storytelling.

What would your readers be surprised to learn about you?

I was very shy as a child.

Someone once gave me a real human skull as a gift.

I've lived in nine states and two countries.

My father built a large treehouse for me and my three siblings when we were children. It was in a small patch of woods, and it had a tower and a secret passageway, and I pretty much lived in it during the summer . . . it was the inspiration for the Sea Witches' conical huts in the Scorch Trees.

IN THIS STAND-ALONE COMPANION NOVEL
TO *THE BONELESS MERCIES*,
APRIL TUCHOLKE SPINS A BOLD, FEMINIST
RETELLING OF THE KING ARTHUR LEGEND

KEEP READING FOR AN EXCERPT.

THE WOLVES

ONE

The Gothi nuns will not travel to remote places, so when the snow sickness sweeps through the forgotten mountain hamlet, or the secluded steading, or the lonely, isolated Hall, we burn our own.

We bury our own.

We thought we were safe, another dark winter behind us. The festival of Ostara had come and gone. Spring had arrived, jade-green buds, emerald-green grass, bright blue skies.

Our steading was in the Middlelands, remote and quiet, far from any sea, far from any major town, far from any jarls with their Great Halls and shifting laws. Here, in the region of Cloven Tell, the soft green Ranger Hills rippled across our horizon, and cold, clear lakes marked our landscape like sparkling jewels.

My sister, Morgunn, and I had spent our childhood running

wild and free without a thought to the world beyond the hills—it was no more real to us than the stories of the Green Women of Elshland or the tales of Frey and the giant Logafell. We were isolated. We were happy.

Aslaug, our cook, used to tell me I had too much happiness in me. She said only witches and Fremish wolf-priests were truly happy, because they cast spells and drank poison, because they made pacts with the gods in pursuit of their own joy.

I'd heard of these magic pacts from the sagas and the songs. I've never stolen an infant, or tricked a jarl into marriage, or slain a sleeping Elver, or burned a village. I've never taken to the air, floating across the night sky, fingers cupping the stars. I've never made all the children of Vorseland scream, as one, in the middle of the night. Yet I've been happy. Happy as a witch. Happy as a wolf.

I'd shrugged off Aslaug's warnings as I'd shrugged off the warnings of Elna, our pretty, apple-cheeked servant, who used to say that the moon was the eye of a great dragon and that one day he would look down and see us and burn our world to ash.

Now Elna was burning to ash, her body on the pile in the east field.

The snow sickness struck a few Middleland villages each winter. It would blow in with a storm and stay as long as the white flakes fell from the sky. It would start with sweating and a fever and end in death. Some people lived, and most people died, and only the gods knew why.

Snow had come in the night and turned the world white again.

At supper, my mother began to shake and sweat until she fell from the bench and lay writhing in pain on the floor beside the hearth fire. The servants began to scream. They knew that only the snow sickness could do this, only the snow sickness could take down such a strong Vorse woman.

I dragged my mother to her bed and awoke at dawn to find her dead in my arms.

The servants died in the night as well. I carried their bodies to the field and set them on fire, gray smoke floating up past the trees.

Gray.

Gray was the color of the winter sky. It was the color of a pair of cooing mourning doves, my father's beard, and the thick wool tunic my mother used to wear on feast days.

Gray was the color of Viggo's eyes.

And now gray was the color of death.

I took a half-empty jug of *Vite* from a table near the main doors of the Hall and drank. I wiped my hand across my mouth and took another sip.

I had two more bodies to see to, and these I would not burn.

I dug two graves by the rowan trees until blisters wept across my palms, stinging, bleeding. I straightened, pressed my hands to my aching lower back and then to my heart.

My heart pushed back. I was alive.

Blood from my palm seeped into the front of my tunic. I wiped my hands on my leather leggings and picked up my shovel. I needed to finish this task before the morning's sorrow could sear itself so deeply into my mind that it would be the only thing I would ever think about. The only thing I would ever remember.

I returned to the Hall, propped open the main doors with two large stones, and then walked slowly to her chamber. My mother had been six feet tall, sinewy, broad-shouldered, made of muscle and steel. I pulled her body out of the bed, strong limbs woven between furs, fingers in tangled hair. I carried her, panting, muscles straining, past the central hearth, past the long feast table, out of the building, into the fresh air.

The Hall smelled of thick smoke—sour, acrid sickness and sweet, rotting death. The air outside smelled of sun and wet earth. It smelled of life.

I glanced toward the five rowan trees in the northeast corner of our estate.

Mother was Elsh. She would go in the ground, not the fire.

The bright sun had melted most of the snow, and my boots were soaked through. Sweat blurred my vision, and my bones ached with my mother's weight.

I set her in the first grave and picked up the shovel. The hole filled slowly.

Now . . .

Viggo.

I'd found the shepherd collapsed outside the Hall at dawn, his tunic covered in blood.

His body should have been in the east field, burning alongside Aslaug and Elna and Ivar the field hand and old Haftor the woodcutter.

The shepherd wasn't Elsh, but I would bury him by my mother all the same.

I tossed the first shovel of half-frozen dirt onto Viggo's body. It fell on his hair, a black clump that would never be washed clean.

I dropped to my knees and howled like wolves on the hunt, crying to the moon.

I yelled my voice into dust . . . and then I rose to my feet and finished burying him.

I knew it was selfish to keep Viggo here with me on the steading, to not burn him in the way of the Vorse. But then, the living are selfish.

When it was done, I threw the shovel into the snow between two of the rowan trees. Let it rust. I would never use it again.

I wasn't full Vorse, and I didn't believe that life was simply a long journey toward a good death. All the same, Viggo had been more than a shepherd, more than my lover, more than a wise, quiet Vorselander who ran across the Ranger Hills with the strength and grace of a young god.

He'd had the heart of a hero, noble, wise, and brave. He deserved a hero's life and a hero's death. Instead, he died alone, in the night, a victim of a passing plague.

I would not let the same fate claim me. If I had a speck of heroism in my heart, then I would find it. I would honor it. I would sacrifice for it.

A memory surfaced. I was a child, ten or eleven, out in the hills with my mother, collecting green winterberries by moonlight for Elsh frost-brew. We stumbled upon a white arctic bear—it came roaring out of a nearby cave, jaws wide, teeth the size of my fist, white fur stained with old blood.

I hid behind my mother and shook with fear. She leaned over slowly, eyes on the bear, and pulled a knife from its sheath on her right calf.

"*Fortune favors brave women*," she said. "*We rise up, while the meek women cower.*" She ran forward and sank her dagger into the bear's throat.

She slept under that bear's snow-white hide for years. It still lay on her empty bed. Each time she caught me looking at it, she reminded me that I had cowered while she killed the bear, that I had flinched when she took its life. It didn't matter to her that I'd only been a child.

"You have a soft heart," she'd say whenever I hesitated to wring a hen's neck or slit a lamb's throat. It wasn't a compliment. "You take too much after your father, Torvi. Your sister is the true Vorse."

I wiped my bleeding palms on the front of my tunic, and then I walked to the cold, fast-moving stream that wove through our farm, down from the Ranger Hills. I tore off my tunic and boots and underclothes—there was no one to see, no one to care. I slid my naked body into the water, feet slipping over stones, limbs pressing into the silky current. I let it wash away all the blood, all the dirt, all the death. I let it cleanse me of my old life.

When I climbed out of the water, I was numb with cold. I ran to the line of laundry strung behind the Hall, near the vegetable garden. Elna never had a chance to gather the clothing before the storm hit. I beat the blood back into my thighs with my palms, and then I grabbed a large wool cloth, wrapped it around myself, and went inside.

I crossed the Hall, leaving a trail of wet footprints. I walked down the east corridor, stopped at the second door, and knocked.

The door opened slowly. "Is it over?"

I nodded, and my sister grabbed me. Her face pressed into my shoulder, and her fingers clenched my tunic at the waist, squeezing the cloth into her fists.